Dedication

This book is dedicated to the unsung heroes—the brave men and women in uniform, both past and present, who tirelessly serve and protect our communities, often at great personal sacrifice. Their dedication to justice, their unwavering commitment to upholding the law, even in the face of overwhelming odds, is an inspiration. This story, though fictional, is a testament to their courage, their resilience, and their unwavering pursuit of truth. It is a tribute to the strength of character, the unwavering resolve, and the sheer grit that it takes to face down injustice, no matter how powerful the opposition. It's for those who've stared into the abyss of corruption and emerged, battered but unbowed, fighting for what's right, even when the system seems rigged against them.

It's also dedicated to those who have endured the trauma of violence and injustice. Their stories, often untold, deserve to be heard and understood. This book attempts to give voice to the silenced, to shine a light on the shadows where injustice thrives. Their strength in the face of adversity, their quiet resilience, their unwavering spirit, even when the world seems to have turned its back, inspires me daily. This is for the survivors, the witnesses, those who have the courage to speak truth to power, those who have lost loved ones to violence and who continue to fight for justice, for those who carry the weight of the world on their shoulders, and yet, still find the strength to carry on. It is for those who believe in a better tomorrow, even when the path seems fraught with darkness and despair.

Finally, this dedication extends to the tireless advocates for justice, those who dedicate their lives to the pursuit of truth and fairness. The lawyers, the investigators, the social workers, the community activists—those who work tirelessly, often behind the scenes, to ensure that justice prevails. This book, a work of fiction, acknowledges the often unseen struggles and triumphs of those who dedicate their lives to fight for what is right, often facing considerable risks and opposition. Their commitment to justice, their unwavering pursuit of truth, and their perseverance in the face of adversity serve as a beacon of hope and inspire us to strive for a more just and equitable world. Their dedication and hard work make our world a better place.

For Lori.

Table of Contents

Chapter 1

Laila remembers The Raid.

The air hung thick with the metallic tang of fear and the acrid bite of gunpowder. Sirens wailed in the distance, a mournful counterpoint to the frantic hammering of my own heart. Flashlights sliced through the darkness, painting the dilapidated warehouse in fleeting, distorted images. Dust motes danced in the beams, swirling like malevolent spirits in a scene ripped straight from a nightmare.

This wasn't the textbook raid we'd meticulously planned.

This was chaos waiting to happen.

"Bet you twenty bucks you trip over your own boots again," muttered Marshal Daniels, nudging me with a crooked grin as he tightened the strap on his vest.

"Only if you don't shoot yourself in the foot first," Carolyn Pryme shot back, her voice dry but carrying a thin edge. Pryme was a whirlwind of controlled aggression, her authority slicing cleaner than any switchblade. She barked orders without hesitation, her sharp voice anchoring us against the rising tide of nerves.

"You two gonna flirt all night or actually watch my six?" another agent, Moreno, chimed in, checking the breach gear strapped to his chest. His smile was forced, too wide, a thin veil over the tension coiling through all of us.
"Relax," Pryme said, tightening her grip on her Glock. "It's just another warehouse full of lowlifes. We've handled worse."
"Yeah," Moreno muttered, scanning the shadows. "Until it's not."
The banter masked our fear, knitted together by long nights, bad coffee, and bullet scars we didn't talk about. We needed it — because the silence waiting behind these doors was far worse.
We'd been tracking the Sal Demarco crew for months, a vicious mob operating out of a network of abandoned warehouses on the industrial outskirts of Philadelphia. Tonight was the culmination of that painstaking investigation — a meticulously planned strike to bring them down.
At least, that was the plan.
Flashlights cut sharper now, the old wood and rusted metal catching the beams in jagged flashes.
The shouts of the other marshals, the crashing of furniture, the guttural growls of the suspects – it all erupted at once, a chaotic symphony swallowed by a deafening roar.

A gunshot.
Sharp. Brutal. Final.
The silence that followed was worse — a vacuum, sucking the breath from my lungs.
My eyes, trained to catch the smallest slivers of danger in the fog of war, locked onto the scene ahead.
Thirteen-year-old Madeline Clark, a scrawny kid with eyes too big for her terrified face, lay sprawled on the grimy concrete floor. Blood blossomed around her like an obscene flower, staining the rough surface a sickening crimson.
Her small body twitched once, twice, then stilled.
Death's cold hand had claimed her.
Dominic Falfor, one of our own Marshals, stood over her — his Glock still smoking, his face frozen in an expression I couldn't quite name.
Shock?
Regret?
Or something darker, something far more sinister?
The question hung heavy in the air, as thick and suffocating as the gunpowder smoke, daring anyone to speak it aloud.
Carolyn's reaction was immediate and visceral. A strangled cry ripped from her throat — a sound of raw, unfiltered grief and fury.
She lunged at Falfor, her voice a venomous

whisper that somehow managed to slice through the clatter around us.

"What the fuck did you do?"

The scene fractured before my eyes. Marshals rushed forward, their faces a mirror of horror and stunned disbelief.

Not the reactions of accomplices — but of witnesses blindsided by betrayal.

This wasn't the takedown we had planned.

It was a bloody, horrifying mess.

Someone had seriously fucked up.

My own response came slower, more deliberate.

Years in the Army had taught me not to rush — to react not just to the immediate threat, but to the bigger picture unfolding behind it. While Carolyn's fury erupted unchecked, mine stayed coiled, clinical.

I moved toward the girl's body, not to check for a pulse — the grim finality was obvious — but to assess the scene with clear eyes.

Details first. Emotions later.

I knelt beside Madeline Clark, careful not to disturb the blood pattern spreading across the concrete.

Her eyes were open — wide, glassy, fixed on a point above us none of us could reach.

She hadn't just been collateral damage.

She had been targeted.

One shot.

High center mass.

Clean. Intentional.

My throat tightened, but I forced it down, cataloging every detail with mechanical precision.

Powder burns. Medium range.

No weapon near her hands.

Only a battered backpack spilled open in the chaos —

a cracked cell phone, a sticker-covered journal, a crushed granola bar, a shattered makeup mirror.

No gun.

No threat.

Nothing a trained Marshal could have mistaken for danger.

Even as I logged the evidence, something inside me splintered — a quiet seam tearing loose at the edges.

But it wasn't just the lifeless girl that held my focus.

It was the flash of movement in the far corner.

A glint of tarnished metal caught in the beam of a shifting flashlight — there, and gone again.

A bribe.

I had seen it.

A fleeting exchange between Falfor and one of the Demarco men, swallowed quickly by the pandemonium.

A small, tarnished object, passed from dirty hand to dirty hand, as easily as breathing. Betrayal, captured in a split-second. Enough to ignite everything that came next.

"Back off Carolyn!" Dominic Falfor barked, "I don't have time for your bullshit. She had something in her hands, I thought". "You thought!" Carolyn spit the words out like poison, "You didn't think Dom…You panicked. You just executed her!"
He stepped back, one hand still tightly gripping his sidearm. His knuckles were white. His breathing quick, shallow. Not adrenaline. Not remorse.

Cover-up mode.

The warehouse, in the aftermath, was pandemonium, yet the memory of that brief transaction played on repeat in my mind, a brutal loop of cold, hard reality. The image of the money, the unspoken promise, the callous disregard for human life – it was too vivid to ignore, too potent to overlook. Madeline's death wasn't an accident; it was a calculated act, a consequence of corruption.

A camera blinked in the corner, mounted near the rafters of the warehouse. Internal surveillance. Standard protocol. Dominic followed my gaze and his jaw tightened. Subtle but telling. He was already working the angles. He'd delete footage, alter timestamps, scrub the narrative clean and unless someone stepped in now, the truth would vanish beneath paperwork, false witness statements and standard procedure.

I stood slowly.

In the immediate aftermath, the scene was a whirlwind of activity. Paramedics arrived, their efforts frantic and futile. The other Marshals secured the remaining suspects, their faces grim and etched with disbelief. The air reeked of fear, regret, and the sharp sting of betrayal. But my focus remained razor-sharp, honed by years in the military and years in law enforcement. I was a soldier, a marshal, a witness. And I knew, with a certainty that chilled me to the bone, that I had just witnessed a cold-blooded murder, not a rogue action, and that Dominic Falfor, our own Marshal, was responsible.

"Don't touch that girl again", I said, low but firm, not to Dominic, but to the entire team. Everyone froze. "She's evidence now and if anyone tampers with her or this scene, I'll make

sure they're wearing orange by morning".
A long silence followed. Then Carolyn stepped to my side. Her face still flushed, but her jaw set. We're logging everything", she said to no one in particular. "Body cams. Timestamped noted. Chain of custody. All of it. You're not burying this Dom. Not this time". Dominic didn't respond. He didn't need to, the story already begun to rewrite itself behind his eyes. But so had mine. And only one of us was willing to walk into a courtroom to defend it.

The subsequent investigation was a whirlwind of interrogations, forensic analysis, and a painstaking reconstruction of the events. The initial reports were

carefully crafted, attempting to paint the shooting as a tragic accident, a regrettable outcome of a dangerous situation. But I had seen the bribe, and I knew the truth. This was more than just a tragic accident; it was a cold-blooded murder fueled by greed and corruption.

Back at my family farm, a sanctuary that usually offered respite from the chaos of my professional life, I wrestled with the decision to speak out. The weight of the truth pressed down on me, a heavy burden amplified by the ghosts of my past. My divorce, the memories of combat, the constant pressure of my job – they all coalesced into a storm raging within me. To speak out would be to expose not just Falfor, but a deep-seated corruption within the system. To remain silent would be to betray Madeline, to betray everything I believed in.

The silence of the Pennsylvania countryside couldn't muffle the internal conflict that tore at me. The rhythmic chirping of crickets and the gentle rustle of leaves couldn't drown out the echoes of that gunshot, the sight of Madeline Clark's lifeless eyes. The farm, normally my solace, became a crucible where I forged my decisions. The serenity of the place, the comforting familiarity of the old farmhouse, provided a stark contrast to the brutal reality I faced. My mother and brothers talked with me and helped me sort things out. It was here, amid the quiet strength of my ancestral home, that I made my decision.

I would testify. My father's legacy, my mother's haven, the home that raised me, the weight of what I had witnessed pressed harder than the autumn skies above. The fields were golden with the last light of the season. Stalks swaying gently in the wind, but there was no peace in me. The land was steady, unchanged. I was not. The old porch creaked beneath my boots as I stood with Simon at my side. The golden retriever had sensed my unrest since I returned, never leaving my heels. He leaned against me now, silent but sure, a steady presence as the war inside me raged on.

To testify would be to strip away the false veil of brotherhood that held federal law enforcement together. It would mean going against the unspoken rule, that you protect your own, no matter what. But how could I protect someone who had stolen the breath from a child?

Inside the house smelled like lemon balm and wood polish. My mother had been cleaning and baking, something sweet and simple. Her nervous way of offering stability when words failed. The kettle whistled low in the background as she poured tea. She set a mug in front of me like a peace offering. “You’ve been quiet”, she said gently as she slid into the chair across from me. “I saw something, Mom, Something I can’t unsee”. Her eyes searched mine. Even in her sixties, Eleanor Wright was sharp. She was more steel than lace. Forged in the courtroom beside my father and tempered by years of raising three headstrong children.

“It was a bad scene”, I added, my voice barely above a whisper, “A kid, thirteen. Shot down like a threat”. She reached across the table putting her hand around mine, “Tell me the worst part”. “It was one of ours”. I answered, “and now I’ve decided to testify to call it what it is …or pretend I didn’t see what I know I did”.

The screen door creaked again. Daniel, my oldest brother, stepped in from the barn. Wiping grease off his hands, his face smudged with engine oil and sun. He looked at me then our mother and knew something was off.

‘Frank call again?” he asked.

“No”, I answered.

“Good. ‘guy’s an asshole”, Thomas added coming in from the back fields, “Let him stay away”.

The mood shifted quickly when mom gave them a look. The same look she used to give the three of us before Dad handed down his verdict at the dinner table.
The four of us sat in the light of the kitchen. The room hummed with age and wisdom. No one needed to ask what the subject was, they already knew.
“You’re scared”, Thomas said finally. He wasn’t accusing me, just naming the truth out loud.

I nodded.

“Then it’s the right thing to do’, Daniel added, “You only get scared or pissed off when something matters”. Daniel knew about those kinds of fear. He was a former F.B. I. agent that was accused of some foul shit himself. He was eventually exonerated but left the service because of all the crap that went with it.

We sat in silence a moment longer. Letting the weight of everything settle. Then Mom rose and walked to the bookshelf by the fireplace. She retrieved a leather-bound folder…Dad's old legal pad.
She set it before me. I flipped through the pages, his handwritten notes, quotes from Supreme Court decisions, musings on justice, underlined passages of personal philosophy. One phrase had been highlighted and rewritten over and over, etched in his precise hand across multiple pages:

"Truth does not serve comfort. It serves justice!"

My throat tightened. I closed the pad and looked up. "I'm going to testify and tell the truth", I had barely completed my statement when my mother gave me a proud, but sad smile.
"Then do it with your back straight, your voice steady and no apologies", she added.
My brother, Thomas, got a beer from the fridge and raised it in the air and toasted, "To Laila, To Courtroom L.A.W." Daniel followed, "To Madeline Clark". I smiled slightly and toasted, "To the Truth!"
Outside the wind shifted. The leaves rustled in a different rhythm. It wasn't peace, but it was purpose.

And that was enough.

The risk was immense.
Falfor was well-connected — protected by a network of influence and corruption that stretched far beyond the local Marshal's office.
Retaliation would be inevitable.
Swift. Brutal.
But the alternative — silence, complicity — was unthinkable.
Madeline's death demanded justice.
My oath demanded it.
My conscience demanded it.
And I, Laila Aurora Wright, would see to it — no matter how long it took, no matter the cost.
The decision hardened into something immovable inside me.
The fear remained — a cold, clammy hand gripping my heart — but it would not deter me.
I would fight.
I would expose the truth, even if it meant losing everything.
This wasn't just about Madeline Clark anymore.
It was about the integrity of the system itself.
The sanctity of justice.
The unwavering commitment to truth that I had sworn to defend.
The battle ahead would be long.
Arduous.
But I was ready.

I was a soldier.
I was a Marshal.
I was a witness.
And I would not be silenced.

Witnessing the Bribe

The warehouse reeked of stale beer, sweat, and something acrid — burnt sugar, maybe. Dust motes hung suspended in the single shaft of moonlight slicing through a grimy window, casting the scene in a macabre spotlight. The air vibrated with the low thrum of adrenaline, punctuated by the ragged breathing of men locked in desperate struggle. My senses, honed by years in the Army and on the force, were hyper-alert, cataloging every detail with clinical precision.

Dominic Falfor, his silhouette stark against the weak light, stood near the back, apart from the chaotic melee of marshals and Demarco's goons.

He wasn't fighting.

He was watching.

Something about him felt wrong — his face, usually a mask of controlled aggression, was oddly slack, vacant.

It was this incongruity that first caught my attention.

Drawn by an instinct I couldn’t fully name, my eyes shifted toward a darker corner.

Two figures: a hulking man with a crumpled face — one of Demarco’s lieutenants — and Falfor.

Their bodies shielded by the shadows, they spoke in hushed tones.
The lieutenant shifted slightly, extending his hand toward Falfor.
In it, a faint gleam of tarnished silver — a small, dainty case, no bigger than a cigarette pack — flashed in the gloom.
Falfor accepted it without hesitation.
A flick of wrists, a near-invisible exchange, practiced and seamless.
And then it was over.
The lieutenant melted back into the shadows, swallowed by the chaos.
It wasn't a transaction.
It was a ritual — a silent communion, honed by years of complicity.
No money flashed.
No loud haggling.
Only a quiet, ritualistic exchange of loyalty and corruption.
The lieutenant's posture — rigid, deferential — spoke volumes.
It wasn't just a bribe.
It was homage.
In that instant, the world slowed.
The cacophony of the raid dulled, fading into a distant hum.
All that remained was the cold metallic glint of that silver case, burning itself into my mind.
This wasn't about raiding a criminal outfit.
This was bigger.
Darker.

Then — the gunshot.
Sharp.
Brutal.
The world snapped back into terrifying clarity.
Madeline Clark collapsed.
The shift in Falfor was immediate — almost theatrical.
Gone was the vacant observer.
In his place stood the professional soldier, reacting with grim efficiency to chaos.
But it wasn't reaction.
It was fulfillment.
Falfor moved like a man completing a task — sealing an agreement.
The ensuing chaos blurred: shouts, flashing lights, the sickening thud of Madeline's small body hitting concrete.
Yet even amid the pandemonium, the image of the bribe — the silver case — remained seared into my memory, as vivid and damning as the gunshot itself.

Paramedics arrived, their efforts frantic but futile.
Other marshals secured the suspects, their faces grim and hollow-eyed.
But I stood apart — silent, still.
A witness not just to a tragedy, but to something far worse.
The initial reports tried to frame it as a tragic accident.
A casualty of chaos.
But I had seen the truth.
Madeline's death wasn't an accident.
It was a consequence — a deliberate, calculated act born from corruption.

Back at my family farm, the place that had always been my refuge, the knowledge pressed on me like a physical weight.

The Pennsylvania countryside — the crickets, the rustling leaves — couldn't muffle the memory of that silver flash, the sharp crack of betrayal.
The farm, usually a sanctuary, became a battleground for my conscience.
The image of Madeline's lifeless eyes haunted every quiet moment.
To speak out was to risk everything.
Falfor was connected, his reach vast and ruthless.
Retaliation wasn't a possibility — it was a certainty.
But to remain silent was unthinkable.
It would be a betrayal — of Madeline, of justice, of the oath I had sworn.
The decision, once made, is solidified into steel.
The fear remained — a cold, constant companion — but it would not silence me.
I would fight.
For Madeline. For the truth.
For the integrity of the system that had betrayed its own soul.
The path ahead would be dangerous.
But I was ready. I reminded myself that
I was a soldier.
I was a Marshal.

I was a witness.
And I would not be silenced.
The fight had begun.

The first rule of warfare: **Secure your intel.**

Before I could accuse Dominic Falfor, before I could even whisper the truth aloud, I needed evidence. Hard evidence. Something stronger than memory, stronger than suspicion.
Because memory could be discredited.
Witnesses could be bought.
But data — cold, unflinching data — was harder to erase.
The internal surveillance footage from the warehouse was my first and only shot.

The Marshal Service kept raid footage archived under layers of protocol and bureaucratic red tape. Usually, the chain of custody was ironclad. But I knew the system — and I knew its cracks.

There was a narrow window between the live feed upload and the official encryption: a gap of hours, maybe less, before the footage was buried under layers of access codes and paperwork... or quietly altered by someone with enough reach.
I had to move.
The sterile white of the hospital room seemed to amplify the silence, a silence that pressed down on me like a physical weight. The smell of antiseptic couldn't mask the lingering scent of gunpowder, a phantom smell clinging to my clothes, a constant

reminder of the horror I had witnessed.

Carolyn, her eyes red-rimmed and swollen, sat beside me, her silence as heavy as mine. We were both exhausted, drained not just physically but emotionally, the weight of what we had seen pressing down on us with an almost unbearable intensity.

My mind replayed the scene in a relentless loop: the flash of metal, the muted crack of the gunshot, the sickening thud of Madeline's body hitting the concrete. Falfor's face, etched with a chilling mixture of panic and calculation, haunted me. His carefully constructed narrative, the attempt to paint himself as a victim, felt like a slap in the face, a grotesque insult to the memory of the girl he had murdered.

The internal conflict began to gnaw at me, a relentless tide pulling at the foundations of my carefully constructed composure. Part of me, the part steeped in years of military training, screamed for order, for discipline, for the adherence to protocol. This part urged me to fall in line, to accept the official narrative, to bury the truth beneath layers of bureaucratic obfuscation. To simply close my eyes and disappear into the anonymity that comes with military silence. It was the ingrained instinct of a soldier, trained to follow orders, to maintain order, to obey authority. It whispered the insidious mantra of "mission accomplished," even when the mission felt terribly, irrevocably wrong. This part of me, though quieter now than in the past, was still very much a part of who I am, a persistent undercurrent to my thoughts.

Another part, however, the part fueled by a lifetime of witnessing injustice, raged against this silence. This voice was less clear, more intuitive, a deep, resonant hum of moral outrage. This voice reminded me of my oath, not just the one I swore to my country, but the unspoken oath I made to myself—to uphold justice, to protect the innocent, to fight against corruption wherever I found it. This wasn't just about a corrupt marshal; it was about a system that allowed such corruption to fester, a system that prioritized appearances over truth. It was about a thirteen-year-old girl who deserved better than a convenient cover-up.

My military background, once a source of strength and stability, now felt like a double-edged sword. The discipline, the unwavering loyalty, the ingrained hierarchy—all of it conflicted with my sense of justice. I had been trained to follow orders, to obey authority, to maintain the chain of command. But in this instance, following orders meant betraying my conscience, betraying a child's memory. To obey authority would be to become complicit in a heinous crime.

The thought of facing Falfor and his supporters, the powerful figures within the system who would undoubtedly try to protect him, sent a chill down my spine. Their influence, their reach, was vast and terrifying. I knew the risks involved in challenging them; I had seen firsthand how the system could crush those who dared to speak truth to power.
Retaliation was not just a possibility; it was a certainty. Yet, the thought of remaining silent, of allowing Falfor to escape justice, was even more unbearable.

Chapter 2

The image of Madeline's lifeless body, the innocence extinguished from her eyes, became a constant, agonizing presence in my mind. Her death was a violation, a senseless act of brutality that demanded retribution, demanded justice. My internal conflict centered on the profound moral weight of what I had witnessed, the weight of her life, the weight of my silence, the weight of my duty. The conflict wasn't just between right and wrong; it was between two fiercely held beliefs: my loyalty to the uniform and my commitment to the truth. It was a deep personal conflict, a battle waged within the confines of my own soul.

Carolyn's presence, though silent, was a source of comfort. Her eyes, despite their redness, held a steely resolve that mirrored my own. She understood the gravity of the situation, the depth of the moral dilemma, as an African American female growing up in tough neighborhoods. The unspoken understanding between us was stronger than words.

We had faced danger together before; this was different. This was personal. This was about more than just another case; it was about the very fabric of justice itself.

The weight of the decision pressed down on me, each moment amplifying the conflict. The quiet hum of the hospital machinery served as a strange, mournful counterpoint to the storm raging within me. I considered the potential consequences: the loss of my job, the threat of physical harm, the social isolation that would surely follow. I pictured my family, my deceased father, my young nieces, the ones I had shielded from the darker aspects of my life.

This was a fight not just for Madeline but also for the future. I needed to ensure that the same thing didn't happen to another child.

Yet, the image of Madeline's lifeless eyes, the silent scream trapped in her frozen expression, pushed the fear aside. It strengthened my resolve. It reminded me that the price of silence was far greater than any potential cost of speaking out. It reaffirmed that the weight of inaction would be far heavier than any risk I might face. My silence would be complicity, my voice, the only hope for justice.

I thought of the farm, my sanctuary, the place where I sought solace and refuge from the turmoil of my life. The farm, with its rolling hills and quiet fields, represented a stark contrast to the grim realities of the courtroom. It represented hope, peace, and the simple, unyielding strength of nature. The thought of the farm gave me strength. It provided the emotional space I needed to accept my decision.

The decision, when it finally came, wasn't a sudden epiphany; it was a slow, agonizing coalescence of duty and conscience. It was the culmination of years of training, of experience, of personal battles fought and won. It was a quiet moment of self-discovery, a decision reached not in the heat of battle, but in the cold, sterile silence of a hospital room. It was a decision born not of bravado, but of quiet, unwavering conviction. I would bear witness. I would speak the truth. I would fight for Madeline. I would fight for justice.

And I would pay whatever the cost might be. The weight of the world felt momentarily lighter, replaced by a steely determination, a cold fire in my soul.

The quiet hum of the machinery faded into the background as a new sound filled my ears: the quiet, resolute thump of my own heart. It was the sound of purpose, of resolve, the steady beat of a warrior preparing for battle. My eyes met Carolyn's; she knew. The unspoken vow passed between us

was stronger than any legal oath. We were in this together. And we would prevail. The long road ahead would be fraught with danger, but we would face it together, our bond strengthened by the gravity of our decision. We would fight for Madeline, for justice, and for the integrity of the system we had both sworn to uphold. The war had begun.
The decision sat heavy but solid within me as Carolyn and I left the hospital, the early morning chill biting at our skin. There would be no going back now. Before the system could bury the truth under layers of official reports and carefully crafted lies, I had one shot to secure the evidence. I didn't have a plan yet — just a drive, a gut-deep certainty. First, I had to move. I had to act. The footage from that warehouse would either save Madeline's memory... or seal her fate forever.

The next morning, just before dawn, I drove to the district evidence facility — a squat, concrete building that smelled of bleach and despair.
The lot was empty except for a battered Crown Vic and a maintenance van idling near the service entrance.
Good. Minimal witnesses.
I wore jeans, boots, and a generic fleece jacket — civilian clothes, easy to forget.
Badge tucked away. The sidearm was holstered out of sight.
I wasn't here as Marshal Wright.
I was here as Laila — soldier, survivor, a woman who couldn't live with letting a child's murder get swept under the rug.

Inside, the fluorescent lights buzzed overhead, casting a sickly pall over the cracked linoleum floor.
The clerk on duty — Evans, a bored kid barely old enough to shave — barely glanced up from his gaming magazine.
"Morning," I said, offering a tired smile. "I'm here to pull body cam footage from last night's raid. Section E, warehouse 41. Incident review."

Evans squinted at me, then at his monitor.
"You're not on the authorization list."
"It's a pending review." I leaned in slightly, dropping my voice to a conspiratorial murmur. "Standard audit. You know how it is — some supervisors don't want paper trails until after it's clean. You'll have the update by end of day."
A lie, wrapped in just enough bureaucratic truth to be believable.
Evans hesitated.
Then shrugged.
"Whatever. Section E's archive's down the hall. Third room on the left. Take a temp keycard."
He slid a chipped plastic card across the counter without another glance.
I slid it into my jacket and nodded.
"Appreciate it."

Inside the archive room, the temperature dropped noticeably — heavy-duty AC to protect the servers.
Rows of blinking machines lined the walls, each humming with stored evidence: footage, reports, audio logs.
Buried somewhere in that digital labyrinth was the key to

everything.
I moved quickly, pulling up the incident logs by date and location.
Warehouse 41.
Timestamp: 0137 hours.
Raid ID: MAR/PHL/2271-Delta.
I inserted a blank encrypted drive into the console and started copying the raw footage.
The progress bar crawled forward.
Each second felt like an eternity.
A soft shuffle echoed from the hallway.
I'm tensed, hand brushing the butt of my Glock under the jacket.
But the footsteps passed by — someone on a different errand.
I exhaled slowly.
The footage completed its transfer with a soft electronic chime.
I yanked the drive free, tucked it deep into an inner pocket, and wiped my prints from the console.

No tracc.

As I walked back toward the exit, Evans called after me without looking up:
"Hey — you forgot to sign out."
"I'll catch it later," I said over my shoulder.
Because if this worked —
If I survived this —

Signing out would be the least of anyone's worries.

The Cover-Up Begins.

The first investigators arrived — faces pale and drawn — meticulously photographing the scene, recording statements.
Flashbulbs illuminated the macabre tableau in stuttering bursts of light.
The preliminary reports already echoed Falfor's version:
A veteran Marshal caught in the heat of battle.
A split-second mistake.
A tragedy, nothing more.
But the memory of the silver case — the silent exchange I had witnessed — burned in my mind.
Not a trick of the light.
Not a misinterpretation.
A bribe.
A contract signed in silence, sealed by the death of a child.
Carolyn and I exchanged subtle glances, imperceptible gestures built over years of trust.
She had seen it too.
We said nothing aloud.
Not yet.
But we knew.
The Pressure Mounts
The hours that followed blurred together — a grinding slog of interviews, forms, and subtle threats.
Every conversation became a battlefield.
Every word, a maneuver.

Every hesitation, a crack to be exploited.
The narrative was being engineered, brick by brick — building Falfor into a hero trapped by circumstance.
Those who hesitated to fall in line found themselves quietly pushed to the margins.
The weight of the truth grew suffocating.
The pressure to conform, overwhelming.
Yet through it all, I worked — meticulously preserving every detail that could undermine the official version:

- The angle of the gunshot.
- The trajectory of the blood spray.
- The scuff marks near Madeline's body.
- The faint smell of gunpowder, drifting from the wrong position, at the wrong range.

Each inconsistency became a weapon.
Each truth, a nail for the coffin of their lie.
Quiet Resolve
By the time the sun began to rise, the warehouse was sealed, the official story locked into place, and the marshals scattered back to their homes.
Content to let the lie settle like dust.
But not me.
I wasn't going home.
Not yet.

I was already planning my next move — quietly, methodically.
The knowledge burned in my gut:
They would erase the evidence if they could.
They would bury Madeline's death under layers of

procedure and polished language.
Unless I stopped them.
The decision didn't come in a dramatic burst of defiance.
It solidified in a slow, creeping certainty.
Not a theatrical revelation — but a quiet, internal shift.
A realignment of everything that mattered.
The sterile white of the hospital room, the cold gleam of the courthouse, the silent weight of Madeline's death — they all receded into a single, focused thought:
I would not be silent.
The fear remained — a cold knot twisting deep in my gut — but it no longer paralyzed me.
It was a dull ache now, a background hum to the insistent rhythm of my resolve.
The potential consequences loomed large.
I could see it all laid out before me:

- The loss of my job — almost a certainty given Falfor's power.
- The threats, subtle at first, then overt.
- The smear campaign — headlines dissecting my past, whispering accusations, twisting old scars into new weapons.

I saw the familiar tactics — the same ones I had once used to dismantle others — now sharpened against me.
My messy divorce, the deployments, the classified missions — all would be twisted, weaponized, distorted into shadows of doubt.
And my family...
My mother, weathered and proud, would carry the worry like another burden slung over her shoulders.

My young nieces would hear the whispered rumors, too young to understand, too old to be shielded completely.
The collateral damage terrified me.
But the alternative — silence — was even more unbearable.
If Falfor escaped justice, another Madeline would die.
And another.
And another.
It wouldn't end with a single death.
It never did.
The image of Madeline's lifeless eyes haunted me, an accusation I could never answer unless I fought.
It wasn’t just about punishing Falfor.
It was about sending a message — to every badge-wearing predator who thought power made them untouchable.
It was about protecting the next child before the bullet left the barrel.
My military training, once a source of conflict, now became my strength.
Discipline.
Planning.
Resilience.
I had survived worse than fear.
I had stood against greater odds.
This fight would be brutal — fought not with bullets and fire, but with evidence and truth.
But the battlefield was no less real.
Carolyn’s quiet presence beside me strengthened my resolve.
We had faced danger before, shoulder to shoulder.

This was different — more personal, more dangerous — but our bond had never been stronger.
And we weren't alone.

Kenneth Fitzgerald, the Assistant District Attorney assigned to the case, understood the stakes.
He knew the risk of challenging an entrenched system.
He saw what we saw — and he stood ready to fight, even if his support had to stay quiet for now.

The thought of facing Falfor in open court, of standing under oath while every part of my life was dissected and attacked, filled me with a sharp, honed apprehension.
But it was a controlled fear.
The kind that sharpened focus, not dulled it.
The kind that real soldiers lived by.

The decision to testify wasn't a choice anymore.
It was a commitment.
A vow.
A declaration of war — against injustice, against corruption, against the silencing of the innocent.
The long road ahead would be brutal.
The threats would come.
The isolation would come.
But I would stand.
For Madeline Clark.
For justice.
For the truth.
I was a soldier.

I was a Marshal.
I was a witness.
And I would not be silenced.

Securing Physical Evidence

The flashing lights of arriving police cars painted the night in a strobe-like frenzy, a stark contrast to the chilling stillness that had settled over the warehouse moments before.
The air hung heavy with the metallic tang of blood and the acrid bite of cordite, lingering ghosts of the violence that had stolen Madeline's life.
Chaos reigned — a maelstrom of uniformed officers, frantic EMTs, and the hushed whispers of onlookers.
Yet amidst the pandemonium, Carolyn and I moved with practiced efficiency.
Military instincts kicked in, clearing away the noise and panic.
This wasn't just a crime scene.
It was a battlefield.
And our mission was clear: secure the evidence before it vanished.
My heart hammered against my ribs, a relentless drumbeat against the backdrop of sirens.
But my movements were precise, deliberate.
I'd seen this before — the frantic rush, the hurried attempts to control the narrative, the subtle, insidious efforts to sanitize the scene.
This was a battle for the truth.

And the first fight was happening now.
Carolyn, her face set and grim, was already establishing a perimeter, her voice sharp enough to slice through the chaos.
She knew, as I did, that the first few minutes after a crime often decided whether justice lived or died.
I pulled my camera, documenting everything:
Madeline's position.
The blood spray pattern.
The angles.
The trajectories.
Each frame was deliberate; each shot a safeguard against the inevitable "lost evidence" or "misplaced files."
My experience as a Ranger — hours spent mapping hostile terrain — served me well now.
Different battlefield.
Same principles: observe, document, secure.

The forensic team arrived next, a welcome reinforcement.
They moved methodically, collecting trace evidence, swabbing surfaces, bagging fibers and microscopic clues.
I absorbed every detail, cataloguing it in my mind — not just as a witness, but as a soldier preparing for the next assault.
We weren't just documenting a murder.
We were building an unbreakable case.

The spent casing gleamed faintly on the concrete, a silent testament to Falfor's guilt.
I photographed it from every angle, then used sterile

forceps to lift it carefully into a pre-labeled evidence bag.
Initials.
Date.
Time.
Precise location.
Every detail meticulously logged.
It wasn't just about following procedure.
It was about honoring a silent promise — to Madeline, and to the principle that truth mattered.
Near Madeline's body, crumpled and stained, lay a small wad of cash.
The bribe.
The physical proof that tied Falfor's corruption to her death.
Carolyn secured it with remarkable calm, documenting the serial numbers, photographing every angle.
The forensic team would conduct deeper analysis later, but the evidence — the rot at the center of it all — was already captured.
Preserving the chain of custody became our next sacred task.
Every piece of evidence was logged, photographed, witnessed.
Every transfer recorded.
We could not allow a single crack for doubt to slip through.
Not in this battle.

The cold night air did nothing to cool the burning rage inside me.
This was more than a raid gone wrong.

This was a systematic attempt to bury a child's murder under layers of sanitized reports and whispered lies.
But not this time.
We were veterans of unseen wars, fighting battles that rarely made headlines.
And we were ready.

Beyond the physical evidence, we gathered witness statements with the same precision.
We interviewed the marshals involved, noting every hesitation, every inconsistency.
We listened carefully to the few civilian witnesses — their shaky voices offering slivers of truth the official reports would try to erase.
Each conversation, each recorded tone of voice, became another thread in a growing tapestry — a narrative of truth that could not easily be unraveled.

Hours melted into a blur of controlled activity.
The crime scene, once a chaotic mess, transformed into an organized space where every piece of evidence had a place, a record, a guardian.
By the time the first rays of dawn stretched across the sky, we had secured a mountain of evidence — enough to bring Falfor down.
But the war was far from over.
The courtroom battle would be brutal.
The pressure to conform would be immense.
The dangers real.
Yet with every carefully documented artifact, we chipped

away at the fortress of lies.
This was more than a case.
It was a battle for the soul of law enforcement itself.
And we had chosen our side.

Witness Interviews

The initial wave of chaos surrounding Madeline's death had subsided, replaced by a chilling quiet punctuated by the occasional click of a camera shutter.
The flashing lights had dimmed. The crowd had thinned.
But the real work was just beginning.
Securing the physical evidence was only half the battle.
The other — perhaps even more critical — half involved the witnesses.
Their testimonies could make or break the case.
And we knew Falfor's influence extended far beyond the warehouse walls.

Our first interviews were with the officers involved in the raid.
Sergeant Miller, his face etched with permanent weariness, went first.
His account was meticulously detailed — almost *too* detailed.
Carolyn and I exchanged a glance.
Miller described the events leading up to the shooting with the measured precision of a man delivering a memorized script.
Madeline Clark's presence was mentioned almost as an afterthought — her death framed as an unfortunate but unavoidable accident.

The sterile precision of his words raised more questions

than it answered.
We pressed him gently at first, then with increasing intensity, probing the inconsistencies, the too-perfect sequencing of events.
His gaze wavered.
The facade cracked.
Sweat beaded at his temple, his hands fidgeting.

Carolyn, ever the master observer, noted every tremor, every flicker of discomfort.
These weren't just words.
They were clues.

Next came Officer Davies, a young officer whose nervous energy filled the room.
His account was a jumbled mess — fragmented memories, glaring contradictions.
Unlike Miller, Davies wasn’t rehearsed.
He was terrified.
He stumbled through answers, contradicting himself, omitting key details.
It was clear he was being pressured.
We shifted tactics, softening our approach, offering reassurance instead of interrogation.
We emphasized his role in bringing justice, the importance of his voice.
Slowly, he opened up.
Davies spoke of whispered warnings among the officers, veiled threats, an ingrained culture of silence.
He revealed that he had seen Falfor take money before the

raid — but fear had kept him quiet.
His fear was still palpable.
But so was his need to be heard.

Civilian witnesses came next — a frail, frightened collection of bystanders caught in the crosshairs of a battle far larger than themselves.
Their accounts were varied. Fragmented. Often conflicting.
Their fear wasn't just about retribution.
It was deeper — a distrust of authority, carefully cultivated and painfully earned.

Mrs. Henderson, an elderly woman living across the street, provided a critical detail.
She claimed to have seen Falfor arguing with a young girl moments before the shooting.
A fact no one else had mentioned.
Premeditation.
Intent.
It was the crack we needed.
Mark Johnson, a young man with darting eyes and a defensive posture, proved more difficult.
He claimed to have seen nothing — despite being in a prime position.
We pressed him, but he remained evasive.
His fear was evident — not of us, but of the power that lurked in Falfor's shadow.

Each interview was a battle.
Each answer, a maneuver.
This wasn't just investigation.
It was psychological warfare.
We weren't just gathering statements.
We were fighting for the soul of the truth.

Carolyn and I leaned on every skill honed through years of military service and law enforcement experience — reading body language, applying pressure, offering empathy where needed, standing firm when necessary.
We were soldiers in a different kind of war — fighting not with weapons, but with words, with patience, with unrelenting resolve.

The day ended with a weary sense of accomplishment.
We had secured crucial testimonies — not perfect, not without gaps — but enough to add significant weight to the case against Falfor.
The system was rigged against us.
The fear was real.
The threats were coming.
But with each truth extracted from fear, each fracture exposed in the facade of silence, we moved closer to justice.
The battle was far from over.
But today — today, we had won a crucial ground.
And the war for Madeline's memory raged on.

Financial Records

The fluorescent lights hummed a monotonous tune in the dimly lit office — a far cry from the vibrant green fields surrounding my family's farm, a place where I usually found solace.
Here, the air hung heavy with stale coffee, exhaustion, and the unspoken weight of what we were about to attempt.
The physical evidence, the testimonies — they were pieces of the puzzle.
But the financial records...
The financial records held the key to understanding the full scale of Falfor's corruption.

Carolyn, pragmatic as ever, had secured a warrant.
Bank accounts.
Credit card statements.
Investment portfolios.
But gaining access to them was another battle altogether.
The first hurdle wasn't technical.
It was bureaucratic — a dense forest of red tape, deliberate misdirection, and stonewalling that slowed every step.
Requests were "lost" in the system.
Approvals were "pending" indefinitely.
Files arrived heavily redacted, pages blank but for legal headers.
Every delay screamed protection.
The system wasn't just slow; it was defending itself.
Carolyn, with her sharp legal mind, countered every obstruction with expert precision —

filing emergency motions, issuing subpoenas, invoking judicial oversight when necessary.
She was relentless — a bulldog gnawing at the machinery until it yielded, inch by agonizing inch.

Finally, after days of trench warfare through the administrative sludge, the dam broke.
The data arrived.
Not a simple spreadsheet —
but a massive, encrypted data dump.
Gigabytes of dense financial transactions, stretching across multiple banks, credit unions, offshore intermediaries, and "anonymous" investment funds.
It wasn't a ledger.
It was a labyrinth.

We dove in.
Every deposit, every withdrawal, every wire transfer had to be scrutinized — not just for irregularities, but for connections.
At first, it was all noise:

- Salary deposits.
- Mortgage payments.
- Grocery runs.

Normal. Boring. Clean.
Then the anomalies surfaced —
small irregularities at first, like static in an otherwise clear signal.

- Large cash deposits, unlinked to any stated income.
- Transfers routed through obscure third-party

processors.
- Withdrawals timed suspiciously close to major raids or operations Falfor had led.

Carolyn flagged each one, her cursor leaving digital scars across the case files.
The financial map started to take shape — and the picture was ugly.

Cross-referencing the bank activity with Falfor's credit card statements painted an even more damning portrait:

- Dinners at five-star restaurants.
- Shopping sprees at luxury boutiques.
- First-class airline tickets to "security conferences" that never existed.
- Hotels stay in cities where no official Marshal Service business had ever been scheduled.

Receipts listed absurdly lavish expenses — private wine tastings, bespoke suit fittings, yacht charters.
It was a lifestyle impossible to support on a Marshal's salary.
The math wasn't just suspicious — it was damning.

And then came the offshore accounts.
Buried under shell corporations, false addresses, and nominee directors, they were carefully constructed layers of misdirection.

But once we found the trail — a single misfiled corporate registration linking an account back to Falfor's known alias

— the house of cards started to collapse.
We uncovered a network of investments tied to known fronts for organized crime — laundering operations, smuggling groups, and black-market arms dealers.
The spiderweb of transactions stretched farther than we had imagined — implicating not just Falfor, but others.
Maybe others wearing badges.

Each revelation struck like a hammer blow.
This wasn't petty graft.
This was systemic corruption, industrial in scale, hidden behind a wall of financial opacity and institutional indifference.

We worked through the nights, fueled by adrenaline, bad coffee, and the relentless need to finish.
Specialized forensic software mapped the data visually — a sprawling digital spiderweb where every line between accounts pulsed with guilt.

- Central hubs revealed connections to shell companies.
- Tangles of transactions showed patterns of concealed movement.
- Link analysis illuminated names we recognized — and others we would need to.

The visual display on the monitor looked almost organic — a diseased organism growing unchecked inside the law.

We compiled the evidence meticulously:

- Timelines.

- Transaction logs.
- Anomalies highlighted and cross-referenced.

The final report wasn't just numbers.
It was a story.
A narrative of greed, betrayal, and criminal conspiracy woven into the very fabric of an agency sworn to uphold the law.
It laid bare not just Falfor's crimes —
but the system that had enabled him.

As dawn broke, casting a pale, cold light across the city, we closed the final case file.
Exhaustion threatened to flatten me, but the grim satisfaction was undeniable.
We had ripped the mask off Falfor's carefully constructed life.
We had pulled the thread that might unravel an entire network of corruption.

The battle was far from over.
Presenting this evidence in court would unleash a storm — not just from Falfor, but from everyone invested in keeping him untouchable.
But now, finally, we had weapons.
The financial records weren't just documents.
They were daggers —
each number, each line, sharpened into truth.
They told a story that could not be spun away or smothered in bureaucratic lies.

A story that would demand justice — for Madeline Clark, and for all the others who had been betrayed.
The war was just beginning.
And we were finally ready.

Building the Case

The digital spiderweb of Falfor's financial crimes, pulsing on Carolyn's screen, shimmered with malevolent complexity.
It was breathtaking — a meticulously woven tapestry of deceit, spanning offshore accounts, shell corporations, coded transactions, and hidden partnerships.
My military training, honed through years of strategic operations, now served a different war — the battle for truth.
Carolyn, with her encyclopedic legal mind and relentless determination, was the perfect counterpart.
Together, we became something greater than the sum of our skills — a force methodical, patient, and unstoppable.
We pieced together the fragments of Falfor's illicit empire, conneccting dots hidden beneath layers of obfuscation.
The large, unexplained deposits in his accounts weren't anomalies.
They were part of a larger machine — a carefully engineered river of dirty money flowing through false fronts.
Following the money trail, we uncovered businesses used as laundering stations — construction firms, logistics companies, nightclubs.

Every transaction uncovered a new layer of criminal enterprise:
drug trafficking, arms smuggling, human trafficking.
Each connection slammed into me like a jolt of adrenaline — a brutal reminder of the scale of corruption we were facing.
Falfor wasn't just another crooked lawman.
He was an operational node in a vast criminal syndicate.

Carolyn dissected every transaction with razor precision, spotting anomalies even the forensic software missed.
Patterns emerged:

- Payments disguised as "consulting fees."
- Transfers masked under corporate mergers.
- Shell corporations registered to dead addresses and fabricated directors.

One strand led to a major figure in the local construction industry — a man with deep political ties.
Falfor had steered lucrative city contracts his way, siphoning kickbacks disguised as business expenses.
Another strand unraveled into offshore accounts hidden behind three layers of shell corporations —
millions siphoned off into the Cayman Islands, Cyprus, and anonymous trusts in Luxembourg.
Using forensic software designed to track terrorist financing, we mapped the tangled flow:
accounts splitting into dozens, converging again, laundered and relaundered until the source blurred.
But we had the thread.
And we pulled.

The deeper we dug, the more sinister the picture became.
This wasn't amateur hour.
Falfor's financial network rivaled those we had seen during counterinsurgency operations abroad.
He had spent years perfecting it — a fortress of deception guarded by layers of false legitimacy.
And yet, we were dismantling it, piece by piece.
The system fought back.
Subtle at first —
missing documents, encrypted files suddenly corrupted, witnesses growing silent overnight.
But as we closed in, the pressure escalated:
sideways glances in the courthouse halls, cryptic warnings left on voicemail, surveillance cars lingering too long near the farm.
We were getting too close.
And they knew it.

Carolyn, unshaken, navigated the legal labyrinth like a veteran general — turning every bureaucratic delay into a legal weapon, every roadblock into evidence of obstruction.
Her network of legal contacts — honest judges, old allies — became our hidden arsenal.
Together, we outmaneuvered them.
Every move forward was a battle won.

But the emotional toll mounted.
The image of Madeline's lifeless body was never far from my mind, a ghost at the edge of every late night, every caffeine-fueled breakthrough.

The stakes were more than professional.
They were personal.
Each discovery — each wire transfer tied to crime, each corrupt official exposed — wasn't just evidence.
It was an act of defiance against the machine that had stolen her life.
And we would not stop.
As the final pieces fell into place, the shape of the case became undeniable.
A financial empire rooted in blood and betrayal.
An infrastructure of corruption that reached higher than we dared to guess.
And then, the final weapon arrived.
An anonymous package, delivered without return address, untraceable.
Inside: a flash drive.
And on it — a recorded phone call.
Falfor's voice.
Clear, cold, deliberate.
Discussing the payoffs.
The raids used as smokescreens.
The murders arranged to silence loose ends.
And worst of all —
speaking candidly with a senior official inside the Marshals Service. Not just corruption. Conspiracy.
At the highest levels.
The implications were staggering.
This wasn't just about Falfor anymore.
This was systemic.
A cancer at the heart of the institution we had sworn to

defend.
The case we had built — the digital maps, the financial trails, the testimonies, the buried transactions — was airtight.
The leaked recording turned it from strong to lethal.
We weren't just bringing down a corrupt Marshal.
We were about to tear the lid off an empire of rot.
The weight of it pressed against my chest —
the knowledge of what came next:
retaliation, betrayal, danger.
But with it came certainty.
We had truth on our side.
And we had no intention of backing down.
The battle wasn't over.
It was just beginning.

Return to the Farm

The sun was low over the rolling hills as I pulled into the long gravel drive, the familiar creak of the gate welcoming me home.

The farmhouse — white paint peeling in spots, porch light buzzing faintly — stood like a stubborn monument to another world, one untouched by city corruption or whispered threats.

At least, it used to be.

Now, even here, the shadows felt longer.

Mom was waiting on the porch, arms crossed, apron dusted with flour from whatever project I had interrupted.

She was a small woman, wiry and tough, with sharp blue eyes that had seen too much to be easily fooled.

Her gaze fixed on me, reading the exhaustion in my shoulders, the grim set of my jaw.

Behind her, my brothers — Thomas and Daniel — hovered like twin sentries, boots scuffing the old wood, their lean frames tense beneath work shirts still stained from the day's labor.

For a moment, no one spoke.

Then Mom's voice broke the silence.

"*You're in trouble, aren't you, Laila*?"

It wasn't a question.

It was a verdict.

Inside, the farmhouse smelled of fresh bread and woodsmoke — but the warmth couldn't quite push back the cold knot tightening in my chest.
Over steaming mugs of coffee, I laid it out for them — not everything, but enough:

- The raid gone wrong.
- Madeline's death.
- The corruption tied to Falfor.
- The investigation Carolyn and I had launched.
- The evidence we had gathered.
- And now, the threats — escalating from whispers to silent warnings left too close to home.

I watched the weight of it settle on them — saw it in the way Thomas's hands clenched around his mug, in the way Daniel's knee bounced under the table, in the way Mom's mouth pressed into a hard, thin line.

"They came by the other night," Daniel muttered, voice low.
I stiffened.
"Who?"
He shrugged, but it wasn't casual.
Nothing about him was casual now.
"Black SUV. Tinted windows. Drove slow past the house around midnight. Twice."
"Nobody we recognized," Thomas added grimly. "Too clean. No plates."
Mom said nothing, just stared into her coffee, the knuckles of her hands white against the ceramic.
I felt the ground shift beneath me — the realization sinking

deeper:
They weren't just threatening *me*.

They were threatening *them*.

"I should leave," I said, pushing the words out before I could second-guess them.
"If I'm not here, they'll have no reason to—"
Mom's hand came down on mine, firm as steel.
"You are *not* running, Laila Aurora Wright," she said sharply.
"Not from them. Not from anyone."
Her voice was low but fierce — the same voice that had soothed skinned knees and defied debt collectors and bureaucrats with equal fury.
"We raised you to stand," she said.
"We knew what kind of woman you were growing up to be. We're not afraid of these bastards."
Daniel leaned forward, elbows on the scarred table.
"We can handle a few threats."
His smile was humorless. "Not the first time someone thought we were easy pickings."
Thomas cracked his knuckles, a sound like gunfire in the quiet room.
"They want a fight?" he said, voice even. "They'll regret bringing it to this door."
I looked at them — my family — and something burned in my throat.

Not fear.

Not guilt.
Pride.
Pride — and the terrible knowledge that no matter how tough they were, no matter how ready, they were now targets in a war they hadn't chosen.
And I had brought it to their doorstep.

Later, as I stood on the porch under the rising stars, Mom joined me, her arms wrapped in an old quilt against the night chill.
"They'll come," she said simply.
I nodded.
"We'll be ready," she added.
And somehow, that simple certainty — delivered without bravado, without fear — steadied me more than any tactical plan ever could.
I wasn't alone.
And when the next battle came —
because it *would* come —
we would face it together.
The quiet hum of the refrigerator in my farmhouse kitchen was a stark contrast to the storm brewing outside — a storm that mirrored the turmoil building inside me.
The investigation into Dominic Falfor's crimes had moved far beyond paperwork and courtrooms.
Now, it was a matter of survival.
The early warnings — misplaced files, hushed courthouse whispers — had mutated into something darker.
The air itself crackled with menace.
It started small.

One evening, while watering the tomato plants, I spotted a beat-up pickup rattling down the long driveway — a stranger behind the wheel, hidden beneath the brim of a weathered cap.

He stopped at the edge of the yard, staring.

Saying nothing.

Daring me to flinch.

I didn't.

But when he finally turned and drove off, the sense of violation lingered long after the taillights faded into the dusk.

Carolyn, ever the pragmatist, moved into action.

Security cameras.

Motion sensors.

Steel-reinforced locks.

Together with my brothers, Daniel and Thomas, we turned the farm into a fortress — hardening the perimeter, documenting every incident, every sign that danger was drawing closer.

The farm, once a sanctuary, now felt like the first line of a battlefield.

The threats escalated.

Late-night phone calls filled with heavy breathing — guttural, rhythmic, designed to mimic the psychological warfare techniques I had been trained to endure.

Calculated, deliberate intimidation, engineered to gnaw at the edges of my focus.

Then came the anonymous packages —
each one containing a single wilted flower.

A quiet but devastating echo of Madeline.

Carolyn cataloged everything meticulously — timestamps, delivery routes, witness statements.
Every threat was evidence.
Every taunt, a nail in Falfor's coffin.
Surveillance footage caught a black sedan lurking at the edge of the property, hidden beneath the skeletal shadows of the tree line.
Too careful.
Too familiar.
They weren't just watching.
They were hunting.
Carolyn urged me to seek police protection.
I resisted at first — instinctively mistrusting the very system we were exposing.
But the threats grew too bold, too direct to ignore.
Daniel and Thomas, furious but practical, insisted on moving Mom off the property — over her protests — to a safer location until this was over.
Watching her leave, small but unbowed, broke something deep inside me.
I had brought this war home.
Detective Miller was assigned to our case — a weary man with eyes too tired to fully trust.
He listened to our report of threats and sabotage with professional detachment, promising to increase patrols.
But beneath the polite words, I sensed his hesitation.
Reluctance.

The quiet rot of a system trying not to see what it didn't want to admit.

The pressure didn't ease.
The calls intensified — vulgar, threatening.
Notes scrawled across my windshield.
Messages slipped under my door.
Each act of harassment felt less like intimidation — and more like a prelude to violence.
The night before we were scheduled to testify, it happened.
The sharp, crystalline sound of shattering glass yanked me awake — primal adrenaline flooding my system.
I crept to the window, heart pounding, and glimpsed a car's headlights disappearing into the night.
The damage was unmistakable:
A large window near the porch, shattered inward — glass sparkling across the wooden floorboards like spilled ice.
A warning, clear and final.
This was no longer a game.
We called Miller again.
This time, he arrived quickly — no detachment now, only the grim acknowledgement that something serious was underway.
The attack changed everything.
Even the skeptics could no longer pretend this was coincidence or paranoia.
We were targets.
And we were out of time.
The next morning, as dawn barely grayed the sky, Carolyn and I stood together at the foot of the courthouse steps.
The building loomed ahead of us — cold, impassive, indifferent.
My heart hammered against my ribs, the ghosts of fear and

resolve warring inside me.
We had the truth.
We had the evidence.
We had the courage.
And we had no intention of backing down.
This wasn't just a trial.
It was a war for the soul of the system itself.
And we were walking into it with eyes wide open.
Ready for whatever came next.

Escape and Reflection...

The old farmhouse stood silent against the encroaching Pennsylvania twilight, a stubborn sentinel in a world that seemed increasingly hostile.
Inside, the air was thick with the scent of woodsmoke and simmering coffee — comforting scents, but they could not mask the sharp undercurrent of fear that clung to my skin.
The farm, once a haven of childhood memories, now felt like a fortress under siege.
The rhythmic tick-tock of the grandfather clock in the hallway marked time with a slow, inexorable patience — a patience I no longer possessed.

I had come here seeking refuge —

a brief escape from the relentless pressure of the Falfor case, from the escalating threats that shadowed my every step.
The rolling hills, the scent of growing things, the soft whisper of the fields — they should have been a balm to my battered soul.
But instead, the peace felt fragile, brittle — a quiet veneer stretched thin over something raw and violent.
The isolation that once comforted now unsettled me.
Every rustle in the trees, every distant howl of a coyote, sent adrenaline lancing through me.
My military instincts, once dormant, were now always just beneath the surface — primed, ready.

Days bled into nights in a monotonous rhythm.
Farm chores offered some anchor —
feeding chickens, checking fences, weeding the stubborn flowerbeds.
Each task a whisper of normalcy in the rising tide of chaos.
Yet under the routine, anxiety thrummed constantly —
a low, electric hum I could never fully silence.

Carolyn's voice crackling through late-night phone calls became my lifeline.
Updates on the case.

Reports of new threats.
Her voice, steady even across the static, was a reminder that I wasn't fighting alone — even when the walls around me felt impossibly far apart.
One afternoon, while clearing an overgrown bed near the porch, my hand brushed against something solid beneath the earth.
A weathered, leather-bound journal.
My grandmother's.
I barely remembered her — only fragments — but as I turned the brittle pages, I found more than family records.
I found stories of battles fought in silence.
Of standing against injustice, even when it cost her dearly.
Of fear, and loss, and defiance written in a careful, looping script.
Her words were a lifeline across decades —
a reminder that resilience ran in my blood.
The farm hadn't just raised crops.
It had raised fighters.
The nights were the hardest.
The farmhouse, strong though it was, felt vulnerable in the dark —
a single light against a sea of black.
Sleep came fitfully, haunted by nightmares:
Madeline's still eyes.
Falfor's sneering grin.
The anonymous threats that seemed to grow

bolder with every passing hour.
I started carrying again —
the heavy weight of the sidearm at my thigh a cold, grim comfort.
A necessity.
A reminder.
And then, one night, the silence shattered.
A series of sharp bangs ripped through the quiet.
I froze, adrenaline surging.
Weapon in hand, I crept to the window.
A car — headlights off — peeled away down the dirt road, its taillights a dying ember in the night.
I sprinted outside, heart hammering against my ribs.
The barn door hung ajar, the lock twisted and broken.
Inside, nothing was taken.
Nothing vandalized.
It wasn't robbery.
It was a message.
A clear, brutal statement:
We can reach you anytime.
Fury eclipsed fear.
This was my home.
My family's legacy.
They had trespassed against something far deeper than land or walls.
They had violated the sanctuary generations

had built with their bare hands.
I called Carolyn immediately.
My voice shook with rage — but not weakness.
Together, we planned.
Hardening defenses. Upgrading surveillance.
Reinforcing every vulnerable point.
The farm became a fortress —
a visible testament that we would not be intimidated.
The days that followed were tense but purposeful.
Every new sensor, every floodlight installed, was an act of defiance.
They would not break me.
Not here.
Not ever.
The farmhouse had changed.
It was no longer simply a place of memory and peace.
It was a front line.
The contrast between the beauty of the hills and the violence that threatened them sharpened my resolve.
The serenity outside masked a growing war within.
And I was ready.
The farm, like me, had weathered storms before.
It would survive this one too.

The fight ahead would be brutal.
But so was I.
And the storm that raged inside me was only just beginning.

.

Chapter 3

Family History

The worn leather-bound journal lay open on the kitchen table, its brittle pages illuminated by the warm, flickering glow of a kerosene lamp.

I traced the faded script with my fingertip, the ink smudging slightly under my touch — as if the past itself were bleeding into the present.

The handwriting was elegant yet strong — a mirror of the woman who had written it.

Elara Wright.

My grandmother.

A figure I had known only through old photographs and whispered stories.

Until now.

The entries were not dated in tidy order, but flowed in an unbroken stream of thought — like the rhythm of the farm itself.

Seasons.

Storms.

Plantings and harvests.

At first glance, it seemed a simple chronicle of rural life.

But woven beneath the mundane details was a quiet, fierce struggle —

a life lived on the edge of survival and defiance.

Elara wrote of the Great Depression:
of debts that crushed families, of storms that stripped the land bare, of neighbors who lost everything.
She documented it all — not with despair, but with a steely resilience that leapt off the pages.
She fought for fair prices for her crops, battled corrupt brokers who tried to shortchange small farmers, organized collective actions when authorities ignored their pleas.
She had been a warrior —
quiet, uncelebrated —
but a warrior all the same.
The parallels to my own fight were impossible to ignore.
Midway through the journal, the tone shifted.
She began writing about "the outsiders" —
businessmen and officials who came with promises, waving contracts and legalese like weapons.
Elara warned of the dangers of trusting those who wore respectability like a mask.
She spoke of underhanded deals, bought sheriffs, land stolen under the guise of progress.
One entry chilled me:
"The ones with power do not fear truth. They fear the ones who survive long enough to *tell* it."
It was more than a reflection.
It was a warning.
And a call to arms.

Tucked between pages, pressed flowers marked the turning points:

- A sprig of goldenrod, fragile but defiant, alongside a description of a legal battle she fought — and lost — but refused to forget.
- A violet, delicate and persistent, marking the death of a beloved friend who had dared to speak out against corruption and paid dearly.

Each flower was a memorial.

Each entry, a manifesto.

As I read, the farm itself transformed in my mind.

It wasn't just fields and barns.

It was *history embodied* —

a living testament to battles fought and sacrifices made by hands now long gone.

Elara's words were not relics.

They were a survival manual.

Near the final pages, her entries grew sparse, the handwriting shaky.

Her health had been failing.

But even as her body weakened, her spirit blazed undimmed.

"Protect the land," she wrote.

"Protect the truth. Protect each other. There is no other way."

And in the last entry, scrawled in a hand that trembled but never faltered:

"When the wolves come, do not hide. Meet them at the gate."

I sat back, closing the journal with reverence, my fingers lingering on the cracked leather cover.
Tears blurred my vision — not from sorrow, but from a fierce, blazing pride.
This fight against Falfor — against the rot infecting the system —
was not just *my* fight.
It was my inheritance.
The blood in my veins, the soil beneath my feet, the stubborn lines etched into my family's history — all of it called me forward.
The farm was no longer a refuge.
It was a fortress.
And I would meet the wolves —
not with fear,
but with the fire of every Wright who had come before me.
The journal was not just memory.
It was strategy.
It was warning.
And it was a promise:
We survive. We fight. We endure.
No matter what storms may come.

The old farmhouse, worn by time but unbowed, stood sentinel against the deepening Pennsylvania twilight — its windows glowing like quiet beacons in the encroaching dark.

Here, the relentless ticking of courtroom clocks, the threat of shadows lurking at every turn, seemed to soften into something distant and small.

Here, at least for a time, Laila Wright could breathe.

Inside, warmth wrapped itself around her like an old quilt.

Sarah — a family friend, a newly minted nurse with a boundless heart and a wicked sense of humor — burst into the kitchen carrying a mug of chamomile tea and a plate piled with blueberry muffins.

"You look like hell," Sarah announced cheerfully, shoving the plate toward Laila. "Eat. Hydrate. Pretend the world doesn't suck for twenty minutes."

Laila chuckled, the sound unfamiliar in her own throat.

Sarah's presence — vibrant, grounding — was a balm against the endless cynicism and fear that had defined her days.

Here, with her, the world narrowed to something manageable.

To tea. To muffins. To simple kindness.

"How's it look?" Sarah asked, her voice casual but edged with concern.

Laila hesitated, weighing what she could safely share.

The details — the rot embedded in the Marshal's Service, the cold terror of Madeline Clark's death, the grinding machine of corruption — felt too toxic to bring here.

"Another long day," she said simply, managing a half-smile.

"But I'm home now."

Sarah nodded, understanding without pressing.

She turned the conversation toward lighter things — her move to Philadelphia, the mess of job hunting, her dreams of someday opening a community clinic, hopefully marrying Thomas.

It was a deliberate lifeline, and Laila clung to it.

Eleanor Wright, Laila's mother — a woman forged by hardship but softened by fierce love — joined them, drying her hands on a kitchen towel.

She said nothing at first, simply enfolding Laila in a hug that spoke volumes.

Strength.

Faith.

Unspoken understanding.

Dinner was simple: roast chicken, mashed potatoes, green beans snapped fresh that morning.

The conversation flowed easily — neighbor gossip, the upcoming county fair, the stubbornness of the new calf born last week.
Ordinary things.
Normal things.
Each small story weaving a fragile cocoon around Laila's battered spirit.
For the first time in days, she tasted food without feeling it catch in her throat.
Later, as the stars stitched themselves across the darkening sky, Laila and her mother sat by the fire —
two women bound by blood and battle scars, separated by years but united by resilience.
The crackle of the flames filled the comfortable silence between them.
Finally, Eleanor spoke, her voice low and sure:
"Your grandmother would be proud of you."
The simple words hit harder than any speech could have.
Laila blinked back the sudden sting in her eyes.
Eleanor's gaze stayed fixed on the fire, her hands cradling a steaming mug like an anchor.
"She fought her battles, same as you. Quietly. Fiercely. Without letting the world turn her hard."

A pause, heavy with memory.
"She didn't just survive, Laila. She made this place — this family — strong enough to weather storms you haven't even seen yet."
The weight of it — the pride, the legacy, the fierce, enduring love — settled in Laila's chest like bedrock.

The days that followed carved new routines:

Sarah's bright chatter filled the mornings, playful and fierce —
a constant reminder that hope wasn't naïve.
It was necessary.
Eleanor, quiet and steadfast, wove stability through the fabric of each day —
baking, tending, reminding Laila without words that strength sometimes wore an apron and smelled of fresh bread. Daniel, Laila's oldest brother — all quiet competence and steady hands — picked up the slack without complaint.
He kept the farm running like clockwork, handling chores, dealing with town matters, ensuring she could focus fully on the case.
His loyalty was silent but unshakable — a shield she hadn't realized how much she needed.
Even Simon, the faithful golden retriever,

seemed to station himself wherever Laila was, a silent sentinel against nightmares and despair. His head in her lap, his steady breathing — an unspoken oath that she wasn't fighting alone. The farm wasn't just land.
It was a living tapestry woven from stubbornness, love, sacrifice, and defiance.
It anchored her.
It reminded her who she was —
and who she was fighting for.
Madeline Clark. Justice. Legacy. The farmhouse walls whispered strength.
The soil held generations of grit and blood and stubborn dreams.
Laila inhaled it.
Let it fortify the cracks inside her.
She wasn't just a Marshal preparing a case.
She was a daughter of this land.
A Wright. A fighter.
And the wolves who had come for her had badly misjudged what it meant to stand against a family built to survive storms.
The battle ahead would be brutal.
But Laila A. Wright —
armed with truth, anchored by love, armored by generations —
was ready for everything.

Strategic Planning.

The crisp morning air bit at Laila's cheeks as she walked the perimeter of the sprawling farm, the dew-kissed grass cool beneath her bare feet.

The rhythmic crunch of dried leaves was a steady, grounding counterpoint to the storm brewing inside her.

The farm — her sanctuary — felt different today.

Charged.

Tense.

The looming trial against Dominic Falfor was a guillotine suspended above her, its blade poised, its shadow stretching long and cold across her life.

She paused beneath the old oak tree, its gnarled arms outstretched toward the pale autumn sky.

Leaning into the rough bark, she closed her eyes and let the farm breathe with her — the scent of damp earth, the distant hum of crickets, the whisper of wind across the fields.

Here, away from courthouse corridors and media clamor, her mind sharpened.

The farm's isolation was no longer just comfort.

It was advantage.

She built the case in her mind like a tactical grid:

- The sequence of the raid.
- The forensic reports.
- The shattered timeline of lies Falfor had constructed.
- The witnesses, the bribes, the cold-eyed execution of a child.

Each fact, each flaw, was mapped, interrogated, weaponized.

Carolyn Pryme's testimony would be a keystone.
Laila replayed their conversations, analyzing every word, every nuance — building a strategy to protect Carolyn on the stand.
She rehearsed counterattacks against the defense's inevitable attempts to discredit them:

- Emotional instability?
- Personal vendetta?
- Insubordination?

She would be ready for every angle, every insinuation.
Carolyn's truth would not be twisted into weakness.

Kenneth Fitzgerald, the ADA, was another critical factor.
He was a man of battered integrity, fighting an uphill battle in a system designed to protect its predators.
Laila rehearsed their strategy sessions in her mind:
the evidence presentation, the critical points, the emotional arcs the jury needed to feel — not just understand.
They needed not a cold recitation of facts.
They needed a story.
A story of betrayal, corruption, and the brutal murder of a child.
A story with no room for doubt.

Days blurred into nights.
Laila pored over reports until her vision blurred — tracing

trajectories, cataloging inconsistencies, memorizing every microscopic detail.

Visualization techniques from her Ranger days returned with force.

She staged mock interrogations against herself, anticipating every cruel trick the defense might use.

She hardened her answers, her posture, her voice — until not even the most brutal cross-examination could crack her resolve.

And all the while, the farm worked with her.

The cycle of planting, tending, harvesting mirrored the building of her case.

Each seed planted was a piece of evidence buried deep.

Each weed pulled was a lie uprooted.

Each stubborn, hard-earned sprout was a truth pushing through hostile soil.

The farm wasn't a background.

It was an ally.

A fortress.

A living reminder of patience, resilience, and inevitability.

At night, beneath a sky thick with stars, Laila wrestled with doubt and fear.

The stakes clawed at her.

Failure meant more than losing a case.

It meant legitimizing the corruption, erasing Madeline's life, emboldening the wolves that prowled unchecked through the halls of justice.

Failure was not an option.

Her strategy crystallized:

- Anchor her testimony to hard, verifiable facts.
- Frame the emotional truth without appearing unstable.
- Anticipate and neutralize every character attack.
- Expose Falfor's greed, brutality, and cowardice with surgical precision.

She would not plead. She would not beg.
She would *demonstrate* — clearly, methodically — that the truth, once seen, could not be unseen.
The farm's silent strength poured into her.
The weathered walls. The stubborn soil.
The memory of ancestors who had survived wars, depressions, betrayals of their own.
Laila Aurora Wright would walk into that courtroom carrying not just evidence —
but generations of unbroken will.
The battle ahead would be vicious.
The enemy entrenched, desperate, and dangerous.
But Laila was ready.
Her strategy was honed.
Her resolve, tempered.
And the truth — ancient, patient, relentless — was on her side.
The soil beneath her feet, the blood in her veins, the fire in her chest —
all carried the same promise:
'We survive. We fight. We endure. And we *Win!*'

Preparing for Court...

The weight of the impending trial settled on Laila like a physical burden, a constant pressure in her chest. The farm, usually a haven, felt less like a sanctuary and more like a staging ground for an imminent battle. She wasn't just preparing a testimony; she was preparing herself, fortifying her mental and emotional defenses against the onslaught she knew was coming. The meticulous planning of her farming activities – the careful planting, the patient tending, the methodical harvesting – had become a mirror to her strategic preparation for the trial. Each seed sown, each crop nurtured, reflected the meticulous attention she paid to every detail of the case.

She spent hours poring over the transcripts of Falfor's interrogation, searching for inconsistencies, for subtle hesitations or evasions that betrayed his lies. Her military training, honed over years of rigorous discipline, served her well. She meticulously noted the discrepancies between his statements and the physical evidence, the subtle shifts in his body language, the micro-expressions that flickered across his face – fleeting betrayals of his inner turmoil. These were not just observations; they were pieces of a puzzle, fragments of a narrative that she would weave into a compelling case against him.

Carolyn's testimony was a cornerstone of the prosecution's strategy. Laila knew the defense would target Carolyn, attempting to undermine her credibility through aggressive cross-examination. They would try to portray her as emotionally unstable, unreliable, or biased. Laila had anticipated this. She spent countless hours with Carolyn, preparing her for the relentless assault that would come. They practiced responses to potential questions, rehearsing scenarios, anticipating every possible angle of attack. Laila helped Carolyn to articulate her experience, to convey the horror she had witnessed, the fear she had felt, in a calm, clear, and convincing manner. She instilled in Carolyn the confidence she needed to withstand the pressure, to stand firm in her account of the events.

But Laila's preparation went beyond simply bolstering Carolyn's testimony. She had to anticipate the defense's strategy as a whole, predicting their lines of questioning, their attempts to discredit her and the other witnesses. She meticulously charted the potential arguments, planning her responses with surgical precision. She was not just presenting facts; she was constructing a narrative, a story that would resonate with the jury on both an emotional and logical level. She knew the power of storytelling, the ability to connect with people on a human level, to move them beyond cold, hard facts.

The isolation of the farm, initially a source of solace, became a crucible where she forged her mental strength. She employed visualization techniques, honed during her years in the Rangers, creating mental simulations of the courtroom, picturing herself under the intense scrutiny of the defense attorney. She rehearsed her answers, adjusting her tone, her posture, her expressions, until her responses flowed effortlessly, confidently, and without hesitation. The solitude allowed her to delve into the deeper aspects of the case, the nuances, the subtle implications that others might miss.

The nights were a battleground within, a constant struggle against self-doubt and the crushing weight of responsibility. She fought against the fear that gnawed at her, the anxiety that threatened to overwhelm her. Yet, in the stillness of the night, surrounded by the familiar comfort of her home, she found the strength to persevere, to fight for the truth, for justice, for Madeline Clark. The image of Madeline's innocent face, her life cut short so cruelly, fueled her resolve, burned away her doubts, and hardened her determination.

She found unexpected allies in the mundane tasks of farm life. The rhythmic planting of seeds, the careful weeding, the meticulous harvesting – these repetitive actions became a form of meditation, a way to channel her energy, to focus her mind, to quiet the chaos within. The farm itself became a symbol of resilience, a testament to the enduring power of life amidst adversity. The cyclical nature of farm life, the constant cycle of growth, decay, and renewal, mirrored the ebb and flow of the legal battle ahead.

Laila's strategy was multifaceted. She would focus not only on the hard facts – the bribe, the murder, the witness testimony – but also on the human element of the case. She would paint a picture of Falfor, not merely as a criminal, but as a man devoid of empathy, a man who had betrayed his oath, his conscience, and his humanity. She would show the jury the callous indifference in his eyes, the chilling lack of remorse in his actions.

She anticipated the defense's attempts to

portray her as biased, emotionally unstable, or even vengeful. She had prepared for this, crafting counterarguments that were both logically sound and emotionally compelling. She would acknowledge her own experiences, her own vulnerabilities, but she would not allow them to be used against her. She would maintain her composure, her professionalism, her unwavering focus on the truth.

The farmhouse became more than just a physical location; it was a strategic command center, a place of planning, preparation, and reflection. It was here, amidst the quiet beauty of the countryside, that Laila forged her armor, not of steel, but of unwavering determination, sharpened intellect, and unyielding resolve. The farm was her ally, her sanctuary, the foundation upon which she would build her victory. The soil of the farm, rich and fertile, nurtured not only the crops but also the seeds of justice she was about to sow in the courtroom. She was ready. The time for planting was over; the time for harvest had arrived. The morning of the trial dawned cold and sharp, the kind of morning that seeped into your bones and sharpened every sense. Laila stood at the edge of the farm's long gravel driveway, the horizon blushing pink and gold, her Marshal's badge clipped firmly to her belt.

A faint mist clung to the fields behind her, veiling the familiar landscape in an eerie quiet that mirrored the gravity of the day ahead.
She loaded her duffel into the back of her government-issued SUV, double-checked the holster under her jacket, and ran her fingers once more over the stack of trial materials riding shotgun. The procedural check — gear, badge, weapon, evidence — steadied her. Each action reinforced a sense of control she knew she would need once the courtroom doors closed behind her.
The drive into the city was uneventful but heavy. She watched the fields give way to suburbs, and suburbs yield to the dense urban heart where the courthouse loomed like a fortress. Her mind drifted occasionally, despite her discipline — flashes of Madeline's lifeless body, the look in Falfor's eyes, the quiet rage she had spent months compressing into something that wouldn't burn her alive.
She parked in a secured lot two blocks from the courthouse. As she stepped out, the weight of public expectation hit her full in the chest — not just justice for Madeline, but justice for every betrayal that men like Falfor represented. She adjusted her jacket, squared her shoulders, and began the walk toward the battle that would define her future.
Courtroom Arrival.

The courthouse loomed ahead, a hulking mass of gray stone against the steel-colored sky. Its broad marble steps, worn smooth by decades of footfalls, stretched before her like a battlefield lined with silent witnesses. Laila tightened her grip on the leather briefcase in her hand, the cold air cutting through her coat as she mounted the first step. Reporters clustered behind barricades across the plaza, their cameras snapping and microphones bobbing in the air like predatory birds scenting blood. She ignored them, her gaze fixed straight ahead, every step deliberate. Inside those walls, Dominic Falfor waited, shielded by a wall of expensive lawyers and institutional rot. But Laila felt no hesitation as she climbed. She carried something far more potent than influence or wealth. She carried the truth. And she would deliver it, no matter the cost. The heavy oak doors creaked open as Laila pushed through, stepping into the cavernous main hall. The fluorescent lights buzzed overhead, casting a sterile glare over the polished floors and the long security checkpoint manned by stone-faced deputies. She moved with mechanical precision — coat off, belt removed, boots slipping through the scanner — her every motion rehearsed in countless airports and warzones. The deputies watched her closely, some with polite detachment, others with a wariness that made her skin prickle. She knew better than to expect allies here. Not all the enemies wore different uniforms. Some hid behind badges. Beyond security, the familiar hush of the courthouse wrapped around her — a silence broken only by the occasional squeak of shoes on linoleum and the distant murmur of legal arguments behind closed doors. Laila adjusted the strap of her briefcase and turned down the hall, her boots striking the floor in slow, deliberate beats. Courtroom Three loomed at the end of the corridor, its heavy double doors closed but humming with tension. She could feel it — the gathering storm, the crackling anticipation of a battle about to be joined. Her throat tightened slightly, but she pushed the nerves down. She had walked into worse arenas than this. She was a soldier before she was a witness. And today, she would fight like both.

The doors opened as she approached, a bailiff holding them wide. Laila stepped inside. The room was stark — pale wood benches, high ceilings, the judge's bench raised like a throne overlooking the battlefield. Her gaze swept the room, locking instantly onto the cluster of men seated at the defense table. Dominic Falfor sat at the center, flanked by his legal team. His posture was relaxed, almost lazy, but his eyes — cold, calculating — found her immediately. For a heartbeat, the noise of the room dimmed, the world narrowing to a razor-thin line between them. He smiled then, slow and mocking, the barest twitch of amusement playing at the corner of his mouth. It was not the smile of an innocent man. It was the smile of a predator who believed the hunt was already over. The heavy double doors at the rear of the courtroom swung open with a solemn creak, and the chatter among the spectators died instantly. Every head turned as Judge Meredith Harlan entered, her black robe billowing slightly with each deliberate step. She was a woman of formidable presence, her sharp gray eyes scanning the room with the quiet authority of someone who had long ago mastered the art of command. The bailiff called the court to order with a brisk, "All rise," and the room obediently stood, the scrape of chairs and shuffle of feet sounding almost like a military drill. Judge Harlan ascended the bench without a word, her gavel striking once against the block — a sound that cracked through the charged air like a starter pistol. "You may be seated," she said, her voice steady, no-nonsense, and unmistakably in control. With the court now officially in session, the battle Laila had been preparing for had begun. The murmur of the courtroom settled into a taut silence as Judge Harlan adjusted her glasses and glanced briefly at the docket. Without ceremony, she shifted her piercing gaze toward the prosecution's table — toward Laila.

"Marshal Wright," the judge said evenly. "You are here under subpoena to provide direct testimony relating to the interrogation of the defendant. You have reviewed the terms of your appearance?"

"Yes, Your Honor," Laila replied, her voice firm but respectful. She remained standing, aware that every movement she made — every breath — was being scrutinized by opposing counsel, by the press huddled in the gallery, by the families sitting stiff-backed behind the barriers.

Judge Harlan gave a slight nod before turning her attention to the defense table, where Falfor sat in a tailored gray suit, his face carefully composed into a mask of injured dignity. His lawyer, a slick operator named Jasper Reeves, whispered something into his ear. Falfor didn't react, only stared ahead, expressionless.

The judge leaned back slightly. "Proceed with opening statements," she said.

The lead prosecutor, Assistant U.S. Attorney Dana Morris, rose smoothly to her feet. She moved with the cool confidence of someone who knew she held a blade sharp enough to cut through lies, but also knew the importance of patience before the first stroke.

"Ladies and gentlemen of the jury," Morris began, her voice measured and clear, "this case is not about technicalities. It's not about mistakes made in good faith. It is about a calculated betrayal — a law enforcement official who violated his oath, corrupted his badge, and cost an innocent woman her life."

As Morris spoke, Laila kept her expression neutral. Inside, though, her muscles coiled with controlled energy. She could feel Falfor's eyes flick toward her now and again — quick, assessing glances — and she met them once, briefly, offering him nothing but the cold professionalism he had once mocked.

Morris continued, laying out the facts: Falfor's unauthorized surveillance operations, the tampering with evidence, the intimidation of witnesses. Each statement built upon the last, weaving a tight net that would be difficult for the defense to unravel.

When the prosecution rested, the judge gave a sharp nod to the defense table.

Jasper Reeves rose, buttoned his jacket with an exaggerated calmness, and offered the jury a rueful smile. "You will hear a lot of harsh words over the next few days," he said. "But you will also come to understand that this case is built on assumptions, misunderstandings, and, frankly, on a vendetta."

Laila didn’t flinch. She knew what was coming. Character attacks, twisted narratives, implied incompetence. It was all part of the strategy: make the witnesses doubt themselves, make the jury doubt the witnesses.

Her turn on the stand was approaching, and she could already feel the weight of it — but she welcomed it. It was the next necessary step. And she had not survived battlefields and broken promises to falter now.

Chapter 4

Opening Statements

The air in the courtroom hung thick with anticipation, a palpable tension that vibrated in the hushed whispers and the rustling of papers. Sunlight, filtered through the high, arched windows, illuminated dust motes dancing in the stillness, a silent ballet against the backdrop of looming legal battle.
The polished mahogany of the judge's bench gleamed under the light, a stark contrast to the worn, somber wood of the jury box where twelve individuals, impassive and watchful, held the fate of Dominic Falfor in their hands.

Assistant District Attorney Kenneth Fitzgerald, a man whose sharp eyes betrayed a mind constantly working, stepped forward. He was known for his meticulous preparation and his ability to connect with a jury on a human level, a skill he honed over years of prosecuting cases that tested the boundaries of justice. His opening statement was a carefully constructed narrative, a slow, deliberate unveiling of the events leading up to Madeline Clark's death. He didn't begin with the brutal fact of the shooting; instead, he painted a picture of

Madeline herself – a bright, vivacious thirteen-year-old, full of life and dreams, suddenly extinguished by a single, fatal gunshot. He described her love for horses, her laughter, her bright, inquisitive eyes – details gleaned from interviews with her family and friends, details meant to tug at the heartstrings of the jury, to humanize the victim and make her loss palpable.

Fitzgerald then shifted his focus to Dominic Falfor, painting a portrait of a man who had betrayed the very oath he swore to uphold. He described Falfor's history within the Marshal Service, highlighting his initial promise and eventual descent into corruption, a subtle erosion of integrity that culminated in the tragic events of that night. He detailed the evidence meticulously, building a logical, sequential narrative supported by forensic reports, witness statements, and the crucial testimony of Laila Wright and Carolyn Pryme. He spoke of the bribe, the hushed transaction witnessed by the young girl, the subsequent raid, and the fatal shot. He didn't shy away from the graphic details, presenting them clinically, objectively, yet with an undercurrent of righteous indignation.

He emphasized the inconsistencies in Falfor's statements, the subtle lies woven into his self-serving narrative. The evidence," Fitzgerald declared, his voice resonating with controlled power, "will show that Dominic Falfor was not acting in the line of duty. He was acting in the service of greed, in the service of corruption. He abused his power, he violated his oath, and he murdered an innocent child. This case is not just about a crime; it's about justice. It's about holding accountable those who betray the public trust, those who abuse the very system designed to protect us. It's about ensuring that Madeline Clark's death will not be in vain." He paused, his gaze sweeping across the jury, his eyes meeting each one in turn.

"We will prove, beyond a reasonable doubt, that Dominic Falfor is guilty of murder."

The silence that followed Fitzgerald's statement was heavy, pregnant with unspoken thoughts and judgments. The defense attorney, a seasoned veteran named Mr. Harrison, a man whose slicked-back hair and tailored suit suggested a mastery of courtroom theatrics, rose slowly. His demeanor was a study in controlled confidence, a stark contrast to Fitzgerald's passionate intensity. He began with a practiced ease, his voice a low, smooth baritone that seemed to lull the courtroom into a false sense of calm.

Harrison's opening statement was a counter-narrative, a carefully crafted defense that aimed to dismantle the prosecution's case piece by piece. He acknowledged the tragedy of Madeline Clark's death, expressing his condolences to the family, but he insisted that Dominic Falfor was not responsible. He portrayed Falfor as a dedicated law enforcement officer, a man who had dedicated his life to serving and protecting his community. He painted a picture of a tense, rapidly evolving situation, where split- second decisions had to be made under pressure, where a young girl, tragically caught in the crossfire, had become an unintended victim.

Harrison skillfully shifted the focus from Falfor's actions to the credibility of the key witnesses. He hinted at the emotional distress of Laila Wright, suggesting that her personal issues and recent divorce might cloud her judgment and impact her testimony. He alluded to potential biases on the part of Carolyn Pryme, questioning her perception of events and her relationship with Laila Wright, implying a conspiracy to frame Falfor. He challenged the evidence presented by Fitzgerald, subtly casting doubt on the forensic reports and minimizing the significance of the bribe, suggesting that it was a misunderstanding, a small act of generosity that had been misinterpreted. He strategically presented alternative explanations for the events, suggesting that the shooting was an unfortunate accident, a tragic but unavoidable consequence of a dangerous situation.

"This case," Harrison asserted, his voice measured and controlled, "is not about justice; it's about misinterpretations and circumstantial evidence. It is about the emotional turmoil of witnesses attempting to rationalize a horrific event. We will show that the prosecution's case is built on speculation and conjecture, not on concrete evidence. We will demonstrate that Dominic Falfor acted appropriately within the confines of his duties, that he made a difficult decision in a dangerous situation, a decision that tragically resulted in the death of an innocent girl. But it was a decision made in the heat of the moment, a decision that was not malicious or intentional." He concluded his opening statement with a confident assurance, a subtle yet powerful declaration of his intention to prove Falfor's innocence. "We will prove that Mr. Falfor is not guilty of murder."

The tension in the courtroom was almost unbearable. The jurors, their faces impassive masks, absorbed the starkly contrasting narratives, weighing the arguments of both sides, the conflicting accounts of events, the subtle jabs and counter-jabs of legal maneuvering. The weight of the case rested heavily on their shoulders, the responsibility of deciding the fate of a man, the resolution of a tragedy that had shaken the very foundations of the community. The courtroom held its breath, anticipating the commencement of the battle, the relentless unfolding of evidence, testimony, and cross-examination that would ultimately determine the truth. The stage was set, the players were in place, and the game, a fight for justice and the truth, had begun. The quiet hum of anticipation was broken only by the rhythmic tick- tock of the clock in the courtroom, a relentless reminder of the time marching towards a verdict – a verdict that would hang heavy in the air long after the final gavel fell. The fight for justice had only just begun, and Laila, from her seat, felt a renewed surge of determination. This was just the first round. The real battle lay ahead. The bailiff stepped forward, a clipboard tucked under one arm, and called the first witness.

"Marshal Laila Aurora Wright," he announced, his voice carrying clearly across the chamber. Laila rose with deliberate calm, smoothing her jacket as she moved toward the stand. Her boots made a measured sound against the polished floor, echoing slightly in the otherwise silent room. She approached the witness box, her posture straight, her expression composed into a mask of professional neutrality.

She took the oath without hesitation, her voice clear and unwavering. "I do."

Sliding into the seat, she folded her hands carefully in her lap, allowing herself one controlled breath as she faced the courtroom — the judge, the jury, the prosecution, the defense, and Dominic Falfor himself.

Kenneth Fitzgerald approached the stand. There was no wasted motion, no unnecessary theatrics. He respected the weight of the moment and treated it accordingly.

"Marshal Wright," Fitzgerald began, his tone professional but edged with gravity, "please state your full name and your current position for the record."

"Laila Aurora Wright," she said steadily. "Deputy United States Marshal, assigned to Special Operations Group."

Fitzgerald nodded, satisfied. He moved closer, but not threateningly so — a gesture of collaboration with the witness rather than intimidation.

"Marshal Wright, how long have you served with the United States Marshals Service?"

"Eleven years, sir."

"And before that?"

"I served in the United States Army," Laila replied, her voice carrying just enough strength to command attention without aggression. "Three tours overseas."

Fitzgerald allowed a brief pause, letting the jury absorb the portrait of dedication and experience. Then he moved into the heart of it.

"On the night of May 14th, you were present at the raid on the East Hollow warehouse. Is that correct?"

"Yes, sir."

"Please describe the events as you observed them."

Laila leaned slightly forward, her mind sifting through the memories with the precision of a soldier cleaning a weapon. No embellishment, no speculation — just fact.

"We had intelligence that a major weapons transaction was taking place. I was assigned to exterior perimeter. Deputy Dominic Falfor was assigned to entry team one. Upon breach, shots were fired. I moved to assist. During the chaos, I observed Dominic Falfor separate from the team and engage an unidentified figure — later identified as Madeline Clark — who had been hiding behind a storage rack. She was unarmed."

A ripple of reaction moved through the courtroom — a slight intake of breath here, a tightened jaw there — but Judge Harlan's stern gaze kept it contained.

Fitzgerald's face was carved from stone. "And what happened next?"

"I witnessed Dominic Falfor fire his weapon at Madeline Clark," Laila said, each word measured and clear. "She collapsed immediately. No warning. No apparent threat."

She could feel Falfor's stare boring into her, but she didn't flinch. She didn't look at him.

The jury leaned forward, just slightly, an almost imperceptible shift — but a telling one.

Fitzgerald gave a small, grim nod. "No further questions at this time, Your Honor."

Judge Harlan turned toward the defense table. "Mr. Harrison?"

The defense attorney rose smoothly, adjusting his cufflinks before approaching the stand. His smile was thin, almost sympathetic, but there was steel behind it.

"Good morning, Marshal Wright," Harrison said, his tone oily with false warmth. "I imagine this has been a difficult experience for you."

Laila said nothing, waiting for the question —

just as she had been trained.
Harrison tilted his head, studying her with the practiced eye of a predator sizing up potential prey.
"Would it be fair to say, Marshal Wright," he continued, "that you were under significant emotional strain at the time of this incident? Personal issues, perhaps? Divorce proceedings, as I understand?"
Objection, Fitzgerald's voice rang out — but Judge Harlan lifted a hand calmly.
"I'll allow a limited inquiry," she said. "Answer the question, Marshal."
Laila met Harrison's gaze squarely. "I was executing my duties as trained and required, regardless of any personal circumstances."
There was no tremor in her voice. No crack in her armor. And the jury saw it.
Harrison's smile tightened minutely, but he pressed on.
"And in the confusion of a firefight, split-second judgments are made, aren't they, Marshal? Mistakes are... inevitable?"
"Yes," Laila replied, still steady. "Which is why we're trained to positively identify targets before discharging our weapons."
The answer cut cleanly through the defense's suggestion of chaos and uncertainty. Several jurors exchanged glances.
Harrison shifted tactics, probing for any

inconsistency, but Laila stayed anchored, methodical, her testimony a bulwark against the defense's creeping doubt.
And through it all, from the corner of her eye, she could feel Dominic Falfor watching her — not with fear, not with regret — but with the cold calculation of a man weighing odds.

The Cross-Examination...

Mr. Harrison, the defense attorney, rose with a slow, deliberate grace, his smile a thin, almost imperceptible line across his lips. He adjusted his glasses, the glint of light off the frames momentarily blinding Laila. His movements were unhurried, predatory — the kind of practiced calm that was far more unnerving than outright aggression. This wasn't a predator pouncing; this was a boa constrictor tightening its coils, inch by suffocating inch.
"Marshal Wright," he began, his voice a low, smooth baritone that curled through the courtroom, "you've described a rather… dramatic series of events. A clandestine bribe, a fatal shooting, a corrupt marshal. Quite a story, isn't it?" His tone was almost casual, deceptively soft, a serpent's whisper meant to lull the prey before the strike.
Laila met his gaze, her own eyes steady, unflinching. Years of military service had forged her composure in fire. "It's the truth, Mr. Harrison," she replied, her voice clear, stripped of anger or fear.
"Truth," he repeated, almost tasting the word. "Such a slippery thing, isn't it? Colored by memory. Shaded by

emotion." He stepped closer to the jury box, angling himself so that his body seemed open, his posture inviting doubt. "Your testimony, Marshal, hinges on your assertion that you witnessed Deputy Falfor accepting a bribe. Let's explore that."

He shifted his weight, hands clasped lightly behind his back — a schoolteacher about to correct a promising but misguided pupil.

"Describe the lighting conditions at the scene," he said, voice low but commanding. "Were they ideal for positive identification?"

Laila kept her tone measured. "It was dark," she admitted, "but there were streetlights along the perimeter. The area where the exchange occurred was illuminated enough to clearly observe the transaction."

"But not the contents of the envelope," Harrison pressed.

"No," Laila acknowledged. "But the context, body language, and the manner of the exchange were all consistent with a covert transfer."

Harrison smiled, almost pitiful. "Body language," he echoed. "Interpretations. Perceptions." He let the words linger, subtle threads of doubt weaving into the jury's mind.

"And you did not intervene," he said smoothly, the rhythm of his speech quickening just enough to draw the jury's attention. "You observed what you believed was a felony — and you chose not to act?"

"We were conducting a broader operation targeting an organized narcotics ring," Laila answered evenly. "Immediate confrontation would have risked compromising an ongoing investigation. Our orders were to monitor and

document until the warrant could be executed."
"Orders," Harrison repeated, his voice now edged with a faint derision. "How convenient. So you watched a crime in progress… and chose paperwork over action?"
Murmurs stirred in the gallery. Judge Harlan silenced them with a pointed look.
Laila kept her eyes forward. "I followed protocol, Mr. Harrison. As required by operational command."
Harrison's lips curved in a semblance of a smile, but his eyes remained cold. He circled like a shark scenting blood. He pivoted without warning. "Let's talk about your emotional state that night," he said. "You were under considerable personal strain, were you not? Divorce proceedings. Recent allegations of misconduct —"
"Objection," Fitzgerald cut in sharply. "Irrelevant and prejudicial."
"Your Honor," Harrison countered, all wounded innocence, "it speaks to the witness's credibility."
Judge Harlan hesitated, then nodded curtly. "I'll allow limited inquiry."
Harrison pounced. "Marshal Wright, would you agree that stress, both personal and professional, can impact perception? Memory?"
Laila felt the sting of anger but suppressed it. "Stress is a factor in any law enforcement operation," she said. "Which is why we're trained to compartmentalize."
"And yet," Harrison said, voice growing softer, more insidious, "the night in question, you witnessed a tragedy.

A young girl's death. You were emotionally compromised."
"I was horrified, yes," Laila said, the memory flashing sharp and brutal. "But I reported what I saw, not what I felt."
"Feelings are powerful, Marshal," Harrison said, his voice a low purr now. "Powerful enough to rewrite memory. Powerful enough to transform uncertainty into certainty."
He let the implication hang in the air before moving to the next blow.
He attacked from another angle, dragging in her military past. Disciplinary records. Internal reviews. Moments pulled from years of honorable service, twisted and distorted into weapons.
"Your record," Harrison said, holding up a printed sheet, "indicates two separate citations for conduct unbecoming while deployed. Care to elaborate?"
Laila sat straighter, keeping her hands folded neatly before her. "Both citations were administrative," she said. "Neither resulted in demotion or discharge. Both were context-dependent judgments made under extreme combat conditions."
"But they were judgments made… under pressure," Harrison said, almost gently.
"Yes," Laila said. "And I survived. And I completed my missions. And I saved lives."
There was steel in her voice now, and a few jurors leaned forward unconsciously, caught by it.
But Harrison was relentless.

He turned back to the fatal night.
"You claim," he said, voice low and coaxing, "that Deputy Falfor fired on an unarmed civilian without provocation. But in the chaos of an armed raid, in the noise, the fear — is it not possible you misinterpreted his intent? That what you perceived was not malice, but mistake?"
Laila let the silence stretch. Then: "Possible? Anything is possible. But what I observed was not fear. It was deliberate. It was execution."
Harrison's smile vanished.
A heavy, charged silence blanketed the room. Even the faint hum of the overhead lights seemed to fade away.
Harrison closed his folder, slowly, methodically. His tone when he spoke again was almost regretful.
"No further questions, Your Honor."
Judge Harlan nodded, her expression unreadable.
"Marshal Wright, you may step down."
Laila rose. Her body felt weighted by invisible chains, but her spine remained straight, her stride measured. She returned to her seat without glancing at the defense table, without seeking affirmation from the prosecution. She needed no applause, no reassurances.
The truth was her shield.
The truth — battered, tested, but unbroken — had survived the first assault.
And as she sat, feeling the eyes of the entire courtroom boring into her, she knew: the real war was only beginning.

The Expert Testimony.

The tension in the courtroom hadn't lessened; it had merely evolved, hardening into a different kind of beast. Where Harrison's cross-examination had been a storm of doubt and insinuation, the next phase promised something colder, sharper — a battle fought with precision instruments instead of bludgeons. Now, the focus turned to the scientific evidence, the hard facts that could either fortify or fracture Laila's testimony.

Dr. Emily Carter, a forensic pathologist renowned for her rigorous methodology and unassailable professionalism, took the stand first. She moved with crisp efficiency, her lab coat replaced by a simple navy blazer that seemed to magnify the clinical detachment in her voice.

Her testimony was a masterclass in clarity. She presented the autopsy findings of Madeline Clark — the trajectory of the bullet, the distribution of powder residue, the precise placement of entry and exit wounds — in language so carefully chosen that even the most scientifically naïve juror could follow. She used simple analogies, projected clean diagrams onto a screen, and never once veered into unnecessary technical jargon.

"Dr. Carter," ADA Fitzgerald asked, "based on

your autopsy, are you able to corroborate Marshal Wright's account of the events?"
"Yes, sir," she answered without hesitation. "The forensic findings — bullet trajectory, wound location, powder stippling — all align with Ms. Wright's statement. The evidence supports her version of events."
Her words landed like hammer blows against Harrison's earlier suggestions of mistaken perception.
When Harrison rose for cross-examination, there was a change in his demeanor — the slick confidence slightly frayed. He challenged her on margins of error, on the variability of human anatomy under stress, on hypothetical miscalculations. But Carter parried each attack deftly, acknowledging the limits of forensic science while emphasizing that none of those margins altered the central conclusion.
"There is always a margin of error in measurements," she conceded coolly, "but none of those margins affect the fundamental findings here. The evidence remains consistent and reliable."
The jury leaned in. The solid ground Harrison had tried to undermine was, for now, firmly intact.
Next came Detective Sergeant Michael Davies of the Pennsylvania State Police Crime Scene Unit. A mountain of a man with a voice like

rolling gravel, Davies spoke with a slow, methodical cadence that demanded attention. He presented the photographic evidence: the location of the body, the position of the shell casing, the layout of the scene, the illumination from surrounding streetlights. He described how the evidence had been collected — gloves, evidence bags, digital time-stamping — highlighting every safeguard designed to prevent contamination or tampering.

"Each item was logged," Davies said, gesturing to the meticulously maintained chain of custody logs. "Every hand that touched it was recorded, timestamped, and verified independently."

Harrison attempted to needle him about potential evidence displacement, about the limitations of forensic photography, but Davies was immovable. He explained that while absolute perfection in a crime scene was impossible, the redundancy of checks and the corroboration between physical evidence and witness statements minimized any reasonable doubt.

"Small movements occur naturally," Davies admitted. "But they don't rewrite the story the scene tells — and this scene tells a consistent story."

The jury watched him with rapt attention. The defense's earlier suggestions of chaos now

seemed feeble in the face of such steady, unshakable testimony.
The final expert called was Dr. Benicio Ramirez, a digital forensics specialist. Unlike the previous witnesses, Ramirez possessed a different kind of presence — sharp, analytical, every answer delivered with rapid, precise articulation. He projected a screen showing recovered text messages, call logs, and geolocation data from Dominic Falfor's confiscated cell phone.
Ramirez carefully explained the data extraction process: using secure forensic imaging, checksum validation, and cryptographic authenticity checks. He demonstrated how the timestamps and GPS coordinates confirmed Laila and Carolyn's observation of Falfor receiving an envelope at the warehouse.
"Even deleted messages," Ramirez explained, tapping the screen, "leave residual data. We recovered these fragments using industry-standard forensic recovery software, cross-verified by hash analysis."
Harrison tried a different tactic — suggesting that outside tampering, hacking, or manipulation could have fabricated evidence.
Ramirez didn't even blink.
"There is no forensic evidence," Ramirez said flatly, "of intrusion, malware, data splicing, or external manipulation. If such activities had

occurred, they would leave detectable forensic footprints. None were present."

His answers dismantled the defense's insinuations with ruthless efficiency.

When Ramirez stepped down, a heavy silence lingered. Even the defense table seemed to sag under the accumulating weight of corroborated, indisputable evidence.

The tide of the trial had shifted.

Not with a single devastating blow, but with the slow, inexorable piling of fact upon fact, until doubt could no longer find safe purchase.

The jurors — some with arms crossed tightly, others leaning forward on their elbows — absorbed the scientific testimony differently than the emotional appeals of earlier. This was harder to refute. Harder to spin.

The prosecution had stitched a tapestry of science behind Laila's words. Where there had once been one woman's testimony vulnerable to character attacks, there now stood an interlocking wall of physical evidence, expert corroboration, and digital trails.

The battle wasn't over.

But for the first time since the trial began, Laila felt a cold, quiet certainty settle in her chest:

The truth was no longer just her burden to bear.

Now, it stood with her — armored in fact, speaking in the language even liars feared most: proof. Tactical Move by the Defense

The air in the courtroom still carried the clinical chill of scientific testimony, but Harrison — ever the predator — was already adapting.

As Dr. Ramirez stepped down, ADA Fitzgerald rose, preparing to rest his expert witness presentation. The prosecution had momentum. The defense needed to fracture it — fast.

Before Fitzgerald could even speak, Harrison was on his feet.

"Your Honor," he said smoothly, "before the prosecution proceeds, the defense would like to request a sidebar."

Judge Harlan's eyes narrowed slightly. She tapped her gavel once — sharp, efficient.

"Counsel, approach."

The attorneys clustered at the bench. The jury, the gallery, even the reporters in the back leaned forward instinctively, sensing a shift.

In hushed, urgent tones, Harrison made his play.

"Your Honor, the defense wishes to call a rebuttal witness out of turn," he said. "New information has come to light — information that directly contradicts Marshal Wright's observations and the forensic interpretations based thereon."

Fitzgerald immediately objected. "Your Honor, the defense has had ample opportunity for discovery. This is a transparent attempt to derail the prosecution's case with procedural ambush."

Judge Harlan gave Harrison a hard look. "Name your witness."

"The defense calls Deputy Marshal Samuel Greaves," Harrison said, his voice calm but charged with purpose. "Greaves was present at the scene on the night in question. His testimony," he added, letting the words fall like loaded dice, "will significantly alter the jury's understanding of the sequence of events."

Fitzgerald bristled. "Greaves' name was never disclosed as a material witness—"

"New statements were obtained last night, Your Honor," Harrison said, almost apologetically. "As per Brady obligations, we are required to disclose material evidence that may be favorable to the defense — and we intend to do so now."

Judge Harlan's expression hardened. She hated surprises — especially those designed to manipulate courtroom flow — but she was bound by law to allow it.

"You will have thirty minutes to prepare your witness," she said tightly. "Court is recessed until then."

The gavel struck the block with a crack that felt almost like gunfire.
The courtroom exploded into murmurs, shocked gasps threading through the crowd.
Fitzgerald turned toward Laila immediately, his face set in grim lines.
"Greaves," he muttered. "We vetted everyone from that night. If he's flipping now—"
Laila swallowed a sour taste rising in her throat. Samuel Greaves had been on the outer perimeter that night — low visibility, limited engagement.
He had seemed loyal. Professional.
But under pressure — or under incentive — loyalties could fracture.
The defense had found their wedge.
The thirty-minute recess felt like a countdown to detonation.
The prosecution scrambled to review the last-minute witness statement. Fitzgerald, furious but controlled, barked orders to his aides, pulling up deployment maps, personnel records, old operation reports.
Laila sat alone for a moment, breathing deeply, forcing herself to think like a soldier again.
Adapt. Overcome. Stay steady.
The defense had bought themselves a window to seed doubt.
And they were about to throw a grenade into everything she had fought to build. Judge

Harlan rapped her gavel once, sharp and percussive.
"Counsel, approach."
Fitzgerald and Harrison moved quickly, their suits brushing in the narrow space before the bench. Laila watched them go, every muscle in her body taut with unspent energy.
The white noise machine at the judge's bench hissed to life — a thin, static buzz designed to keep the jury from overhearing.
"Mr. Harrison," Judge Harlan said, her voice low but fierce. "Explain yourself."
Harrison's expression was almost placid. "Your Honor, last night, the defense was approached by Deputy Marshal Samuel Greaves. He provided a sworn statement indicating he witnessed different events at the East Hollow warehouse raid — events that call into question the prosecution's narrative."
"Different events," Fitzgerald repeated tightly, disbelief flashing across his face. "Greaves was interviewed months ago. He gave no such account. This is a stunt."
Harrison spread his hands — the picture of reluctant necessity. "New recollections surfaced, Your Honor. Traumatic incidents often cause delayed memory retrieval. We have an obligation under Brady to present potentially exculpatory evidence."

Fitzgerald leaned forward, barely keeping his voice in check. "The defense is trying to backdoor surprise testimony to manufacture reasonable doubt. This violates the spirit of discovery—"

"I'm aware," Judge Harlan cut in. She fixed Harrison with a gaze that could have cracked stone. "When exactly did this 'recollection' surface?"

"Late yesterday evening, Your Honor," Harrison said smoothly. "We notified the prosecution first thing this morning. The statement was signed under penalty of perjury."

Judge Harlan's fingers drummed once against the bench. She hated being cornered — but Harrison had left her little choice. Suppressing a potentially exculpatory witness, however dubious, would be grounds for immediate appeal.

The law was clear.

Even if the tactic reeked of manipulation.

"You will provide the prosecution with a copy of the statement immediately," she ordered. "And you will limit your direct examination to the contents of that statement. No fishing expeditions."

Harrison inclined his head, all faux humility. "Of course, Your Honor."

Judge Harlan turned to Fitzgerald.

"You'll have thirty minutes to review and

prepare cross."
Fitzgerald's jaw flexed, but he nodded curtly.
Judge Harlan lowered her voice even further.
"Make no mistake, gentlemen: I will not tolerate grandstanding. If either of you abuses this court's patience, sanctions will follow."
She banged the gavel again, ending the sidebar.
The static hiss stopped. The courtroom noise returned like a rising tide — whispers, rustling papers, shifting chairs.
The jury watched, puzzled but alert.
The battle had shifted, and everyone knew it.
Laila caught Fitzgerald's glance as he returned to the table. It wasn't reassurance he gave her — it was a soldier's grim acknowledgment:
Brace for impact.

Carolyn's Testimony

Carolyn Pryme, her posture rigid and her jaw set in a hard line, stepped into the witness box. Her uniform, immaculate and pressed, seemed heavier today, a tangible reminder of the weight she carried — not just as a Marshal, but as a keeper of memory and truth.
The courtroom, which had thrummed with scientific certainties during the expert testimony, now fell into a tense, aching silence. Only the rhythmic tick of the wall clock marked the passage of time, each second a slow drumbeat toward revelation.

Carolyn's gaze swept the room, steady and searching. When her eyes met Laila's, there was a flash of unspoken understanding between them: We carry this together.
Assistant District Attorney Fitzgerald approached, his face composed into a mask of calm professionalism. His steps were measured, his voice low and respectful when he spoke, offering Carolyn the dignity she deserved.
"Marshal Pryme," he began, "please state your name and your current position within the U.S. Marshals Service."
Carolyn answered with the precision of long habit. Her voice was clear but edged with quiet gravity, recounting her years of service, her credentials, her numerous commendations.
Every fact she laid down was another stone in the foundation of her credibility — not boastful, not defensive, simply irrefutable.
Fitzgerald guided her gently, deliberately, through the night Madeline Clark died.
The raid.
The objective.
The layout.
He moved slowly, methodically, never rushing her, allowing Carolyn to paint the night in meticulous strokes.
Carolyn described the atmosphere: the flickering streetlights, the uneven shadows, the chemical smell of damp concrete. She recounted the team's careful entry into the warehouse, the tension crackling in the air, the brief radio exchanges clipped and precise.

When Fitzgerald finally steered her toward the heart of the matter — the bribe — the courtroom seemed to hold its breath.

"I observed Deputy Falfor in a side corridor," Carolyn said, her voice tightening. "He was speaking to an unidentified man. I saw the man hand him an envelope. Falfor glanced around, then tucked the envelope into his jacket."

Fitzgerald's next question was soft but deadly.

"Could you identify the contents of the envelope?"

"No," Carolyn admitted. "But based on the context, and the later recovery of similar cash denominations at the scene, it was consistent with a bribe."

She went on, her voice cool but underpinned with palpable disgust, describing Falfor's furtive glances, his stiff posture, the way guilt seemed to radiate off him like heat haze.

Then came the fatal moment.

"Did you witness the shooting itself, Marshal Pryme?" Fitzgerald asked quietly.

Carolyn nodded once, her throat working.

"Yes, sir."

The room felt airless.

"Please," Fitzgerald prompted, "tell the court what you saw."

Carolyn's voice dropped lower, but her words grew sharper, carved from granite.

"I saw Madeline Clark step into the corridor," she said. "She looked… terrified. She froze. She wasn't armed. She posed no threat.

Deputy Falfor raised his weapon.

There was a moment — a heartbeat — where he could have lowered it.
But he didn't.
He fired."
The jury sat motionless, expressions frozen somewhere between horror and disbelief.
Carolyn described the way Madeline crumpled to the ground, the smell of burnt gunpowder sharp and acrid, the way the echoes of the shot seemed to linger longer than they should have.
She described the chaotic aftermath — the screaming, the radios bursting to life, the desperate, futile rush to save a child already gone.
Her testimony wasn't florid. It didn't need to be.
The sheer *truth* of it was its own force.
Then Harrison rose.
The defense attorney's usual slick composure had cracked slightly at the edges.
There was a new urgency to him, a sharpened aggression masked under professional veneer.
"Marshal Pryme," he began, his voice almost affable, "you've given a very… evocative account. But human memory is fallible, is it not?"
Carolyn met his gaze with the steadiness of a soldier staring down incoming fire.
"It can be," she agreed. "Which is why we train to observe under stress."
Harrison smiled thinly and launched into his assault — hammering her on lighting conditions, angles, distances. He pointed out minor discrepancies between her written report

and today's testimony: the position of a hallway light, the number of seconds between Falfor drawing his weapon and firing.
Carolyn answered without hesitation.
She acknowledged the minor inconsistencies — and then framed them perfectly.
"Small details can blur under stress," she said. "But the core facts remain unchanged.
Madeline Clark was unarmed.
Deputy Falfor shot her."
Harrison's attacks grew more desperate.
He tried to suggest Carolyn hadn't seen the shooting directly, that her perspective might have been obscured, that she might have been relying on assumption rather than observation.
Carolyn's calm never wavered.
"I had a clear line of sight," she said. "I saw what I saw."
He pivoted then — fast, sharp — trying to sow discord between Carolyn and Laila.
"Marshal Pryme," Harrison said, voice dripping with insinuation, "your account today differs slightly from Marshal Wright's, doesn't it? Different positioning. Different timing. Doesn't that suggest a coordinated attempt to craft a narrative?"
Carolyn's expression didn't flicker.
"No," she said. "It suggests two people saw the same tragic event from different angles.
We didn't collaborate.
We lived it."
The jury shifted, visibly moved by the simple strength of

her words.
Harrison’s attacks faltered. His final questions became increasingly scattershot, probing for anything — *anything* — that could salvage his momentum.
Carolyn, seasoned and unwavering, answered each blow with quiet defiance, standing as an immovable pillar in the swirling storm.
When Fitzgerald finally rose for redirect, it was almost unnecessary. Carolyn had done the work herself.
Her testimony stood intact — scarred perhaps by the battle, but unbroken.
When she stepped down from the witness box, a strange energy lingered in the air.
Not relief.
Not triumph.
Something heavier.
A collective understanding that the truth, once spoken with such clarity and courage, was a force unto itself.
Laila caught her eye as Carolyn returned to the prosecution table.
No words were needed.
Their fight was far from over —
but today, they had stood their ground.
And it showed. ADA Fitzgerald rose slowly from his chair, his face composed, but his eyes sharp and calculating. He moved toward the witness box with a deliberate calm, letting the jury absorb the contrast between his measured approach and Harrison's frantic final assaults.
He stopped just short of the stand, giving Carolyn the space to breathe, to settle.

"Marshal Pryme," Fitzgerald began, his voice steady, "you've acknowledged that under high-stress conditions, some minor sensory details — things like lighting, distances — may blur. Correct?"
"Yes, sir," Carolyn answered crisply.
"But in your professional judgment," Fitzgerald pressed, "is there any doubt in your mind — *any doubt at all* — about what you saw Deputy Falfor do that night?"
Carolyn didn't hesitate.
Her voice, when she answered, was clear enough to cut glass.
"No, sir.
I witnessed Deputy Falfor fire upon an unarmed civilian."
A subtle ripple moved through the jury — not an audible sound, but a collective exhalation, a settling of certainty among them.
Fitzgerald nodded once, sharply.
"No further questions, Your Honor."
Judge Harlan inclined her head approvingly.
"Marshal Pryme, you are dismissed."
Carolyn stood, gave the judge a respectful nod, and stepped down from the witness box — not victorious, not triumphant — but carrying the solid, immovable weight of truth with her.
As she returned to the prosecution's table, the subtle momentum in the courtroom shifted once again.
The jury had heard emotion.
They had heard science.

And now they had heard human witness — unwavering, undeniable.
And the defense, for all its tactics, could not unspeak what had been said.

Unexpected Witness

The tension in the courtroom, thick enough to cut with a knife, hadn't eased after Carolyn Pryme's devastating testimony. If anything, it had sharpened into something brittle and dangerous. The rhythmic tick of the clock seemed to hammer against the fragile calm, each second a drumbeat of inevitability.
Then — movement.
A figure, slight and unassuming, was ushered through the side door by a bailiff. Heads turned.
A low murmur rippled across the room, rising into a hushed, disbelieving buzz.
The woman was small, almost frail, but her eyes — bright, sharp, unflinching — held a presence that dwarfed her stature.
Mrs. Eleanor Vance.
Madeline Clark's neighbor.
A woman known, until this very moment, only for her quiet life and her love of gardening.
Neither the defense nor the prosecution had anticipated her appearance. Even Fitzgerald, ever-controlled, tensed slightly as he rose.
But his training held:
Adapt. Pivot. Control.

He approached the witness stand cautiously, allowing the gravity of the moment to settle over the courtroom.
"Mrs. Vance," Fitzgerald said, his voice pitched low, almost coaxing, "please state your name and address for the record."
Mrs. Vance's voice, though soft, carried a fierce, unshakable conviction.
She provided her name and address, her gaze never once wavering.
She spoke briefly of her years living next to the Clark family, painting Madeline as a bright, spirited girl — full of life, full of promise. Every word made the loss sharper, more real, a blow to the heart of the courtroom.
Then, carefully, Fitzgerald brought her to the night in question.
"Mrs. Vance," he said gently, "did you see or hear anything unusual on the night of May 14th?"
Mrs. Vance's hands tightened slightly on the rail. Her eyes clouded for just a moment — memory and grief warring in her gaze — but her voice, when it came, was firm.
She spoke of the distant sirens first, then the sharp, staccato pops of gunfire cutting through the night.
She described hesitation — fear — before she moved to her window, drawn by a sense that something was terribly wrong.
And there, through the thin veil of night and streetlamps, she saw him.
Dominic Falfor.
Not outside. Not with his team.
Inside the Clark residence.

Moments before the shots rang out.
A gasp rippled through the gallery.
Several jurors visibly stiffened.
Mrs. Vance described Falfor's appearance — his hurried movements, his pale, agitated face. She recalled details with astonishing clarity: the way he clutched something close to his body, the way he glanced over his shoulder with the furtive energy of a man fleeing guilt.
Her words painted an image no amount of cross-examination could easily undo.
It didn't just support Laila and Carolyn's testimony — it *rewrote the map.*
It placed Falfor at the scene.
Alone.
Agitated.
Moments before a young girl's death.
Fitzgerald asked few further questions, understanding instinctively that her testimony needed no embellishment.
Then Harrison rose.
The defense attorney's face was pale, drawn tight across his features. His voice, when he began cross-examination, lacked its usual oily composure.
He struck at Mrs. Vance quickly, almost desperately — questioning her eyesight, her vantage point, the lighting conditions.
"Mrs. Vance," Harrison said sharply, "you were viewing from across the street, through a window, at night. Isn't it possible — likely even — that you were mistaken about what you saw?"
Mrs. Vance did not flinch.

Her reply came calm and sure:
"No, sir. I know what I saw."
He attacked again, suggesting fear might have distorted her memory, that adrenaline and distance could have combined to create false impressions.
But she met every challenge with unwavering steadiness.
He pointed to minor inconsistencies — the color of Falfor's jacket, the angle at which he stood — but each time, Mrs. Vance calmly corrected or contextualized the detail without faltering from her central truth.
At one point, Harrison grew visibly frustrated, slapping a hand lightly against the defense table.
"How can you be so certain?" he demanded.
Mrs. Vance's reply was soft — devastating in its simplicity.
"Because a mother knows when something terrible is about to happen.
And that night, when I saw Deputy Falfor, I knew."
The silence that followed was absolute.
Harrison tried a few more attacks — that she was influenced by news reports, that memory was malleable — but his momentum was gone.
The more he pushed, the smaller he looked, the more credible Mrs. Vance became.
Her calm, her quiet strength, stood as an unassailable fortress against his desperation.
When Harrison finally slumped into his seat, defeated, it was not merely Mrs. Vance's testimony that had dealt the blow.

It was her truth — simple, human, undeniable — that shattered the defense's carefully crafted illusions.
The courtroom felt different now.
Heavier.
More certain.
The jury had seen too much. Heard too much.
Falfor's web of lies was unraveling strand by strand.
And an unassuming neighbor — a woman no one had thought to fear — had become the sharpest weapon of all.
The battle was not over.
But for the first time, it was clear who was winning.
Courtroom Recess:
Dialogue Between Laila and Carolyn
The moment the judge banged the gavel and declared a recess, the courtroom dissolved into a low, chaotic murmur — jurors filing out under bailiff escort, reporters scribbling notes furiously, the gallery buzzing with speculation.
Laila stood slowly, the adrenaline of the morning making her muscles feel strangely stiff. Carolyn approached from the other side of the prosecution table, her uniform neat but her face lined with tension.
They met in the narrow hallway just outside the courtroom, leaning in close, speaking in low voices meant for no one else.
Laila was the first to break the silence.
"You held up strong," she said quietly, folding her arms across her chest. "Took everything he threw at you and made him look like a rookie."
Carolyn gave a dry, humorless chuckle.
"Feels like I've been run over by a truck anyway," she

muttered, glancing toward the closed doors as if expecting Harrison to come storming through them.
There was a brief silence. The hum of fluorescent lights overhead seemed unnaturally loud.
"I hate how close he got," Laila said finally, her voice tightening. "Twisting everything... even the good parts. Makes you question if the jury even sees the truth anymore."
Carolyn shifted, her boots scuffing softly against the tile. "They saw," she said, her tone low but certain. "Especially after Mrs. Vance. You could feel it. The way they looked at Falfor afterward... they know he's lying."
Laila rubbed the back of her neck, the old scar from a training injury throbbing in the familiar way it did when stress tightened her whole frame.
"I kept second-guessing everything on the stand," she admitted. "Every answer. Every word. Like any crack would be enough for Harrison to pry it wide open."
Carolyn nodded grimly.
"Same."
She paused, her gaze steady.
"But you didn't crack, Laila. Neither of us did. They tried to rattle us, but we're still standing."
Laila gave a tight smile, the corners of her mouth barely moving.
"Yeah," she said softly. "For now."
Another pause.
From down the hall came the faint sound of reporters gathering near the elevators, voices rising, snippets of commentary about "a dramatic shift in the trial" and

“devastating witness testimony.”
Carolyn leaned closer, dropping her voice further.
"Listen," she said, her tone shifting, hardening. "Harrison's not done swinging. He’s bleeding, but he’ll get desperate. He’ll go for blood if he has to."
Laila nodded, the old combat instinct stirring in her chest — the knowledge that wounded enemies could be the most dangerous.
"Let him try," she said. Her voice was low, steady, and ironclad.
"We finish this."
Carolyn smiled then — a real one, small but fierce.
"Side by side," she said.
"Always," Laila answered.
The call to reconvene echoed faintly from the courtroom doors.
Their brief moment of uneasy peace ended.
They straightened their jackets. Squared their shoulders.
And together, they walked back into the storm.

Chapter 5

Closing Arguments

The air in the courtroom crackled with a raw, electric tension, a current that pulsed through the walls, the floors, the rows of rigid wooden benches. Every breath, every shift of movement, seemed magnified in the charged silence.

The jury sat motionless, twelve individuals bearing the invisible weight of the truth they had witnessed unfold. Their faces were drawn, lined with exhaustion, yet their eyes remained sharp, pinned on the final battleground that was about to be contested.

After weeks of testimony, of emotional confessions and forensic certainties, the trial had reached its inevitable climax.

The closing arguments.

The final chance to define the story, the final plea for justice.

Assistant District Attorney Kenneth Fitzgerald rose from his chair.

There was no grandstanding in him — no theatrics, no sweeping gestures. His power came from restraint, from the calm authority of a man carrying the burden of truth in his hands.

He approached the jury, his steps deliberate, his expression solemn.

He began not with evidence, but with memory.

With Madeline Clark.

He spoke softly, painting her with words: a vibrant, inquisitive soul, full of dreams and small joys, extinguished before her life could even begin. He spoke of the family left to grieve, of the empty seat at the dinner table, the unopened birthday cards, the horses she would never ride again.
His voice was steady, but it carried a deep, aching sorrow that resonated through the silent room.

Then, methodically, he laid out the case.

He recounted the testimony of Marshal Laila Wright — detailed, unwavering even under brutal cross-examination. He honored the courage of Carolyn Pryme, a veteran standing alone against corruption. He wove in the devastating appearance of Mrs. Eleanor Vance, the unexpected voice who had shattered the defense's web of lies.

He did not rant.
He did not shout.
He let the facts — relentless, irrefutable — speak louder than any flourish could.

Each piece of evidence, each corroborated witness, built a lattice of truth around Dominic Falfor's actions.
A truth the defense had desperately tried to fracture — and failed.

Fitzgerald turned briefly toward Harrison's table, not in accusation, but in acknowledgment of the games played there: the manipulation of doubt, the desperate appeals to human fallibility.

He reminded the jury that reasonable doubt did not mean the absence of all doubt.
It meant doubt based on reason, not speculation.

And here, in this case, there was no reasonable doubt left.

He spoke of Laila and Carolyn's courage, not just as professionals, but as citizens who refused to be silent.
He spoke of the cost of truth-telling — reputations risked, futures imperiled — and the integrity it demanded from everyone, including the twelve sitting in judgment.

He closed with no dramatics.
Just truth, laid bare:

"Justice for Madeline Clark," he said, his voice carrying through the hushed courtroom. "Justice for a community betrayed by one of its own. Justice that demands you find Dominic Falfor guilty."

Then he sat down slowly, his eyes never leaving the jury.

There was a pause — not long, but heavy — before Harrison rose.

The defense attorney's movements were stiff, mechanical, as if he were forcing his body to obey when his mind had already admitted defeat.

His closing was an echo of earlier desperation.

He spoke of Dominic Falfor's years of service.
He spoke of the chaos of raids, the burden of split-second decisions.

He tried — feebly — to paint the witnesses as biased,

their memories unreliable. He clung to the suggestion that Mrs. Vance's account might be flawed, distorted by fear and time.
He invoked the sacred concept of reasonable doubt like a shield against the tidal wave of evidence drowning his client.

But the power was gone from his words.
The jury had seen too much.
Heard too much.

And no amount of rhetorical fog could obscure the truth that now blazed clear before them.

When Harrison finally sat, his face was pale, his hands trembling slightly on the defense table.

The silence that followed was absolute.

Judge Harlan's voice broke it only briefly, instructing the jury with final reminders of their solemn duty.

Then they filed out — twelve citizens stepping into a separate chamber, carrying with them the fate of a man, the weight of a child's death, and the integrity of a broken system waiting for redemption.

The courtroom remained frozen.

Reporters scratched hurried notes.
Families clasped hands.
Even the air seemed reluctant to move.

Outside the tall windows, the sun had dipped low, casting long shadows across the marble floors — a mirror of the long shadow this trial had cast over everyone involved.

The wait began.

And with it, the silent, relentless counting of each tick of the clock, marking the slow, inevitable march toward judgment.

The final chapter had not yet been written.
But its shape — heavy with truth, sharpened by courage — was already carved into the heart of the waiting room.

Jury Deliberations...

The deliberation room was small, almost claustrophobic, the air thick with the unspoken weight of responsibility.
Twelve individuals — ordinary citizens pulled from their lives into the crucible of justice — now held the fate of Dominic Falfor in their hands.

The fluorescent lights buzzed overhead, a harsh, mechanical sound that grated against the raw nerves stretched taut within the room.
Each juror carried their own burden — memories of testimony, flashes of evidence, lingering questions — stitched into their weary faces.

At the head of the table sat Harold Miller, a retired history teacher whose kind demeanor masked a spine of iron. He had taught generations about moral courage; now, he was called to practice it.

Silence ruled at first, a heavy, reverent pause

acknowledging the magnitude of the decision before them.

Then Martha Jenkins, the librarian with the meticulous mind, broke it — her voice quiet but steady.

"Let's start with the timeline," she said, spreading her color-coded notes across the table.

Slowly, the dam broke.
Carefully at first — reviewing witness accounts, reconstructing the night minute by minute.
The discussion circled Laila Wright's testimony: its unwavering precision, her military bearing under cross-examination.
Her credibility, many agreed, had survived Harrison's relentless assault intact.

Carolyn Pryme's account brought more complexity.
Some questioned her emotional involvement, her friendship with Laila, her grief.
But those questions collapsed under the weight of her detailed recollections — corroborations too precise, too grounded to dismiss.

The forensic evidence became the next battlefield:
Ballistics. Blood spatter. Trajectory.
Arguments flared — concerns over chain of custody, potential contamination — but were quickly met by the cold, methodical trail of documentation the forensic team had laid out.

Then came the debate over Mrs. Eleanor Vance.

Some jurors hesitated.
Could a woman observing from across the street — at

night, through fear — be trusted?
But others pointed to the precision of her description, the logic of her account, and most importantly, the fact that her story fit perfectly into the gaps others had left.

And more than that —
It exposed the rot underneath Falfor's facade.

Hours passed.
Coffee cooled untouched.
Tempers frayed.

At one point, Sarah Chen, a young mother of two, broke down briefly, her voice shaking as she recalled Madeline Clark's frozen, terrified figure.

"I keep seeing her," Sarah whispered, wiping at her eyes. "Just a kid. She didn't stand a chance."

The jurors fell into a heavy silence — not from indecision, but from the crushing sorrow that permeated the case.

They pressed on.

Gradually, doubt eroded under the steady flow of logic, evidence, and truth.
Harold Miller steered them gently but firmly, always bringing the discussion back to the heart of their duty.

Was there reasonable doubt?

Not speculation.
Not discomfort.
Real, rational doubt.

The answer, when it finally settled in the room, was

undeniable.

Late into the night, as fatigue threatened to blunt their sharpness, a subtle consensus emerged — first in glances, then in nods, then in quiet, solemn affirmations.

There was no rush to judgment.
No bloodlust.
Only a shared understanding that justice demanded a verdict, even when the truth carried its own terrible sorrow.

Harold Miller stood, the creak of his chair cutting through the exhausted stillness.

He looked around the table — seeing not strangers anymore, but twelve people bound by an unspoken oath to truth.

"We have reached a verdict," he said quietly.

Relief swept through the room, muted but profound.

The weight, for a moment, lifted.
The burden was no less heavy, but it was now shared equally among them — a burden they had faced head-on, with care, with conscience.

The silence that followed was different now — not of fear or indecision, but of solemn finality.

The verdict was sealed.

And outside that small, claustrophobic room, a city — and a courtroom filled with waiting hearts — would soon hear their judgment.

The Verdict.

The courtroom was packed to the walls. Every seat was filled, every aisle crowded with observers leaning forward, straining to capture the moment when fate would be sealed.

The air itself seemed to vibrate with tension, thick and oppressive like the heavy stillness before a storm. Journalists lined the back, cameras flashing sporadically, a muted staccato of shutters clicking through the room's pregnant silence.

In the front row sat Madeline Clark's family — faces pale, drawn tight with grief and quiet, simmering rage.
Their hands gripped each other tightly, their eyes fixed unblinking on the jury box, searching for any clue, any shift, that might reveal the verdict before the words were spoken.

Across the aisle, Dominic Falfor sat rigid, his hands clenched tight atop the defense table.
His face, carefully composed through weeks of brutal testimony, now betrayed the smallest cracks — a twitch of the jaw, a blink too slow.
His once-crisp suit hung slightly wrinkled against his frame, the confident air he had carried into the trial now hollowed out, replaced by something smaller. More desperate.

His attorney leaned in close, whispering urgently — words meant to steel him for the worst, or perhaps simply to brace for impact.

Falfor barely moved, his eyes fixed forward, seeing something no one else could.

At the prosecution table, Laila Wright and Carolyn Pryme sat side by side, their hands clasped beneath the table in silent solidarity.
Laila's outward calm — the soldier's discipline — held fast, but her pulse hammered so hard in her ears it drowned out the room.
Beside her, Carolyn trembled slightly, her grip on Laila's hand fierce, almost bruising.
The shared strain of the trial, of reliving their worst moments on the stand, sat heavy between them — but also the shared pride that they had made it this far.

ADA Kenneth Fitzgerald sat forward, his jaw tight, his fingertips pressed lightly against the polished wood table.
He had built the case brick by brick, testimony by testimony.
But no amount of evidence ever made the final judgment certain.

The silence inside the courtroom was a living thing. Only the grandfather clock's slow, relentless ticking marked time's passage — each second an agony.

Then the bailiff called for order.

The murmuring crowd stilled.
The gavel echoed sharply across the room.

The jury filed back in, their faces solemn, their steps measured.

Harold Miller, the foreman, rose with a single sheet

of paper trembling faintly in his hand.
The room seemed to hold its breath.

He cleared his throat, then spoke —
each word crisp, carrying the heavy finality of judgment.

"We, the jury, find the defendant, Dominic Falfor, guilty on all counts."

A collective gasp rippled through the courtroom — sharp, immediate, almost physical in its release. Whispers surged like a tide, quickly suppressed by the stern gaze of the judge.

Madeline's mother buried her face in her husband's shoulder, her quiet sobs piercing the heavy silence. Others reached for tissues, for each other, for anything solid enough to hold onto.

At the prosecution table, Fitzgerald allowed himself a single exhale — quiet, controlled — before straightening again.
Victory, yes.
But hard-won. Bitter in its necessity.

Falfor sat motionless, frozen in a posture of disbelief. For a long, stretched moment, he did not move.
Then his shoulders sagged — the defeat seeping into his bones, draining away the last vestiges of arrogance.
His lawyer leaned closer, murmuring something urgent, but Falfor didn't respond.
It was over.

Laila and Carolyn exchanged a glance — no words, no gestures needed.

It was all there in their eyes:
Relief. Exhaustion. Victory. Hard-won. Deserved.

The judge, his face grave, thanked the jury for their service and formally adjourned the trial.
The courtroom broke into movement — reporters racing for the doors, conversations rising in volume, families embracing, officials quietly packing up.

The electric tension of before was replaced by a heavy, solemn buzz — a collective exhale after weeks of unbearable holding-in.

But for Laila and Carolyn, the moment wasn't wholly celebratory. "Do you feel like we won anything?" Carolyn asked. "Truth". Laila replied.

The verdict was a victory — a bright crack of light in the long night — but the road ahead remained uncertain.
Their courage had exposed rot not just in one man, but in a system many still wished to protect.
Retaliation, whispers, isolation — they knew all of it could still come.

Their fight was not finished.

As they stepped outside, into the cold Pennsylvania air, the courthouse looming behind them like a stone sentinel, the sun was just breaking over the horizon.
Long shadows stretched ahead, but so too did the first fragile light of day.

Laila released Carolyn's hand, only to clap her gently on the shoulder instead.

"We did it," she said, voice low, steady.

Carolyn smiled — a real, weary smile — and nodded.

"We did," she whispered.

Their fight had carved scars they would carry forever. But for today, they had chosen to stand. They had chosen truth over fear.

The weight of the verdict, the burden of justice — they carried it together.

And they were ready for whatever came next.

Aftermath of the Verdict...

The courthouse doors swung shut behind them — heavy oak sealing away the whirlwind of the trial behind them. Outside, the Pennsylvania autumn pressed close — the sun a pale disc in a washed-out sky, long shadows stretching across the worn pavement.
For Laila Wright and Carolyn Pryme, the world beyond the courtroom felt altered.
The air was crisper, cleaner — but the burden on their shoulders remained.
The initial wave of relief that had crashed over them when the verdict was read had already begun to ebb.
In its place settled a deeper exhaustion — a bone-deep weariness that no verdict could erase.
Carolyn leaned heavily on Laila's arm, her steps slow, her gaze downcast.
The usual color in her cheeks was gone, her face pale and hollowed by the toll of weeks spent under a relentless emotional siege.
Laila, soldier as always, steadied her silently — feeling the

tremor in Carolyn's hand, the sag in her frame.
She squeezed her partner's fingers tightly, a silent reassurance:
Still standing. Still here.
Around them, the courthouse steps were a hive of activity. Cameras flashed. Reporters barked questions. Spectators pressed close, kept at bay only by a flimsy cordon of uniformed deputies.
Ahead, a small podium had been hastily set up at the foot of the stairs — a row of microphones bristling from its surface like steel reeds.
The press conference was inevitable.
ADA Kenneth Fitzgerald was already there, adjusting his jacket, conferring with his team.
His face, grim and measured, betrayed none of the exhaustion Laila could see in his eyes.
The bailiff beckoned them forward, and together Laila and Carolyn made their way to stand just behind Fitzgerald — not at the podium itself, but close enough for the cameras to catch them.
Symbols of the battle fought.
Symbols of what justice demanded.
Fitzgerald stepped up to the microphones. The flashbulbs popped wildly. The murmuring crowd fell silent.
He cleared his throat once — then spoke, his voice carrying with the weight of victory and solemnity.
"Today," he began, "justice was served."
He spoke briefly — no grand speeches, no theatrics — about the courage of the witnesses, the importance of accountability, the painful cost of truth.

He named Madeline Clark, giving her life dignity in death, refusing to let her be reduced to a case file or courtroom statistic.
He thanked the jury, the investigative teams, and finally, with a glance back toward Laila and Carolyn, he spoke of those who had risked everything to stand for what was right.
"Their courage," Fitzgerald said firmly, "reminds us that no badge, no title, no position places anyone above the law."
He fielded a few quick questions — terse, carefully measured answers about potential appeals, about broader investigations hinted at but not detailed.
When asked about retaliation against witnesses, he was blunt:
"We are aware of the risks," Fitzgerald said. "And we will not allow intimidation to silence the truth."
The press surged forward, shouting more questions, but Fitzgerald raised a hand, signaling an end.
The courthouse steps erupted into noise once more as the team retreated.
Laila and Carolyn didn't speak as they walked through the crowd — they didn't need to.
Their silence was their armor.
The drive back to the farm was subdued.
Rain misted against the windshield, the world outside blurring into gray smears.
The road wound past bare trees, empty fields — familiar ground rendered unfamiliar by the weight of the past few weeks.

At the farm, they slipped into the kitchen like soldiers returning from a battle.
The kettle whistled. The fireplace crackled.
Simple, grounding sounds.
They ate quietly — not out of sadness, but out of sheer emotional depletion.
The trial had wrung them out, leaving behind only the raw, undeniable reality of survival.
Later, they sat by the fire — mugs of tea cradled between their palms — watching the flames dance across the rough brick hearth.
The heat should have been comforting.
Instead, it was a reminder of the burning intensity they had just endured.
Laila stared into the fire, seeing flashes of the courtroom:
The jury foreman's steady voice.
Falfor's face sagging under the weight of judgment.
Madeline Clark's bright, vanished smile.
Carolyn spoke first, her voice barely a whisper:
"Do you think they'll try something?"
It was the question that had haunted them both — unspoken until now.
Laila didn't hesitate.
"Maybe," she said simply. "But we're ready.
Whatever comes, we stand."
Carolyn nodded slowly, drawing strength from Laila's certainty, even as her hands trembled slightly around her mug.
The shadows flickered along the walls — long, distorted shapes shifting with every pop of the logs.

Victory had come.
But so had the realization that the system they had cracked open would not collapse quietly.
There would be consequences.
There would be more battles.
More nights like this, staring into uncertain futures.
Yet there was also something else —
a steel-hard certainty woven between them, stronger than fear.
They had chosen this path.
Together.
Outside, the storm passed.
The wind eased.
And somewhere beyond the darkness, dawn was waiting.

The Long Road to Justice.

The rain continued its relentless assault on the Pennsylvania landscape, drumming against the windows like a thousand tiny hammers.
Outside, the world seemed wrapped in gray, blurred and indistinct — mirroring the storm raging quietly within Laila Wright.
The verdict — a hard-won, brutal victory — felt less like a triumph and more like a pause between battles.
Dominic Falfor's conviction was a crack in the wall.
But the wall itself — built on decades of corruption, fear, and silence — still stood.
Inside the farmhouse, Carolyn Pryme was already moving,

her phone pressed tightly to her ear as she paced the worn wooden floorboards.
The whispers she'd caught in the courthouse corridors — veiled threats, careful warnings, coded messages passed between shadows — had ignited a cold urgency in her.
Each call she made was a tightrope walk: a plea for support disguised as casual conversation, a quiet search for safe harbors among uncertain allies.
Laila sought refuge in her grandfather's study — a place heavy with the smell of old leather and yellowing paper.
The thick, weathered books lining the shelves had always offered her a kind of anchor: lessons of history, of principle, of endurance.
Her fingers traced the spines as if drawing strength from the quiet ghosts of generations who had fought their own battles for truth.
The rain battered against the glass.
The fire hissed in the hearth.
The farmhouse, once a sanctuary, had become a fortress.
Every creak of wood, every pair of headlights sweeping past on the road, set their nerves singing.
Days bled into weeks.
The farm's fences were reinforced.
Surveillance cameras hidden in the tree line.
Emergency protocols rehearsed in low voices under the cover of night.
Their existence became a tense, careful ballet — outwardly normal, inwardly primed for war.
Carolyn wore her exhaustion plainly now.

The bright spark that usually danced behind her eyes had dimmed, replaced by a wary calculation Laila recognized all too well — the look of a soldier scanning every crowd, every alley, for danger.
One evening, as the fire threw long, restless shadows against the walls, Carolyn finally voiced the fear that had wrapped itself around both their hearts.
"What if we haven't seen the last of it, Laila?"
Her voice cracked, barely audible above the crackling logs.
"What if this is just the beginning?"
Laila didn't speak immediately.
She turned, caught Carolyn's gaze — raw, stripped of armor — and simply placed her hand over hers.
"Then we fight," she said, her voice low and steady.
"Together. Like always."
The simple certainty of her words was a lifeline.
Carolyn's grip tightened.
Their bond — tested, battered, reforged in fire — had become a shield against everything the world might throw at them next.
The victory against Falfor had been only the first step.
The evidence they had unearthed, the testimony given, pointed to something far darker, far more entrenched.
A network of corruption reaching deep into the veins of the Marshal's Service itself.
And so they turned from survival to pursuit.
Laila, drawing on years of tactical and investigative experience, began to assemble the fragments — mapping names, dates, unexplained transfers of power and money.
Piecing together a shadow operation that had thrived in the

cracks of a system meant to protect.
Carolyn moved just as deftly through the corridors of bureaucracy, leaning on trusted allies, tapping old favors, piecing together the invisible resistance gathering within the Service.
Every conversation was a risk.
Every question a potential trigger.
But the two of them moved with relentless purpose — an unspoken understanding that the price of standing down now would be far greater than the risks they faced pressing forward.
What they uncovered was staggering:
A network of senior officials shielding each other, manipulating cases, burying inconvenient truths.
Falfor had been a symptom.
The disease ran far deeper.
The system did not bend easily.
Resistance came in subtle forms:
Bureaucratic inertia.
Misdirection.
Warnings passed through unofficial channels, daring them to turn back.
But they didn't.
Each piece of evidence recovered was another crack in the edifice.
Each whistleblower convinced, another crack.
Each hidden file uncovered, another crack.
The long road to justice had never been paved with easy victories.
It was carved, inch by painful inch, by those willing to

stand when standing meant sacrifice.
The fight ahead would be dirtier.
Harder.
Longer.
But as Laila and Carolyn sat by the fire that night, the rain softening into mist outside, they knew one thing with absolute clarity:
They were not finished.
Not by a long shot.
And together, armed with truth and forged by loyalty, they would keep carving cracks into the wall — until it finally, inevitably, came crashing down.

The Family, Banter, and Warnings.

The scent of fresh bread and roasted meat filled the farmhouse kitchen, clashing with the undercurrent of tension that neither time nor distance could erase.
Rain beat against the windows, a steady drumroll that added a strange intimacy to the old house.
Laila sat at the kitchen table, peeling an apple with mechanical precision, her mind elsewhere.
Carolyn lounged nearby, tossing a ball of foil from hand to hand, a mischievous glint returning — if only briefly — to her tired eyes.
It was a small, fragile attempt at normalcy.
The front door swung open with a bang, letting in a blast of cold air — and two laughing figures.
Daniel and Thomas Wright, Laila's older brothers, stumbled inside, carrying bundles of firewood and trailing

the wet, earthy smell of rain-soaked clothes.

"Hey, city girls," Daniel called out, shaking rain from his hair like a dog. "We heard you needed rescuing."

"Rescuing?" Carolyn smirked, standing to plant her hands on her hips. "Please. You two couldn't rescue a cat out of a puddle."

Thomas grinned, stripping off his jacket.

"We do make better scenery, though."

Carolyn laughed — a real laugh, short and bright, a break in the gloom.

She gave a theatrical once-over at both brothers.

"Scenery?" she said, pretending to appraise them. "Hmm. Maybe if we squint."

Daniel clutched his chest dramatically.

"Wounded. Crushed. Betrayed by a federal officer."

Laila shook her head, a half-smile tugging at her mouth.

"She flirts with everyone when she's stressed," she deadpanned.

"And when I'm not stressed," Carolyn added brightly, winking at Thomas, who nearly dropped the firewood.

The kitchen erupted in laughter — not loud, not wild — but real.

A precious crack of light piercing the heavy clouds pressing down around them.

Their mother, Eleanor Wright, emerged from the pantry with a dish towel slung over one shoulder, her face stern but soft around the eyes.

The laughter faded slightly when she entered — not out of fear, but respect.

She crossed to Laila’s side, setting a gentle hand on her shoulder.

"Come walk with me, sweetheart," she said quietly.

Laila nodded, rising smoothly.

The kitchen chatter picked up behind them again — Daniel teasing Carolyn, Thomas burning himself slightly on a kettle — but the hallway where Eleanor led her was quieter, shadowed and still.

They paused near the big picture window overlooking the back fields.

Beyond the misted glass, the rain blurred the world into a watercolor haze.

Eleanor studied her daughter carefully, the way only a mother could.

"You're worried," she said.

Not a question. A fact.

Laila sighed, crossing her arms tightly over her chest.

Her soldier's mask faltered just slightly in the dim light.

"It's not over, Mama," she said. "We hit something bigger than we realized. And they're angry. They're scared."

Eleanor said nothing, just waited.

"Threats have started," Laila continued, her voice low. "Not accidents. Not random. Purposeful. Targeted."

Eleanor nodded slowly, as if she'd already known somehow.

Mothers often did.

"You think they'll come here?," she asked.

Laila hesitated — then nodded once, sharply.

"Maybe not tonight. Maybe not tomorrow. But they will. They want to remind us we're never safe."

Eleanor's hand squeezed Laila's arm gently.
"You're not alone, Laila.
Not in this house. Not in this family."
Tears pricked the back of Laila's eyes — unwelcome, unexpected.
She blinked them back fiercely.
"We know how to defend ourselves," Eleanor added, her voice soft but steely. "You taught us well. You and your father both. He was a stubborn but fierce man, and he loved us."
They stood together, watching the fields blur into the rainy distance, two generations of strength welded together by love and stubbornness and hard-earned wisdom.
When they returned to the kitchen, Carolyn was still holding court with Daniel and Thomas — both brothers clearly enjoying the distraction she provided, their laughter louder now.
But under the surface, they all knew.
The laughter was a shield.
The family was a fortress.
And the outside storm,
inevitable,
was coming.

Retaliation Attempts.

The quiet hum of the refrigerator was the only sound in the farmhouse kitchen as Laila stared out the window, the pre- dawn darkness clinging to the Pennsylvania countryside like a shroud. Carolyn's breath hitched beside her, a soft gasp that spoke volumes of the unspoken anxieties that gnawed at them both. The guilty verdict against Falfor had felt like a pyrrhic victory, a fleeting moment of triumph overshadowed by the looming shadow of retaliation.

That shadow had begun to materialize in subtle ways. Anonymous calls, late at night, filled with heavy breathing and disconnected lines. A slashed tire on Carolyn's car, discovered one morning as she prepared for work. A flickering light in the distance, seen only momentarily in the periphery, a suggestion of something watching, lurking in the darkness. These were not the actions of random vandals; these were deliberate, calculated threats, designed to instill fear, to test their resolve.

One evening, while Laila was meticulously reviewing the case files, a package arrived. No return address, just a plain brown wrapper. Inside, nestled amidst layers of packing peanuts, was a single, wilted red rose. The thorns were carefully removed, but the petals were bruised, almost decaying, a macabre mockery of romance. A chilling message, handwritten on a scrap of paper, accompanied the flower: "Justice is a two-way street."

Carolyn's color drained as she read the note. Her hand trembled as she held it up to the light, searching for an identifying mark, a clue, anything that could lead them to the sender. "This isn't just intimidation, Laila," she whispered, her voice laced with a chilling certainty. "This is a warning."

Laila's military training kicked in, a reflexive response honed over years of combat and high-stakes investigations. She carefully examined the rose, the paper, the packaging, looking for fingerprints, trace evidence, any sign of the sender's identity. She meticulously documented everything, taking photographs, collecting samples, her mind racing through various scenarios, formulating countermeasures.

The next few days were a blur of heightened awareness, a constant state of vigilance. Laila and Carolyn traded off shifts, one always on alert while the other slept, their senses sharpened, their instincts honed to a razor's edge. The farm, once a sanctuary, had transformed into a fortress, their daily routine carefully structured around security protocols, their movements planned and deliberate.

They fortified the property, installing motion detectors, improving lighting, reinforcing doors and windows. Laila, drawing on her military experience, designed a rudimentary security system, utilizing readily available resources and their existing knowledge of the property's layout. Carolyn, using her contacts within the law enforcement system, discreetly requested additional surveillance and police patrols in the area, though she was met with vague reassurances and little concrete assistance. The subtle resistance, the veiled indifference, only fueled their suspicions of deeper collusion.

One night, a vehicle approached the farm, its headlights cutting through the darkness, illuminating the farmhouse in a stark glare. They had been expecting it, prepared for it, yet the anticipation did little to dampen the surge of adrenaline as the vehicle stopped at the edge of the property. Laila and Carolyn, armed and ready, watched from behind reinforced windows, their hearts pounding in unison. The vehicle remained for what seemed like an eternity, its occupants unseen, its intentions unclear. Then, just as suddenly as it had arrived, it departed, disappearing into the night, leaving behind only silence and lingering fear.

The following days brought more subtle threats, more disturbing messages. Anonymous packages arrived at their workplaces, each containing a different grim memento – a single bullet, a broken watch, a charred photograph of Madeline Clark. The messages were clear: they were being hunted. The system, the very institution they had tried to reform, had turned against them.

Their investigation into Falfor had unearthed a vast network of corruption within the Marshal's service, reaching far beyond the reach of their immediate investigation. Their pursuit of justice had not only exposed Falfor, but it had also inadvertently angered powerful figures, those with the resources and influence to unleash a relentless campaign of harassment and intimidation.

Carolyn's network of contacts began to dry up. Calls went unanswered, messages were ignored. The walls of the system seemed to close in, reinforcing their initial fear and suspicion. The lack of support from within the system forced Laila and Carolyn to operate alone, relying solely on their skills, their instincts, and their unwavering bond.

Laila sought the help of her old military contacts, men and women who understood the realities of clandestine operations and covert threats. She relayed the details of the escalating threats, the subtle patterns of harassment, the deliberate ambiguity of the messages. They shared their knowledge, their resources, providing advice and support, but their involvement was necessarily clandestine, carefully veiled from official scrutiny.

The escalating threat level brought a new dimension to their investigation, a desperate race against time to uncover the source of the retaliation before they became victims. Their search for truth and justice had become a fight for survival. The lines between hunter and hunted had blurred, and the consequences of their actions loomed larger than ever before. The battle for justice had become a fight for their own lives, a relentless pursuit in which every shadow held potential danger and every moment could be their last. The farm, once a refuge, had become a battleground, and the war was far from over. The quiet nights were punctuated by the sounds of vigilance, the constant hum of anxiety, the chilling reality of their perilous situation. The fight for truth and justice had taken on a new urgency; it was now a matter of survival.

Chapter 6

Internal Affairs Investigation

The initial wave of public outrage following Falfor's conviction eventually ebbed, replaced by something far more unsettling:
Silence.

The media, once rabid in its coverage, turned its attention elsewhere, leaving Laila and Carolyn exposed, vulnerable in the vacuum.
The farmhouse, once a haven, now seemed to echo with a deeper, darker unease.
It wasn't just the external threats that gnawed at them — it was the growing, suffocating absence of support from the very system they had served.

The Marshal Service, eager to contain the damage, announced a sweeping Internal Affairs investigation. Official statements brimmed with promises of reform and accountability.
But behind closed doors, it felt less like a pursuit of justice and more like a carefully choreographed exercise in damage control.

Agent Miller was assigned to lead the inquiry — a man whose every line and movement seemed etched with weary cynicism.
A veteran investigator, yes — but one whose disillusionment clung to him like a second skin.

When he first arrived at the farm, Laila studied him

closely:
The heavy coat.
The worn leather case.
The exhausted, watchful eyes.

And something else — a quiet hostility barely hidden behind the professional veneer.

Their first interviews were civil on the surface.
But beneath the polite questions and clipped notes, Laila sensed the real purpose.

They weren't being investigated as witnesses.
They were being investigated as threats.

Miller's questions were precise scalpels, not hammers.
Not about Falfor's crimes — but about them.
Their motivations. Their personal lives. Their judgment.

"We're looking into systemic failures," Miller said flatly, reclining in a chair that groaned under his weight.
"How could a man like Falfor operate for so long without anyone noticing?"

But Laila heard the unspoken accusation:
How could you let it happen? Why did you have to bring it to light?

Carolyn answered carefully, but even she — sharp, composed Carolyn — was showing cracks.
The relentless nature of the questioning, the deliberate pressure tactics, wore them down, hour by hour, session by session.

Miller magnified trivial inconsistencies — a shift in timeline phrasing, a forgotten detail about a meeting location — blowing them out of proportion, weaving a narrative of doubt.

The pressure wasn't just professional.
It was personal.

The subtle suggestion that their bond — the sisterhood forged through survival — was somehow suspect, inappropriate, tarnished.
It was a slow bleed of credibility, a way to isolate them, erode their foundation.

The investigation's scope expanded outward.

Background checks.
Financial audits.
Work histories combed line by line.

Miller's team dredged up records of suspicious transfers, buried complaints, and cover-ups spanning years — perhaps decades.

They unearthed chilling patterns:
Marshals quietly shuffled between posts.
Internal investigations abruptly closed without findings.
Promotions granted to those who looked the other way.

The rot wasn't isolated.

It was systemic.

And the deeper Laila and Carolyn dug — and the more they watched Miller *not* dig — the more certain they became:

Falfor wasn't the disease.
He was a symptom.

As the investigation ground on, the threats escalated.

Late-night phone calls.
Packages left on their porch — a single bullet, a shredded photograph of Madeline Clark, a charred child's toy.

A silent promise: *We see you.*

Their families weren't spared either.
Pictures of Laila's brothers.
Carolyn's sister's address — sent anonymously.

Each new threat hammered home the truth:
They were not just witnesses anymore.
They were enemies to be eliminated.

Miller acknowledged the threats with a shrug and a half-hearted promise to "review security protocols." But no additional protection materialized.
No new patrols.
No assurances.

Only silence.

The farmhouse bristled with new alarms, reinforced locks, hidden cameras — all built by their own hands. The Service, the institution they had once believed in, had turned its back.

At night, Laila lay awake, listening to the farmhouse settle — every creak a potential intruder.
Carolyn's room, just down the hall, sometimes glowed faintly into the early hours — her light left on, the quiet evidence of a woman who no longer

trusted the dark.

The Internal Affairs investigation dragged on — a slow, suffocating noose tightening around them.

The system was protecting itself.
And Laila and Carolyn — inconvenient, disloyal truth-tellers — were marked for erasure.

The war for justice had become a war for survival.

And survival, they realized now, would mean stepping far outside the rules they had once sworn to uphold.

The old rules had already been broken.

Now it was their turn.

Media Scrutiny...

The verdict against Dominic Falfor sent shockwaves across the nation.
Cable news dedicated hours of airtime dissecting every detail of the trial.
Talk shows debated endlessly.
Social media exploded with outrage.
The image of Madeline Clark — a smiling thirteen-year-old, frozen forever in time — became the face of a national reckoning.
#JusticeForMadeline
#CleanUpLawEnforcement
#AccountabilityNow
Hashtags blazed across screens, fueling a digital storm of anger, grief, and demands for systemic reform.

Editorials thundered from major newspapers, questioning the efficacy of internal investigations, condemning the "blue wall of silence," calling for sweeping changes not just in the Marshal Service, but across all law enforcement agencies.
What began as the downfall of one corrupt officer rapidly metastasized into a broader indictment of the system itself.
At first, Laila Wright and Carolyn Pryme stood at the heart of a hurricane of praise.
They were hailed as heroes.
Whistleblowers.
Symbols of courage against impossible odds.
Profile pieces lauded their bravery.
They sat, reluctantly but dutifully, for interview after interview — their faces becoming fixtures on screens and magazine covers.
For a brief moment, they were the nation's champions.
Proof that integrity could still survive in the corridors of power.
But that spotlight burned bright.
And then it began to turn.
The constant scrutiny wore them down.
Every word they spoke was dissected.
Every hesitation magnified.
Every nuance twisted by commentators eager for a new narrative.
And slowly, the questions shifted.
What had they known — and when?
Had they acted out of duty — or ambition?
Was there a personal vendetta motivating their courage?

Carolyn saw it first.
"They're trying to flip the script," she said one night, staring bleakly at the television as a panel of talking heads speculated about their 'possible biases.'
"They're setting us up to fall."
Investigative journalists — emboldened, or perhaps instructed — began digging deeper.
Into Laila's military past.
Into Carolyn's internal service records.
Into minor administrative complaints, professional rivalries, even past personal relationships.
Suddenly, it wasn't just about Falfor's crimes.
It was about *them*.
Their flaws.
Their imperfections.
Their supposed "motives."
Meanwhile, the threats that had once been whispered grew louder, bolder.
Anonymous messages escalated from veiled warnings to overt promises of harm.
Photos of Laila's brothers arriving in unmarked envelopes.
Details about Carolyn's sister's job posted online.
Unmarked vehicles idling outside the farmhouse in the dead of night.
The system, it seemed, had decided to fight back.
Not with open violence — not yet — but with character assassination and silent terror.
Agent Miller, leading the Internal Affairs inquiry, sharpened his assault.

No longer bothering with courtesy, he drilled into their testimonies, magnifying minor discrepancies into suggestions of deceit.
He implied professional jealousy.
He hinted at personal entanglements clouding judgment.
And the media — hungry for blood, always ready to turn on yesterday's heroes — amplified every insinuation.
Laila recognized the strategy.
Classic counterinsurgency tactics:
Isolate the target.
Discredit the source.
Destroy the symbol.
But recognition didn't make it any less effective.
Support drained away.
Sympathy curdled into suspicion.
They were no longer symbols of hope.
They were liabilities.
Inconvenient witnesses in a system desperate to cleanse itself — not by reform, but by burying the truth along with them.
Onc evening, sitting by the fire as rain lashed against the windows, Carolyn broke the thick, exhausted silence.
"It's not just Falfor they're protecting," she said quietly. "It's everything behind him."
Laila nodded slowly, staring into the flames.
Her voice was steel.
"And that's exactly what we're going to tear down."
The farmhouse — once their fortress — now felt more like an outpost under siege.
The war wasn't over.

It had simply changed fronts.

Emotional Toll

The quiet of Laila's Pennsylvania farmhouse, once a refuge from the chaos of her life, now felt like a cage.
The rhythmic chirping of crickets — once a lullaby — was drowned beneath the ever-present hum of anxiety that thrummed under her skin.
Sleep offered no reprieve.
Nightmares stalked her, pulling her back again and again to Madeline Clark's lifeless eyes.
Carolyn bore the strain just as deeply.
The bright energy that had once lit up her every movement was dulled now, her sharp gaze clouded with a weariness that seeped into her bones.
The bond they had forged — a brotherhood born not of blood, but of battle — was tested daily by the relentless pressure and growing isolation.
The first wave of public support had ebbed away like a retreating tide, leaving them exposed on the rocky shore.
The media, once eager to champion them, now dissected their every word, their every expression, twisting nuances into suspicion.
Each minor discrepancy in their testimonies, each hesitation under the relentless questioning of Agent Miller, was seized upon, magnified, weaponized.
Every new headline seemed less about justice and more about doubt.
The righteous fire that had once fueled them flickered low.

Laila found herself replaying the trial in endless loops — searching for mistakes, for missteps, for moments where she might have handed the enemy ammunition.
The certainty she had once carried like armor eroded under the grind of scrutiny and isolation.
Carolyn, ever pragmatic, tried to maintain routines, but the cracks showed.
Her appetite withered.
Her easy laughter disappeared.
The hollow spaces beneath her eyes grew deeper with every sleepless night.
The threats gnawed at them — anonymous calls, veiled warnings, familiar faces in unfamiliar cars parked just out of sight.
The silence between each new intimidation was almost worse than the acts themselves.
The farmhouse, once a sanctuary, became a fortress under siege.
Friends and family — initially vocal in their support — began to pull away.
Fear, Laila understood.
People feared contamination, feared retaliation, feared standing too close to those who had dared to stand at all.
Even here, among the soft fields and misty hills of her childhood, Laila found no real peace.
The earth still smelled the same.
The seasons still turned in their slow, patient way.
But the soil that had once grounded her now felt fragile beneath her feet.
The psychological toll deepened.

Both women battled PTSD — the sudden jolts of adrenaline from creaking floorboards, the way shadows seemed to lurch alive in the corners of their vision, the crushing chest-tightness when the wind slammed the screen door too hard.

Trained as they were to endure hardship, this was different.

This was personal.

This wasn't survival under fire.

It was survival under silence.

Isolation weaponized into a slow, grinding siege.

Simple tasks became monumental.

Carolyn, once so decisive, found herself standing in the kitchen unsure of what to do next, paralyzed by a tidal wave of anxiety she could not name or fend off.

Laila battled demons far older.

The horrors of war — images she had long ago locked away — bled into the present:

The sharp crack of gunfire imagined at the creak of the barn.

The endless funerals reawakened by a single glimpse of Madeline's photo on a newspaper left at the general store.

Their friendship strained under the weight.

There were arguments — sharp words thrown and regretted, long silences filled with things too painful to say.

Moments where resentment — not at each other, but at their shared circumstances — cracked the surface of their bond.

Yet the bond held.

Frayed, battered, bent almost to breaking — but held.

They didn't speak of loyalty anymore.

They lived it.
It was in the way Carolyn passed Laila her coffee, knowing without asking she hadn't slept.
It was in the way Laila double-checked every door and window before letting Carolyn sleep, wordlessly taking the first watch.
It was in the way, night after night, they both kept rising.
The aftermath of the trial was not the clean victory the public had imagined.
It was a daily battle — a relentless, grinding war against despair, against betrayal, against the slow bleed of faith.
Their lives were no longer measured in court victories or media accolades.
They were measured in survival.
And survival, for now, was enough.
The farmhouse remained quiet.
The crickets sang.
The shadows still danced along the walls.
But so did something else —
A quiet, unkillable fire.
They would endure.
They would fight.
Because that was who they were.
Because surrender, even now, even broken and battered, was never an option.

The Professional Ramifications…

The whispers started subtly, like the rustle of dry

leaves across an abandoned courtyard.
At first, they were easy to dismiss — quiet murmurs in hallway corners, glances exchanged across crowded cafeterias.
But soon, the whispers grew louder, sharper, unavoidable.

Their testimonies, once celebrated as acts of defiant heroism, were now subjected to a brutal dissection. Every hesitation, every small inconsistency — natural in any high-pressure situation — was magnified into supposed evidence of instability, or worse, deceit.

The internal affairs investigation, led by the methodical and merciless Agent Miller, felt less like a pursuit of truth and more like an orchestrated purge. Each question he asked carried a blade's edge:
Not demanding confession — but planting seeds of doubt, drip by drip, into the minds of their superiors and peers.

Miller never accused openly.
He didn't need to.
The power of insinuation did the work for him.

The Marshal Service — once their home, their brotherhood — turned cold and brittle around them.

Colleagues who had once stood shoulder to shoulder with them now avoided eye contact.
Partners found excuses to reassign.
Opportunities vanished under vague explanations about "restructuring" and "review periods."

Their reputations, once sterling, were left to rot in the silent judgment of empty break rooms and unanswered phone calls.

The rot spread beyond the Service.
Other agencies — ATF, FBI, local departments — hesitated to cooperate with Laila and Carolyn.
Collaboration offers dried up.
Background whispers began to tarnish every corner of their professional worlds.

Laila's military service — once a badge of honor — was now twisted against her.

"Combat stress."
"Hypervigilance."
"Difficulty distinguishing civilian threat levels."

The very discipline and battlefield-tested clarity that once made her an asset now became a weapon to undermine her.

Carolyn, who had built her career on meticulous professionalism, fared no better.
Her partnership with Laila — once praised as a model of efficiency — was recast as suspicious collusion, a "troublesome" alliance that called her judgment into question.

The effect was devastating.

Career advancement opportunities disappeared overnight.
Promotions were quietly shelved.
Mentorships evaporated.

Doors once open were now bolted shut.

And lurking just beyond the professional shunning were the legal threats — growing like storm clouds on the horizon.

Civil suits loomed, not just from Falfor's allies, but shockingly, from Madeline Clark's grieving family. A family manipulated by a shifting public narrative, now desperate for closure — and vulnerable to those offering easy targets for their rage.

The possibility of financial ruin, of years entangled in costly litigation, became a grim reality.
Every court summons, every notice, every whispered warning felt like another lash across an already battered spirit.

The psychological toll deepened.

Fear, once a background hum, became a constant companion.
Fear of losing everything.
Fear of dying anonymously in a system designed to erase inconvenient heroes.

The professional network that had once buoyed them had rotted into an invisible prison of suspicion and betrayal.

And so they turned inward, relying only on each other and leaning a little on their families.

Their bond — battered, strained, silent — remained intact.
Not by the warmth of camaraderie, but by necessity.
By sheer survival instinct.

They spoke less now.
Each understood the other's exhaustion without needing words.

At night, as the rain whispered against the farmhouse windows and the shadows shifted across the fields, the weight of isolation pressed down harder.

The bright futures they had once imagined — leadership, innovation, change — were gone.

What remained was survival.

The farmhouse — their fortress — had become a symbol of all they had lost.
A hollow place filled not with peace, but with the bitter echo of a fight they had dared to start.

The system had exacted its price.

But it had not yet broken them.

Not completely.

And somewhere deep within the silence, beneath the exhaustion and despair, something fierce still smoldered:

The knowledge that they had told the truth.

The knowledge that the battle wasn't over.

It had simply moved to a new front.

And they were still standing.

First Offensive: Part One Gathering Evidence

The farmhouse had gone cold.

Not from the weather — the spring air outside was

soft and sweet — but from the realization that waiting would only end in death.

Laila sat at the old kitchen table, boots scuffing against worn wood, while Carolyn pinned a large sheet of butcher paper to the wall.

On it, they had begun to draw the real map.

Not one of territory or terrain — but of power.

Each name they knew.
Each whisper they'd heard.
Each "coincidental" promotion, "unexplained" transfer, "lost" internal complaint.

“They buried the bodies in paperwork,” Carolyn muttered, marking lines in black ink between names.

“Then we'll exhume them.” Laila’s voice was iron.

They knew they couldn’t rely on public appeals anymore.
They needed facts.
Documents.
Voices.

Hard evidence.

It was the only shield left.

They divided the targets.

Carolyn would dig inside the Marshal Service — exploiting old favors, forgotten access codes, invisible loopholes that hadn't yet been sealed against her.

Laila would reach outward — calling on former military contacts skilled in cyber operations and surveillance.

Quiet.
Efficient.
Deadly precise.

They would find the rot at the roots.

The first missions were small.

A late-night visit to a shuttered evidence locker in Harrisburg — a warehouse supposedly decommissioned, where files from old internal affairs investigations were quietly "misplaced."

Carolyn, wearing dark jeans and a borrowed maintenance uniform, slipped inside using a security code still assigned to her profile — overlooked in the Service's half-hearted attempt to erase her.

Inside, the air was thick with dust and neglect.

She found it buried in an unmarked box.

A series of internal memos from six years earlier — showing warnings raised about Dominic Falfor's conduct.

Warnings ignored.
Suppressed.
Reassigned.

She photographed everything.

Not just Falfor — but a dozen other names linked to the same network.

Back at the farmhouse, under the flicker of the storm lantern, they catalogued their first evidence:

- Internal complaints were deleted without investigation.

- Early accusations of excessive force dismissed.
- Supervisors who rubber-stamped promotions without background checks.

It wasn't enough to break the dam yet.

But it was proof the cracks had always been there.

Next came the riskier move:
Tracking the "ghost files."

Files supposedly purged from digital records, but which Laila knew — from her time in Army Intelligence — often left traces on internal backup servers.

She called in a favor.

A former cyber-warfare specialist named Beckett — a ghost even within military circles.

They arranged a meeting in the parking lot of an abandoned strip mall, under the cover of a rainstorm.

Beckett was wary.

"You sure you wanna poke this bear?"
He lit a cigarette with shaking fingers. "This ain't leaking to the Times. You're talking about institutions that make people disappear."

Laila didn't flinch.

"I don't need it leaked. I need it retrieved."

Beckett gave a grim smile.

"You always were terrible at asking nicely."

He agreed to try.

One week.

One chance.

No promises.

As he drove away into the mist, Carolyn leaned against the hood of the truck, pulling her jacket tight against the cold.

"You trust him?" she asked.

Laila watched the taillights disappear.

"No," she said.
"But I trust the dirt more."

They both knew:
Once they pulled those files, they couldn't undo it.

There would be no hiding.
No retreat.

They were now committed.

The first shots of the real war had been fired — and this time, they were aiming first.

The rain had thickened into a steady, heavy curtain by the time Laila and Carolyn returned to the farmhouse.

They worked in silence, scanning and cataloguing everything they'd recovered so far.
The stolen documents.
The ghost memos.
The names.

The growing web on their butcher-paper map now stretched across almost the entire wall.

Not just Falfor.

Supervisors.
Deputy Marshals.
Internal Affairs agents.

Even an Assistant Director.

A conspiracy years in the making, rooted deep and wide.

Carolyn circled three names in red ink.

“These three. They coordinated Falfor’s last assignment.”

Laila leaned closer.

“Gatekeepers.”

Carolyn nodded grimly.

"And one of them’s still in Harrisburg."

They exchanged a look.
Silent agreement.

Time to press.

David Rourke.

Deputy Section Chief.
Mid-level.
Ambitious.
Vulnerable.

They tracked him to a downtown steakhouse after hours — one frequented by federal employees who didn’t want official meetings on official record.

He wasn’t alone.

Three other Marshals — ones linked to the web — sat with him, nursing scotches, laughing too loudly.

Carolyn, dressed down in civilian clothes, took a booth near the back.

Laila lingered at the bar, pretending to nurse a beer.

They watched.

Listened.

It didn't take long.

Rourke, already two drinks deep, started to brag — low, bitter, boasting — about how Falfor had been "set up to fail."
About "making an example of someone expendable."
About "sacrificing a few pawns to save the king."

Carolyn leaned closer, her heart hammering.

She pressed record on her burner phone, sliding it behind a napkin holder.

Every word Rourke said was a nail in the coffin.
Not enough for court yet — but enough to terrify the right people.

Enough to force mistakes.

As Rourke stumbled toward the restroom, Laila followed.

Intercepted him just inside the hallway.

Her voice was low.
Neutral.

"Deputy Chief."

Rourke blinked, trying to focus.

"I know what you did," Laila said.

He paled instantly.
A bead of sweat rolled down his temple.

"Leave it alone," he hissed.

"You don’t know who you're really messing with."

"Then enlighten me."

He glanced over her shoulder — checking for help, finding none.

"They're bigger than the Service," he whispered. "You're already dead. You just don't know it yet."

Laila let him stumble away.

She didn’t need more.

Sometimes panic spoke louder than confession.

Back at the farmhouse, they stitched the recording into their growing evidence archive.

Each piece added more weight.

More danger.

Carolyn clicked through the files Beckett had begun to unlock from the Marshal Service's supposedly purged servers.

It was worse than they feared.

Not just complaints.

Not just misconduct.

Connections to private security firms.
Illegal asset seizures.
Unreported deaths.

And always — always — the same handful of names turning up at the edges.

Laila rubbed a hand over her face, exhaustion dragging at her bones.

"We’re sitting on a damn bomb."

Carolyn nodded grimly.

"Question is — where do we detonate it?"

The answer came sooner than they wanted.

A knock at the farmhouse door.

Three sharp raps.
Not friendly.
Not hesitant.

Laila's instincts screamed.

She motioned Carolyn back into the kitchen, drawing her sidearm from beneath her sweatshirt.

Another knock — harder this time.

She moved to the window, staying low.

A dark SUV idled just beyond the porch light.
Government plates.

A figure in a dark jacket stood at the threshold — hands empty, posture careful.

Not a hit squad.

At least, not yet.

Laila eased the door open a crack.

The man outside raised a badge slowly.

"Special Agent Nathan Reddick," he said quietly.
"Office of Inspector General."

Laila didn't move.

"We need to talk," Reddick said.
"Before you get yourselves killed."

First Offensive: Part Two Exposing the Network.

The farmhouse living room had become a battlefield of silences.

Special Agent Nathan Reddick stood just inside the door, damp from the rain, his badge still visible but his posture cautious — a man who understood just how thin the ice beneath him was.

Carolyn kept her hand near the grip of her concealed weapon.
Laila remained stone-faced.

"We don't trust easily these days," Laila said, her voice flat.

Reddick nodded once.
"Good. You shouldn't."

He took a seat by the window, careful to angle himself so he could see both exits without seeming to.

"You two dug into something bigger than you realize. Falfor was expendable. The people running this... they're not."

He pulled a flash drive from his pocket and slid it across the table.

"Proof of life."

Carolyn picked it up warily, plugging it into the burner laptop.

Encrypted files loaded instantly.

Photos.
Financial ledgers.
Maps.
Names.

Confirmation of what they'd begun to piece together — and hints of even deeper corruption tied to federal contracts, private prisons, narcotics interdiction programs.

"Why help us?" Laila asked.

Reddick's jaw tightened.

"Because if this doesn't come down the right way, the system eats itself alive."

He leaned forward, voice dropping.

"You've got about a week before they stop playing cute and start playing lethal. We leak this smart, targeted... or we all go down together."

Laila and Carolyn exchanged a long look.

Trust was still out of reach.

But necessity wasn't.

They planned in whispers, huddled over the kitchen table as a cold dawn crept over the fields.

The leak had to be surgical — not a mass dump, not an anonymous upload that could be discredited or buried.

"One source," Carolyn said, tapping her pen against the table. "One journalist. Someone with enough reach to survive the first hit."

"And someone they can't buy off," Laila added grimly.

They compiled a list.
Cross-checked affiliations.
Ruled out the obvious puppets.

Finally, they settled on Erin Haldane — a stubborn investigative reporter with a track record of surviving lawsuits, smear campaigns, and even an assassination attempt during a cartel investigation.

"Risky," Carolyn murmured.
"But it's better than waiting to get buried."

Reddick agreed to broker the first meeting.
Neutral ground.
Minimal exposure.

It was a dangerous gambit.

But doing nothing was suicide.

The meeting place was a parking structure beneath an abandoned mall twenty miles outside Harrisburg — a decaying concrete shell perfect for clandestine transactions.

Laila and Carolyn arrived early, scanning the perimeter with sharp, practiced eyes.
Carolyn drove a battered pickup.
Laila had an untraceable burner phone and a compact .45 tucked into a side holster.

Erin Haldane was due in fifteen minutes.

Reddick hadn't shown yet — though he promised he would.

The only other signs of life were a few rats and the dripping echo of rain leaking through the cracked ceiling.

Too quiet.

Laila felt it first — the subtle vibration beneath her boots, the shift in the stillness.

“Company,” she murmured.

Carolyn’s hand slid to the Glock under her jacket.

A black SUV emerged from the far ramp, tires hissing against wet concrete.

Not Reddick’s car.

Not Erin’s.

Three figures piled out — no badges, no hesitation.

Guns up.

Laila and Carolyn moved instantly, instincts overriding thought.

Carolyn shoved open the passenger door, diving behind the engine block as the first shots rang out — the deafening crack of suppressed 9mm rounds cutting through the air.

Laila rolled low, returning fire with two quick, disciplined shots — forcing the attackers to scatter.

Concrete chipped and screamed as bullets tore into the walls around them.

"Trap!" Carolyn shouted.

"No shit!" Laila snapped back, ducking another volley.

They moved together, years of training in perfect

synchronicity.

Carolyn laid down cover fire, her rounds slamming into the SUV's fender, sending the assailants scrambling for better angles.

Laila sprinted for a concrete pillar, using the brief window of chaos to flank.

A round grazed her shoulder — a burning kiss of pain — but she didn't slow.

She caught one of the attackers in her sights — a man in tactical black, no insignia — and dropped him with two center-mass shots.

Another muzzle flashed to her right.

Carolyn pivoted smoothly, firing once, twice — and another enemy crumpled behind a stack of cinderblocks.

For a heartbeat, the parking deck was still.

Then tires screeched overhead.

Another vehicle.

Backup incoming.

"Out!" Laila barked.

They fell back together, weaving between crumbling concrete barriers, hearts hammering, muscles burning.

Shots ricocheted around them — close enough that Laila could smell the cordite.

They reached the stairwell exit just as a second wave of gunfire shattered the windshield of the pickup.

No time to mourn it.

They slammed through the door into the stairwell, boots pounding against the corroded steel steps, adrenaline fueling every breathless heartbeat.

Carolyn kicked open the emergency exit at the top.

They burst out into the gray, rain-slicked morning — alive, bruised, bloodied but breathing.

Their truck was a wreck.

Their meeting was compromised.

And the enemy was no longer content to just smear their names.

They wanted them dead.

Aftermath: Back to Strategy.

They drove a stolen service van they'd hotwired from the abandoned mall parking lot.

Silent.

Gritting their teeth against pain.

Neither spoke until the farmhouse lights finally blinked into view, a small beacon against the endless gray.

Inside, Laila peeled off her soaked jacket, wincing at the graze along her shoulder — a raw, angry welt.

Carolyn pressed a towel against it, her face tight with worry.

"They're escalating fast."

Laila nodded grimly, breathing through the pain.

"Means we're close to something."

Carolyn dumped the burner phones into the wood stove, watching the flames consume them.

"Plan's still alive," she said. "New location. New contact window. We don't stop."

Laila leaned heavily against the counter, exhaustion threatening to drag her under.

But her eyes — her eyes burned with renewed fire.

"No. We don't stop."

She crossed to the butcher paper map, redrawing lines, adjusting targets.

The enemy had made their move.

Now it was their turn.

And next time, they would hit first.

Hard.

Part Two: The System Fights Back.

The first sign that things had escalated beyond bureaucratic warfare came with the black SUV parked a little too perfectly across from Laila's farmhouse. It was there at dawn and still there at midnight, windows blacked out, its occupants invisible but their message crystal clear.

"You're being watched," Carolyn said grimly, setting a steaming cup of coffee on the farmhouse table between them.

Her hand hovered over the holstered Glock at her hip, an old habit from her years in tactical ops. "And they're not playing fair anymore."

Laila nodded, her jaw tight. She'd known it was only a matter of time. They were getting too close, pulling too many threads, and someone in the higher echelons had decided intimidation was easier than answering uncomfortable questions.

The real test came two days later.

It was supposed to be a simple retrieval — a backup drive hidden in a rented storage unit across state lines. The drive contained raw footage from courthouse surveillance cameras, footage that had mysteriously been "corrupted" in the official files but which the private security contractor had kept a copy of.

Evidence that could not just clear their names — but expose a web of corruption so tangled it would shake the Marshal's Service to its core.

Laila and Carolyn approached the facility at dusk. The place was deserted, the last slanting rays of sunlight casting long shadows across the cracked asphalt. Carolyn handled the lock — a quick flick of her wrist and the padlock snapped open, no time wasted.

The storage unit's door rattled up halfway before they froze.

Movement inside.

Laila's instincts screamed — she ducked, dragging Carolyn down with her just as the first shot cracked the silence like a thunderclap.

BANG!

A slug tore through the flimsy aluminum siding behind them, sending shards of metal whirling. Without thinking, Laila rolled, drew her sidearm, and returned fire — two quick shots toward the muzzle flash she'd seen.

Carolyn was already moving, flanking left, her own weapon spitting concise, disciplined rounds.

Another shooter revealed himself near the rear exit of the facility — a dark-clad figure with a short-barreled rifle. He squeezed off a burst — too high, panic overtaking training — and Laila felt the rounds zing overhead, snapping through the dry evening air.

"Two shooters!" Carolyn barked, her voice steady.

"Copy!" Laila called back, sliding behind a rusting metal dumpster for cover.

She exhaled slowly, narrowing her world to the iron sights of her weapon and the rhythm of her heartbeat. In combat, clarity came.

A shadow darted between two units — Laila tracked it — one breath, steady hands — squeezed the trigger.

The figure stumbled, weapon clattering to the ground.

"Got one!" she hissed.

The second shooter broke and ran, vanishing into the maze of storage units beyond. Carolyn started after him, but Laila grabbed her arm.

"Not why we're here," she said tersely.

Carolyn nodded. Professional. Focused.

They found the drive quickly, right where it was supposed to be — inside a hollowed-out HVAC vent. Laila stuffed it into her jacket and they retreated fast, keeping low and moving silent.

Only when they were miles away, tearing down backroads with headlights off, did Laila allow herself to speak.

"They're not just trying to scare us anymore," she said.

Carolyn checked the side mirror, then the rearview, scanning for tails. "They're trying to erase us."

"And they're sloppy," Laila added. "That wasn't standard Marshals Service protocol back there. Those guys were mercs. Hired hands."

Carolyn smiled grimly. "Good. Means they're desperate and expendable".

The farmhouse was too hot now. Too exposed. If they were being monitored she could keep her family out of harms way. Laila drove past it without stopping, heading instead to an old safehouse she hadn't used since her ranger days.

They needed time. They needed space. And they needed a plan.

The system was fighting back.

But so were they.

The safehouse was a relic from another life — a squat stone cabin buried deep in the Appalachian foothills, shielded from prying eyes by dense pines and crumbling forest roads.

Inside, the air was thick with dust and the lingering scent of cedar and gun oil. Laila locked and barred the door behind them, checking windows and corners like second nature.

Carolyn powered up a battered laptop they had grabbed from a Faraday cage box. No wireless cards. No microphones. No cameras. It looked ancient — because it was. And that made it invisible.

Laila set the drive on the rough-hewn table between them.

"Moment of truth," Carolyn said, inserting it.

The screen flickered to life.
Folders. Files. Video clips timestamped for the day of Madeline Reyes' testimony — and her death.

Carolyn opened the first file.

At first, it was what they expected — courtroom footage. Madeline sitting on the witness stand, calm and precise, even under cross-examination. Laila felt her chest tighten at the sight of her friend, so alive, so brave.

Then —
At the far edge of the screen — a figure.

A man in a Marshal's uniform, standing where no Marshal should have been — close to the secured evidence room door.

He wasn't assigned to security.
He wasn't supposed to be there.

Carolyn froze the frame. Zoomed.

The resolution wasn't perfect, but it was good enough.

"That's Pearson," Laila said, her voice low and dangerous.

Deputy Chief Marshal Anthony Pearson — a man so high up the food chain that even Internal Affairs rarely touched him.
A man who had publicly wept at Madeline Clark's funeral.
A man now caught on camera tampering with secured evidence.

Carolyn scrolled forward.

They watched, grim-faced, as Pearson disappeared into the evidence room for nearly twenty minutes — emerging with a satchel he hadn't gone in with.

Minutes later, the chain of custody logs — supposedly "lost" — were entered with forged signatures.

Laila leaned back, closing her eyes.

"It's worse than we thought," she said.

Carolyn didn't answer immediately. She was scrubbing through another clip.

A different camera angle.

This one showed Agent Miller — the so-called Internal Affairs investigator leading the inquisition against them — laughing with Pearson in the courthouse parking lot.

Time-stamped three hours before Madeline’s death.

Carolyn exhaled slowly, like a punch had been driven into her gut.

"Son of a bitch," she muttered.

Laila stood, pacing. Energy crackled off her in sharp, volatile bursts.

"This isn’t about covering up Falfor’s corruption," she said. "It’s bigger. It’s systemic."

"They're cleaning house," Carolyn agreed. "Anyone who threatens the machine… disappears."

They sat in silence for a moment, the weight of revelation settling over them like a funeral shroud.

Finally, Carolyn asked, "What’s the move?"

Laila’s hands curled into fists at her sides. Her training screamed at her to plan, to compartmentalize, to strike with surgical precision.

"We can’t go to IA," she said. "They're compromised."

"FBI?" Carolyn offered, though her tone made it clear she didn’t believe in that path either.

Laila shook her head. "Even with Daniels’s contacts it would still be too slow. Too political."

She stopped pacing. Looked at Carolyn dead in the eye.

"We need to take it public. Everything. All at once. So fast and so loud they can't shut it down."

Carolyn gave a grim smile.

"Guerrilla lawfare," she said. "Expose them before they can finish silencing us."

Laila nodded.

"It’s the only chance we've got."

Preparing to Leak Evidence.

The next hours were a blur of activity.

- Laila and Carolyn made copies of the drive, storing backups in dead drops scattered across three states.
- They drafted a statement — careful, fact-based, devastatingly precise — naming names, times, dates.
- They compiled the video clips into a streamlined exposé, complete with analysis overlays and chain of custody documentation.

But time was against them.

They knew they had been seen at the storage facility. They knew there would be retaliation.

It came faster than expected.

Just after midnight, as Laila was double-checking an upload to an encrypted server, Carolyn snapped her head up.

"Vehicle," she whispered.

Laila killed the laptop’s power immediately, plunging the room into darkness.

They moved instinctively — grabbing weapons, taking up defensive positions.

Outside, the faint hum of an engine cut through the still night air, growing louder.

Headlights slashed through the woods.

Two SUVs this time.

No insignia. No markings.

But Laila didn't need to see badges to know what they were.

Not rescue.

Not reinforcements.

Elimination squads.

The first round struck the front door like a battering ram.

Boom!

Splinters exploded inward. The old wood, reinforced but ancient, cracked but held — barely.

"They're not knocking," Carolyn said grimly, crouched behind an overturned oak table.

Laila checked her pistol — full mag, one chambered — and tucked two more spare mags into her jeans pocket. She moved to the rear window, peeking through the cracked blinds.

Two figures, tactical gear, moving in slow and deliberate. Suppressors on their rifles. Professional.

Not mercs this time.
No — these were Marshals.

Dirty ones.

"We can't let them pin us down here," Laila hissed.

Carolyn nodded. "Back door?"

"They'll have it covered."

"Then we go through them."

The front door groaned again under a second impact. No more time.

Laila moved first, smooth and silent.
She thumbed the latch on a homemade flashbang — a trick she learned overseas — and hurled it through a side window.

The *pop* was small but blinding in the darkened woods.

Yells. Shuffling.

Laila kicked the side door open and sprinted out, low and fast. Carolyn covered her, popping two precise shots at the stunned figures regrouping near the SUV.

One went down hard, clutching his leg.

The other dove for cover, firing blind.

Laila didn't hesitate.
She kept moving, zigzagging across the uneven ground, every step calculated.

More gunfire erupted — controlled bursts, meant to suppress rather than kill immediately.

They wanted to capture them alive.

Bad mistake.

Carolyn followed, her weapon barking sharp, economical shots that kept heads down.

They reached the tree line and dropped flat,

concealed by the thick brush.

"Visuals?" Carolyn whispered.

Laila scanned. Two near the front door. One behind the left SUV. Maybe one more unseen.

"Four minimum," she said.

"Five," Carolyn corrected, nodding toward a faint glimmer of movement on the roof of the cabin — a sniper position.

Laila grimaced. "They're thorough."

"We need to split them," Carolyn said. "Force them to think we're escaping."

Laila's mind raced.

There was an old dry creek bed that ran fifty yards from the backside of the cabin to the woods beyond — shallow now, but cover was cover.

"If we bolt west," Laila said, "they'll chase. We pick them off one by one."

Carolyn smiled grimly. "Classic ranger snipe-and-scoot."

"Exactly."

They moved, fast and silent.

Another burst of fire chased them — wild, inaccurate. The shooters were frustrated. Good.

At the creek bed, Laila dropped into the ditch, the hard-packed dirt jarring her knees. Carolyn hit the ground next to her, already sighting down her pistol.

"Three on pursuit," Carolyn said calmly.

"Fourth is hanging back, trying to box us."

"Fifth?"

"Holding sniper cover."

Laila gritted her teeth. "We deal with the three first."

The first pursuer rounded a copse of trees, muzzle raised — but too slow.

Laila's first shot caught him high in the chest.
He staggered back, armor catching the round — but Carolyn's second shot found the seam at his collarbone.

Down.

The other two hesitated — a fatal mistake.

Laila vaulted up, closing the distance in a flash.
A sharp, brutal takedown — a knee to the gut, an elbow to the jaw — and the second man went sprawling, unconscious before he hit the dirt.

The third ran.

Carolyn dropped him with a single round to the thigh.

They heard a sharp whistle — coded — from the SUV.
The sniper repositioning.

"They're pulling back!" Carolyn said.

Laila shook her head.

"No — repositioning to trap us."

A low rumble reached their ears.
Another vehicle.
More reinforcements.

Laila's mind raced.

They couldn't hold this ground.

"Time to disappear," she said.

Carolyn looked dubious. "Options?"

"Creek runs downhill. Caves about a half-mile south."

Carolyn grinned fiercely.

"Then let's go."

They sprinted, using the shallow ditch as a shield, vanishing into the thick, wild forest.

Behind them, the cabin burst into flames — the Marshals torching it to cover their tracks, to make sure no evidence survived.

But it was too late.

The drive was already backed up.
The statement already queued for distribution.
The truth — their truth — would see daylight.

If they could survive the night.

The caves were a temporary ghost shelter — enough to catch their breath, but not a place to stay long.
Dawn bled faint light through the cracks overhead as Laila wiped soot and ash from her face, checking the backup sat-phone hidden deep in her pack.

The drive was safe — uploaded to an anonymous drop server in three separate countries.
Their names were still on the "Wanted" list internally, tagged as rogue agents.

Good.

It would make what came next easier.

"This isn't defense anymore," Laila said, her voice

low and lethal. "We flip the board."

Carolyn leaned against the cave wall, cracking her knuckles.

"About damn time."

They outlined the offensive in sharp, clipped bursts of strategy — a plan formed from two different schools of survival.

Laila's Norway training focused on destabilization —

- Psychological pressure.
- Deception operations.
- Economic and personal strikes against enemy logistics.

Carolyn's street instincts honed an unforgiving edge —

- Hit fast, hit dirty.
- Create confusion.
- Control the narrative with fear and perception.

Together, they would dismantle the machine that tried to erase them.

First Offensive Strike: "Takedown of the Handler"

Their first target was the weakest link — a handler named Drew Kantor, a corrupt logistics officer who quietly funneled resources to Pearson's black ops teams.

They tracked him to a private club outside Richmond — a place where secrets flowed more freely than liquor.

Laila played point — slipping inside in the early evening dressed not like a Marshal, but like a wandering executive looking for a drink.
Her body language screamed *non-threatening*.
Norwegian training emphasized camouflage in plain sight — social invisibility.

Carolyn circled outside, watching for Kantor's usual exit points, noting the guards, the rhythms of security.
She already had her entry options mapped:

- The delivery door.
- The unguarded second-story window.
- Or, if necessary, a classic gang-style strongarm through the service alley.

Inside, Laila spotted Kantor almost immediately — bloated on stolen power, laughing too loudly, drink in hand.

Easy.

She waited, blending in — watching him drink past caution.

When he stumbled toward the private restrooms, she was there, brushing against him "accidentally."

Soft. Forgettable.

Except for the tiny black capsule she slipped into his jacket pocket.

Outside, Carolyn watched her phone screen blink once — the signal.
The tracker was live.

Kantor never knew he was tagged.

Second Offensive Strike: "Bleeding the System"

Over the next forty-eight hours, they made his life hell.

Using a burner laptop, Carolyn spoofed emails from Kantor's account — sending fake leaks to Internal Affairs and Pearson's office.
Anonymous tips reported Kantor's bank accounts receiving illicit funds.
Security footage — real and doctored — placed him at scenes he couldn't explain.

By the third day, Pearson's paranoia turned inward.

Kantor was grabbed by his own people, dragged into an interrogation black site.
Exactly what Laila and Carolyn had planned.

Destabilization Phase One: complete.

Preparing for the Kill-stroke, they moved quickly now, momentum on their side.

At a battered diner off I-85, they met with Deputy Marshal Eli Vance — one of the few remaining clean officers, a man whose sister had once been saved by Madeline Reyes.

Vance looked rough — bloodshot eyes, hand trembling around his coffee mug.

"You're asking me to commit treason," he said in a raw whisper.

"No," Laila corrected him. "We're asking you to honor your oath."

Carolyn leaned in. "If we don't bring them down, nobody else will."

Vance stared at them for a long moment — weighing life, career, honor — then nodded.

"What do you need?" he asked.

Laila slid a flash drive across the table.

"Access to the command center downtown," she said.
"One hour window.
No questions.
No witnesses."

Vance exhaled slowly.

"I can do that."

Carolyn smiled — a cold, feral grin.

"Then let's burn this mother down."

Chapter 7

Marshal L.A.W. Unleashed.

The city glittered under a rain-slicked sky, neon lights bleeding into oily puddles across the pavement. From their vantage point across the street, Laila and Carolyn studied the Marshal Service's regional headquarters — a monolith of glass and steel, cold and imposing against the dark.

Vance's coded text came at exactly 0300 hours.

Now. Window open. One hour. Go.

No second chances.

Laila pulled her dark tactical jacket tighter, the Kevlar vest beneath it pressing against her ribs like a silent oath.

Carolyn checked her weapons — twin Glocks, suppressed. A knife strapped low against her thigh. They moved like wraiths through the shadows, slipping into the underground loading dock just as a garbage truck pulled away, leaving the service gate slowly grinding closed behind it.

Carolyn jammed the closing sensor with a sliver of metal — classic street trick — and they slid inside before anyone noticed.

Inside, the sterile corridors buzzed with the low thrum of fluorescent lights.

Most of the building was dark — skeleton crew at best.

The opulence of daytime operations — gleaming badges, polished boots, gleaming conference rooms — was stripped bare at night.

Predators hunted best in darkness.

They moved fast, silent — checking corners, syncing their steps with the lazy sweeps of security patrols.

On the 12th floor, they hit their first checkpoint — two guards, bored and lazy, chatting about football.

Carolyn moved first — a whisper of motion, a twist of her wrist — and one man sagged to the floor, unconscious.
Laila took the other, a quick nerve strike sending him into dreamless sleep.

No alarms.
No mess.

They continued upward, bypassing elevators — too risky — taking narrow maintenance shafts and back staircases.

At the 18th floor, the heart of the beast, Laila paused.

"This is it," she whispered.

Carolyn nodded once.

They breached the door — and walked straight into hell.

Ambush

Pearson was waiting.

Not just Pearson.

Miller.

And six more — full tactical loadouts — rifles raised.

The floor was stripped bare — furniture cleared, lights off, only the green glow of emergency exit signs illuminating the trap.

"You really thought you could beat us?" Pearson sneered, stepping forward, pistol dangling loosely from his hand.

Carolyn smiled lazily, unafraid.

"Looks like we're standing here, and you're still talking," she said.

Pearson's smile faltered.

Miller barked, "On your knees, hands behind your heads, now!"

Laila's mind raced, calculating.

Too many guns.
Too many angles.

A frontal fight was suicide.

But she didn't need to win this fight.

She needed to change the battlefield.

Her fingers flicked a tiny switch on her belt — a remote.
One of the few things she still owed Norway for.

Outside, at the building's main generator, a blacked-out drone detonated a carefully placed EMP device.

The world flickered.

Then plunged into darkness.

The Night Falls

Chaos.

Shouts.
Swearing.
The clatter of weapons fumbling in the sudden blackness.

Laila and Carolyn moved like phantoms.

Flashlights swung wildly, too slow to track them.

Laila disarmed the nearest tactical agent with a brutal wristlock and elbow strike, the suppressed pop of Carolyn's Glock silencing another trying to call for backup.

Pearson fired blindly, bullets sparking off steel and concrete.

Miller screamed orders that no one could follow.

In the confusion, Laila reached the primary server room door — already pre-wired by Vance to unlock during the EMP breach.

The servers flickered — battery backups kicking on — just long enough for her to yank the drive containing the core surveillance logs, financial records, and encrypted black site orders.

The smoking gun.

Behind her, Carolyn fought with ruthless precision — a dance of dirty street fighting and surgical strikes.

It wasn't pretty.

It was effective.

When the emergency lights finally limped back on — dim red glow bathing the floor — Pearson and Miller stood alone, panting, disarmed, surrounded by their fallen men.

And Laila and Carolyn stood before them.

Alive.

Victorious.

Final Exposure

By 0500, the files were broadcast.

Anonymous drops to:

- Major media outlets.
- Federal oversight committees.
- Whistleblower organizations.

Chain of custody documentation, financial records, witness testimony — everything Pearson's cabal had tried to bury — laid bare before the nation.

Madeline Clark's death.
The forged chain of custody.
The secret renditions.
The black money slush funds.

Public outrage exploded like wildfire.

By noon, Pearson and Miller were in custody, frog-marched out of the shattered command center in full view of the press they could no longer control.

Laila and Carolyn watched from a rooftop across the street, cloaked in shadows.

Not cheering.
Not celebrating.

Just standing.

Silent.

Solemn.

Free

The quiet of the Pennsylvania farmhouse, once a refuge, now felt like a suffocating cage. The weight of the past few months pressed down on Laila, a physical burden as heavy as the silence. The vibrant fields outside seemed muted, drained of color, a mirror to the emptiness inside her.

Her military training — once her strength — now mocked her. Discipline, resilience, focus: all felt distant. Sleep was no escape; nightmares of the raid and Madeline Clark's terrified eyes shattered any hope of rest. Even awake, adrenaline lingered like phantom pain, her muscles aching, her senses on high alert. Every creak of the old house, every rustle of leaves, triggered a jolt of fear.

But Laila was a soldier. She remembered how to fight — not just enemies, but herself.

She started small: short walks across the farm, forcing her breath into a steady rhythm. Each step became a small act of defiance against the chaos inside. Gradually, she pushed further — calisthenics at first, then jogging the perimeter of the fields. Her body protested, but she welcomed the burn, grounding herself in the tangible pain of recovery.

Yoga followed, a discipline she once scoffed at but now embraced. Stretching, mindfulness, breath control — it slowed the racing thoughts, soothed the knots in her shoulders and spine. In the stillness, she found the beginnings of peace.

Physical healing was tangible. Emotional healing was not.

Guilt gnawed at her relentlessly. Had she missed something? Could she have saved Madeline? The questions battered her daily.

After weeks of resisting, Laila sought help. She found a therapist — a woman with a gentle voice and sharp mind — who helped her unpack the layers of trauma and guilt. Therapy was hard. Some days it felt impossible. But slowly, she learned to shift her perspective: from self-recrimination toward self-compassion.

Carolyn became her anchor. Bound by shared scars, they trained together, laughed together, survived together. In Carolyn's fierce loyalty and blunt humor, Laila found a vital lifeline — a bond forged in fire and refusal to fall.

She also reconnected with her family. Her mother, once distant with worry and confusion, came to understand the depth of her wounds. Both of her brothers, veterans, were familiar with PTSD. Their steady presence, their unconditional support, helped ground her — a reminder of the life still waiting beyond the shadows.

The farm, her family, Carolyn, and her own iron will became the pillars of her recovery.

It was slow. It was brutal. But Laila was a fighter. She had survived battlefields on foreign soil — she would not be broken by betrayal at home.

The scars would remain, but they would no longer define her. They would be marks of survival — testaments to her strength.

She started to think not of what was lost, but what could be rebuilt.
One breath.
One step.
One day at a time.

The road to healing was long and winding — but Laila was ready to walk it.

Carolyn's Recovery

The city never slept, and neither did Carolyn — not really.

After everything, the noise, the lights, the endless movement offered a strange kind of comfort. The chaos outside matched the chaos inside her head. Sirens, shouting, the hum of traffic — it kept her anchored, reminded her she was still alive.

But survival wasn't the same as healing. Being from the 'hood' taught her that.

Carolyn moved into a small apartment above a rundown gym on the east side, a place where the rent was cheap and the questions were few. She spent hours pounding heavy bags, lifting weights until her muscles trembled, pushing her body harder than she had even in the Service. The sweat and the bruises were real — unlike the nightmares, unlike the guilt that gnawed at her when she lay awake at 3 a.m.

Her recovery was less about reflection and more about *defiance.*
The world had tried to break her. She refused to let it.

Therapy wasn't her first choice, but she made herself go. Once a week, a gruff ex-cop turned counselor peeled back the layers she kept hidden — the rage, the helplessness, the grief for the friends lost and the world betrayed.

"You don't have to forgive them," he said once. "You just have to stop letting them live rent-free in your head."

It stuck.

So Carolyn fought back the only way she knew:

- By rebuilding her body.
- By taking back control of her mind.
- By planning for the next time — because there would always be a next time.

She started volunteering at a youth center, teaching self-defense classes to girls who had seen too much of the city's darkness. Watching them find their strength gave Carolyn a purpose again — something clean to hold onto in a world that felt permanently stained.

And when the darkness crept in — the memories, the what-ifs, the endless questions — she didn't pretend it wasn't there.

She just kept moving. One fight at a time.

The courtroom's sterile atmosphere had faded, replaced by the earthy scent of the Pennsylvania farm. Yet the echoes of the trial lingered — phantom pains that clung to Laila and Carolyn like second skins. Carolyn, ever practical, had suggested the retreat, but the farmhouse's silence, meant to soothe, only amplified their shared anxieties. The weight of what they had endured — the betrayal, the violence, the loss — hung heavy in the air.

Laila struggled with the haunting image of Madeline's terrified eyes. Logic, her old refuge, offered no comfort. Nightmares shredded her sleep; during the day, flashes of memory ambushed her without warning.

Carolyn coped differently — retreating into routine, drowning herself in paperwork. But the dam eventually broke. One late evening, hunched over legal briefs, Carolyn finally confessed her sleepless nights, her gnawing self-doubt. Had they missed something? Could they have done more?

Their real healing began in that raw honesty.

Sitting together on the porch swing, tears falling in silence, they let the weight of their fears and guilt surface. Carolyn spoke of past losses, hidden anxieties. Laila shared wounds she'd kept buried for years — her divorce, the isolation she had worn like armor.

Their bond deepened in those shared vulnerabilities.

They spent days walking the farm fields, talking not about the trial, but about life — hopes, regrets, dreams long shelved. In the crisp autumn air, the rhythm of their steps became a kind of therapy. The laughter they slowly rediscovered was tentative but real.

One evening, beside a crackling fire, Laila finally voiced the fear that haunted her most:
That she might never feel whole again.

"I feel... detached," she whispered. "Like I'm fading."
Carolyn rested a hand over hers, steady, unwavering.
"It's not weakness," Carolyn said softly. "It's part of healing.

And you're not alone."

With Carolyn's support, Laila found the courage to seek professional help. It wasn't easy. Years of military culture had taught her to equate vulnerability with weakness. But therapy — patient, painful, persistent — helped her start peeling back the layers of guilt and grief. She learned to manage anxiety, to challenge the self-blame that threatened to consume her.

Recovery wasn't about erasing the scars; it was about learning to live with them.

Meanwhile, Carolyn forged her own path to healing. She reconnected with old friends, allowing herself to be vulnerable without shame. She found strength not in pretending to be unbreakable, but in embracing the fractures honestly.

Together, Laila and Carolyn created a new rhythm — supporting each other through setbacks, celebrating small victories. They learned each other's triggers, recognized when to push and when to simply be present.

The farm, once oppressive, transformed into a sanctuary again.
The rolling fields no longer spoke of isolation, but of hope.

The scars they carried would always remain. But they bore them now not as wounds, but as testaments:
To survival.
To resilience.
To the fierce, unbreakable bond between two women who had walked through hell and refused to stay there.

Whatever the future held, they would face it together — stronger than ever.

The weeks following the trial blurred into exhaustion and unsettling quiet. The adrenaline that had carried them through battle drained away, leaving a hollow ache. The Pennsylvania farm, once a symbol of refuge, now mirrored the emptiness inside them. Silence pressed heavy, broken only by the mournful cry of distant owls and the rustle of dry leaves.

Laila withdrew further into herself. Nightmares — brutal replays of Madeline's death — shredded her sleep, and waking hours offered no relief. Detachment crept in, a terrifying numbness that both comforted and scared her. Her military instincts, once her salvation, now felt like shackles, binding her to routines that offered no peace.

Carolyn saw the decline and refused to stand by. Their bond, forged through blood and betrayal, demanded action. She gently urged Laila to seek help — facing initial resistance from Laila's ingrained stoicism and the heavy stigma surrounding mental health.

It took weeks of quiet persuasion and constant support before Laila agreed.

Therapy became the first true turning point.

Dr. Emily Carter, a trauma specialist, listened patiently without judgment. She helped Laila understand that the nightmares, detachment, and guilt were not signs of weakness but normal responses to extraordinary trauma. Through breathing exercises, mindfulness practices, and cognitive therapy, Laila slowly began unwinding the tight knots of guilt and grief that choked her.

Progress was slow, agonizing at times. But each session peeled back another layer of pain — offering space for healing to take root.

Outside therapy, Carolyn encouraged Laila to rebuild personal connections. Tentatively, Laila reached out to her estranged family. There were awkward beginnings, tentative conversations — but eventually, her parents' unconditional love and her brother's quiet, steady presence became vital anchors. Ordinary moments — shared meals, laughter over small things — started stitching her back together.

Carolyn, too, leaned on her own circle. Friends she had once kept at arm's length now offered a listening ear without expectation. Vulnerability became strength, not weakness.

Healing wasn't a straight line.
Some days the nightmares returned sharper than ever. Some mornings the guilt felt heavier than it had at the start.

But they faced it — together.

They built new routines:

- Laila, pushing her body through grueling but empowering physical training.
- Carolyn, tending a vibrant garden on the farm, finding peace in nurturing new life.

They leaned on each other openly, without masks or pretense.
Victories, no matter how small, were celebrated.

Setbacks were met with compassion, not judgment.

Their bond deepened into something rare — not just forged by trauma, but strengthened by chosen trust.

One evening, sitting on the porch swing as the sun dipped low, Laila spoke aloud what both of them felt:

"We're not victims," she said, voice firm despite the tears shining in her eyes. "We’re survivors. And we’re still standing."

Carolyn squeezed her hand.

"Damn right we are," she whispered.

Months later, the farmhouse no longer felt like a prison.

It was a sanctuary again — a testament to resilience, to shared healing, and to a future they were ready to face.

The scars remained, yes.
But thcy were no longer wounds — they were badges of survival, stitched together with loyalty, hope, and fierce determination.

The echoes of the courtroom still whispered.
But the melody of their recovery — strong, stubborn, unbroken — rose far louder.

Rediscovering Peace.

The rhythmic creak of the porch swing became a comforting mantra, no longer a reminder of unease but a song of resilience. The Pennsylvania countryside, once overshadowed by courtroom horrors, embraced Laila with quiet familiarity. The farm, her family's legacy, was not just a sanctuary — it was now a living canvas for healing. Each sunrise painted breathtaking hues across the sky, slowly washing away the darkness inside her. Simple sensations — the scent of freshly turned earth, the rustle of leaves, the chirping of crickets — became profound sources of peace. She spent hours by the creek, its murmuring flow mirroring her own slow, steady path toward recovery.

Her days found a gentle rhythm. Helping her father with chores grounded her — milking cows, tending fields, feeling life continue through her hands. These daily tasks, once routine, now became sacred acts of reconnection.

Evenings brought family meals around the worn kitchen table, laughter and simple conversation knitting frayed threads back together. Her parents' quiet presence, her brother's silent strength — these were the anchors that kept her steady.

Physical training, once torturous, became a reclaiming of strength.

Each run across the fields, each burning pushup, re-forged her body and her spirit, transforming pain into resilience.

Carolyn became a permanent fixture in this new life. Their bond, born in fire, deepened into something unbreakable.

Carolyn's visits brought energy and laughter — helping Laila's mother in the garden, long walks across golden fields, quiet hours sitting by the creek, speaking without needing to fill every silence.

Together, they planted an herb garden — bright with scent and color, a symbol of renewal. They built a small chicken coop, their daily care adding a steady, simple rhythm to their days. Carolyn's practical spirit brought new order to the farm, weaving healing into every corner.

The legal battles rumbled in the background, but the farm became their buffer — a place untouched by courtrooms and chaos.

One afternoon, tending the herbs, Laila spotted a family of deer grazing peacefully across the field. The sight struck her with unexpected force — a symbol of survival, of moving forward. It became a silent promise to herself: to live, to grow, to fight for the future without being trapped by the past.

The memories of Madeline never left.

The nightmares came still — but less often, their grip weakened by time, therapy, and shared strength.

Laila channeled her grief into purpose, advocating for better training and reforms within law enforcement. She no longer sought to erase the pain — but to weave it into her story, allowing it to fuel change.

Carolyn, too, found a new focus. Their ordeal deepened her commitment to justice, driving her to advocate for support systems for those navigating trauma within the legal system.

Together, they rebuilt their lives.

The farm became not just a place of refuge but a symbol of endurance — a living testament to their friendship, their healing, and their renewed sense of purpose.

One evening, the two of them sat on the porch swing, watching the sky bleed into twilight.

The swing creaked a steady rhythm beneath them — no longer carrying the echoes of trauma, but the heartbeat of lives reclaimed.

They didn't speak much.

They didn't need to.

Peace wasn't the absence of pain.

It was this:

Hope blooming quietly against the scars.

The steadfast light of two souls who had walked through fire — and kept walking.

Reflecting on the Past.

The crisp autumn air carried the scent of woodsmoke and decaying leaves, a far cry from the sterile antiseptic sting of the courtroom that lingered in Laila's mind. She sat on the porch swing, its gentle creak blending with the hum of cicadas. Beside her, Carolyn cradled a mug of steaming tea.

Between them, silence stretched comfortably — a silence born not of awkwardness, but of understanding.

"Remember that first day?" Carolyn finally murmured, her voice soft, touched with the same melancholy Laila felt. "Standing in that courtroom, staring down Falfor… it felt like the world was holding its breath."

Laila nodded, memories flickering to life. Falfor's smug, remorseless expression. Madeline's wide, terrified eyes. The crumbling illusion of a justice system meant to protect but too often used to destroy.

"And the look on Madeline's face," Laila whispered, her voice catching. That image would never leave her. Nor would the fire of anger that still smoldered in her chest.

Carolyn reached across the swing, resting a hand over Laila's.
"We told the truth," she said quietly. "We fought. And we're still standing."

The words offered some comfort — but not complete absolution. The appeal process dragged on, a grim reminder that justice was never guaranteed.

"It's bigger than Falfor now," Laila said, her gaze sweeping the rolling fields. "It's about everything he stood for. The broken system we saw firsthand."

Carolyn nodded. "Which means we have work to do."

It wasn't just talk. In the weeks since the trial, the two of them began laying the foundations for something bigger — a program to support victims of police misconduct, to advocate for reforms from within. Grief was slowly transforming into determination, pain into purpose.

The farm became their sanctuary — and their forge.

Together, they tended the herb garden, took long walks through the fields, worked side by side helping Laila's father with chores. Carolyn's steady, practical energy helped anchor Laila when nightmares and flashbacks tried to drag her back into darkness.

In time, Laila's family joined their healing too.

One evening, Eleanor — Laila's mother — and her two brothers gathered with them on the porch. They sat wrapped in quilts, sipping cider as the sky shifted from gold to deep indigo.

There were no lectures, no forced reassurances. Only presence.

"I worried for you," Eleanor said finally, her voice gentle but unwavering. "But I see you now — stronger than ever. Not untouched, but unbroken."

Her brothers — both rugged and stoic — nodded in agreement, one clapping Laila lightly on the shoulder, the other offering Carolyn a rare, genuine smile. The simple, wordless solidarity washed over Laila like a balm.

The weight she had carried alone — fear that her trauma had tainted the family — began to lift.

Later that night, unable to sleep, Laila wandered into the attic and stumbled upon a forgotten trunk. Inside, wrapped in a faded quilt, she found a battered leather journal.

Her grandmother's.

The entries were dated during the war years — a young woman raising a family while the world burned. The handwriting was small but firm, the words filled with quiet strength, moments of fear, resilience, hope.

One passage caught Laila's breath:

"When the world feels too heavy, plant your feet in the earth. Remember who you are. Remember who you fight for."

Laila closed the journal, feeling the weight of her grandmother's legacy settle warmly around her shoulders.

Strength wasn't the absence of fear. It was the decision to keep moving, even when afraid.

The next day, she showed the journal to Carolyn, Eleanor, and her brothers. They gathered by the creek, the sun dappling through the trees.

Reading those words aloud, Laila felt the last, stubborn remnants of doubt begin to dissolve.

They were not broken.

They were *reborn.*

Whatever battles lay ahead — in courtrooms, in city halls, in the quiet, private corners of their own hearts — they would face them.

Together.

The steady creak of the porch swing that evening was no longer a counterpoint to grief.
It was the heartbeat of lives reclaimed, hope rekindled, and purpose renewed.

The fight for justice wasn't over.

It was just beginning.

Rediscovery

The farmhouse breathed with the quiet rhythms of night: the distant lowing of cattle, the occasional creak of settling wood, the whisper of wind across the fields. Inside, the old clock ticked steadily, marking time Laila could no longer feel.

She sat alone by the living room window, a mug of tea cooling in her hands, forgotten.

The farm stretched out before her under the silver wash of moonlight — familiar, steadfast — yet she felt detached from it, like a ghost watching a world she no longer belonged to.

The trial was over.
Falfor's face, that smug, hollow smirk, was no longer looming.
Madeline's memory was honored.

And yet...

The emptiness lingered.

What right do I have to help others, she thought bitterly. *I couldn't even save her.*

The darkness outside blurred with the darkness inside her. For all the victories they'd clawed from the jaws of injustice, Laila couldn't escape the gnawing feeling that she was irreparably broken — a shattered blade, dulled beyond use.

She closed her eyes, willing herself to find peace, but only questions flooded in.

Was survival enough?
Could she truly build something new from the ashes of what they'd lost?
Or was this quiet farm life all that was left — a safe, slow fading away?

The soft creak of floorboards startled her.

Eleanor stood at the edge of the room, wrapped in a shawl, her hair a silver halo in the moonlight.

"You're not sleeping," her mother said gently.

Laila managed a small, brittle smile. "Didn't mean to wake you."

"You didn't." Eleanor crossed the room without hurry and sat down beside her, folding her hands in her lap. "I woke because I felt you thinking too loud."

Laila huffed a soft breath, almost a laugh, almost a sob. "Is it that obvious?"

Eleanor's smile was sad but knowing.
"You carry too much, baby girl. Always have."

They sat in silence for a long moment, the night wrapping around them like a familiar quilt.

Finally, Eleanor reached into the pocket of her shawl and pulled out the worn leather journal — Laila's grandmother's words, heavy with life lived hard and well.

"I was reading this earlier," Eleanor said, setting it between them. "Your grandmother knew something about brokenness. About doubt."

She opened the journal to a page marked with a faded ribbon.

Her voice was quiet as she read:

"A wound does not destroy the body's purpose. It is proof that we have stood, that we have fought, and that we are still needed. Scars are not signs of weakness. They are the maps of the battles we survived — and the wisdom we earned."

Laila swallowed hard, blinking against the sudden burn in her eyes.

"I don't feel wise," she said hoarsely.

Eleanor's hand covered hers — warm, strong.

"Maybe wisdom isn't something you feel. Maybe it's something you earn every time you get back up." She squeezed Laila's hand gently. "You're not broken. You're *tempered.* Stronger at the places where you thought you'd shatter."

The dam inside Laila cracked — just a little — and she leaned into her mother's steady presence, letting the weight of unspoken fears slip from her shoulders for the first time in what felt like years.

"You're not alone, Laila," Eleanor said softly. "Not now. Not ever."

The old clock ticked on.
Outside, the first hint of dawn tinted the horizon with soft gray.

And inside, slowly, carefully, something began to knit itself back together.

Not erasing the scars.
Honoring them.

Tomorrow would bring new doubts. New challenges.

But for the first time in a long time, Laila felt she wouldn't face them alone.

And maybe — just maybe — she was strong enough to help someone else find their way, too.

The town market bustled with late-autumn energy, a mixture of earthy scents — hay, cider, damp leaves — blending with the chatter of neighbors catching up before winter set in. Booths lined the square, overflowing with squash, apples, handwoven blankets.

Laila adjusted the basket on her arm, filled with jars of homemade preserves and bunches of dried herbs from the garden she and Carolyn had spent weeks tending. Carolyn trailed beside her, sipping a steaming coffee, her sharp eyes scanning the crowd with old habits she hadn't quite shed.

It felt good to be out among people again.
Normal.
Almost.

But normalcy was fragile.

Raised voices shattered the calm.

Near the edge of the square, by a pickup truck laden with pumpkins, a small crowd had gathered — murmuring, tense.

"—Saw him sneakin' around!" barked an older man in a battered cap, jabbing a finger at a young farmhand in dusty overalls. The boy — barely more than seventeen — stood stiff and wide-eyed, his hands raised slightly in confused protest.

"I wasn't stealin' nothin'!" he said, his voice cracking.

"Liar," another man snapped. "Caught you red-handed!"

The sheriff's deputy — a heavyset man with thinning hair — seemed more interested in nodding along with the accusers than actually investigating. His hand hovered near his holstered weapon, a clear intimidation tactic.

Laila felt her stomach knot instantly.

It was too familiar.
The mob mentality.
The presumption of guilt.

Carolyn muttered beside her, low and dangerous, "Here we go again."

For a heartbeat, Laila froze.

Is it my place? Should I just let it go?

Old fears whispered. *You can't save everyone.*

But another voice — quieter, steadier — rose within her.

You don't have to save everyone. Just don't look away.

Before she knew it, her boots were moving.

Carolyn followed without hesitation, setting her coffee down on a crate as they approached.

"Excuse me," Laila said, her voice calm but firm. "What's going on here?"

The crowd shifted, wary. Outsiders weren't often welcomed in these parts — but Laila's stance, her steady gaze, gave them pause.

"Thief," the older man grunted. "Tried to take from Jacobson's truck."

"That's not true!" the farmhand protested again, desperation thick in his voice. "I dropped my wallet! I was just pickin' it up!"

"Any witnesses?" Carolyn asked coolly, folding her arms across her chest.

The deputy looked uncomfortable. "No, but—"

"No witnesses," Carolyn repeated, her voice sharpening.

"Maybe we should check the truck first," Laila said evenly, turning toward the owner's pickup without waiting for permission. Carolyn flanked her.

There — half-buried beneath a scattering of dropped hay and a stray gourd — lay a battered leather wallet, its edges cracked from use.

Laila picked it up carefully and flipped it open — inside were a worn school ID card, a few crumpled bills, and a library card.

She turned back toward the crowd.

"This belongs to him," she said, holding the wallet aloft. "Dropped, not stolen."

An uncomfortable shuffling rippled through the gathering.

The boy's eyes filled with tears — a mix of relief and humiliation.

The deputy shifted, clearing his throat. "Maybe we... jumped the gun."

Laila held his gaze steadily until he looked away.

Without another word, she handed the wallet back to the boy. His hands trembled slightly as he took it.

"Thank you, ma'am," he whispered.

"You're welcome," she said gently. "Next time, make sure someone's with you when you're loading or unloading. And don't be afraid to stand up for yourself."

He nodded, eyes wide with a gratitude that stabbed Laila deep — gratitude that someone had seen him, had *believed* him.

As the crowd dispersed, embarrassed and grumbling, Carolyn clapped Laila lightly on the shoulder.

"Feels good, doesn't it?" she said.

Laila watched the boy retreat to the far end of the market, head down, wallet clutched tightly.

It wasn't a court battle.
It wasn't headlines or sweeping reforms.

But it mattered.

"It's not enough," Laila said quietly, "but it's a start."

Carolyn smiled — it was a slow, fierce thing that made Laila's green eyes spark with life.
"Everything big starts small. Except for this one guy I dated, he…"

"I don't need to know Carolyn"

Both women enjoyed a laugh and took a breath.

They resumed their shopping, but the world felt different now.
Laila's chest felt lighter.
Not whole — not yet — but mending.

And somewhere deep inside, a seed of an idea, tiny and persistent, began to take root.

Maybe they weren't done fighting after all.

Maybe they were just getting started.

Chapter 8

The First Discussion.

The kitchen was warm with the scent of apple pie cooling on the counter and the faint crackle of the wood stove. Outside, the last of the market day's bustle had faded into silence, the stars bleeding through the dark velvet sky.

Laila leaned against the counter, nursing a chipped mug of black coffee. Carolyn sat at the table, idly flipping through a worn farming almanac, her boots kicked off and feet tucked beneath her chair.

Neither spoke for a long time.

The peace was welcome.
But it wasn't empty.
It thrummed with the weight of the day — small in the grand scheme, yet heavy with meaning.

Finally, Carolyn broke the silence.

"You felt it too, didn't you?" she said, not looking up from the book.

Laila took a slow sip of coffee, then nodded. "Yeah."

"Helping that kid," Carolyn continued, setting the almanac aside. "It mattered. Even if it was just a stupid wallet and a bunch of pumpkins."

"It wasn't just the wallet," Laila said softly. She set the mug down and crossed to the window, looking out over the fields silvered with frost. "It was about someone believing him. About someone standing up when it would've been easier to walk away."

Carolyn leaned back, folding her arms behind her head.

"Been thinking about that a lot lately," she said. "How easy it is to disappear after something like… after everything."

Laila turned, catching the flicker of sadness in her friend's eyes.

"And how easy it would be to stay disappeared," she finished.

Carolyn shrugged. "Safe. Quiet. Simple."
She grinned crookedly. "Boring as hell."

That pulled a reluctant chuckle from Laila.

They fell into a comfortable silence again, the kind that needed no filling.

But the seed had been planted.

"You ever think about doing something more?" Carolyn asked after a moment, voice casual but edged with something sharper. "Not back in the Marshals. Not chasing badges. Just... helping. Where it counts."

Laila thought about it.

Really thought about it.

About the brokenness they had seen — the cracks in the system, the lives crushed under machinery that cared more about image than justice.

About the faces that still haunted her: Madeline Clark. The boy at the market. So many others.

"I don’t know where to start," she admitted.

"Doesn’t have to be big," Carolyn said. "At least not at first."

Laila frowned, crossing back to the table and sitting down across from her.
"You're serious."

Carolyn’s grin widened.

"As a heart attack."

She leaned forward, her voice dropping.

"Think about it. We’re on leave from the DOJ. We know the system. We know its blind spots, its pressure points. We’ve got skills — investigative, legal, tactical. Hell, you could out-argue a federal judge if you wanted."

"And you could probably outfight half the academy," Laila said wryly.

"Exactly," Carolyn said, raising her mug in a mock toast. "We’re like... Swiss Army knives. Angry, tired Swiss Army knives with a grudge and some free time."

Laila laughed, the sound surprising herself.

It felt good.

Real.

"But seriously," Carolyn continued, softer now, "we can help people who don’t have anyone else. People who'd otherwise fall through the cracks."

Laila sat back, the idea circling in her mind like a hawk riding thermals.

She didn’t have all the answers.
She wasn’t even sure she was ready.

But something inside her stirred — a deep, steady certainty she hadn’t felt in a long time.

Hope.

Not the naive kind.
The hard-won, bloodied kind that knows the price of change — and chooses to pay it anyway.

"I’ll think about it," she said finally.

Carolyn nodded, unfazed. "Good. I wasn’t expecting a signed contract tonight."

They grinned at each other — a flash of the old fire sparking between them.

Outside, a shooting star stitched a silver line across the sky.

A sign?

Maybe.

Or maybe just a reminder:
Some journeys didn’t need maps.
They only needed a first step.

And Laila — scarred, stubborn, still standing — was ready to start walking again.

The next morning dawned pale and cold, a silver mist curling along the edges of the fields. Inside the farmhouse, Laila and Carolyn took their first, tentative steps toward building something new.

It started at the kitchen table — cluttered with notebooks, laptops, and half-drunk mugs of coffee.

Carolyn tapped her pen against a legal pad filled with furious, slanted handwriting.

"Turns out," she said dryly, "starting a nonprofit is about as easy as getting a hippo through airport security."

Laila snorted, flipping through yet another government website on her laptop.
"Forms. Fees. Filing statuses. Compliance audits. And don't even get me started on the grant application language."

Carolyn tossed her pen onto the table with exaggerated disgust.
"I thought we were just gonna save the world, not drown in paperwork."

"We can't just wing it," Laila said, though she felt the same overwhelming frustration tightening in her chest. "If we're serious about this... we have to do it right. Otherwise it's just another good idea that goes nowhere."

Carolyn leaned back in her chair, tipping onto two legs, balancing precariously.

"So. What are we thinking? Mission statement? Target demographic? Services?"

"First step," Laila said, pulling a notebook toward her, "is figuring out exactly what we're offering."

She wrote carefully, the words deliberate:

- Legal advocacy for victims of official misconduct.
- Support services: counseling referrals, media protection strategies.
- Law enforcement reform education: de-escalation techniques, ethics workshops.
- Community outreach: raising awareness about systemic abuse.

Carolyn whistled low.

"Ambitious."

Laila smiled tightly. "It has to be."

They brainstormed for hours — scribbling ideas, scratching them out, arguing, laughing, revising.

Some things were clear:

- They needed lawyers.
- They needed licensed counselors.
- They needed connections — and funding.

Some things were murkier:

- How to stay independent without alienating the people they needed to work with at the D.O.J.
- How to protect the privacy of the victims who would come to them.

By mid-afternoon, the farmhouse looked like a war

zone of papers, laptops, and whiteboard sketches.

Carolyn collapsed into an armchair, groaning dramatically.
"My brain is leaking out my ears. Where's one of those brothers of yours to give me a massage with those strong farm hands?"

Laila laughed — really laughed — for the first time in days.

It wasn't easy.

It wasn't glamorous.

But it was theirs.

Later That Night

They sat outside under a blanket of stars, sipping hot cider, exhausted but strangely energized.

"I was thinking," Carolyn said, her voice thoughtful, "about what we should call this thing."

Laila tipped her head back, gazing up at the dark sky.
"Yeah?"

"Needs to be something... simple. Something people can remember. Something that says what we are without sounding like another cold, bureaucratic alphabet soup."

Laila smiled.

Earlier that week, she had reread more of her grandmother's journal. One phrase had stayed with her — written in faded ink across a page filled with stories of hardship and stubborn hope:

Be the light they can walk toward when everything

else is dark.

She turned the phrase over in her mind, tasting its weight.

"How about..." she said slowly, "The Lantern Project?"

Carolyn sat up straighter.

A slow grin spread across her face as she nodded slowly digesting the name.

"I like it."

"The Lantern Project," Laila repeated, feeling the name settle deep in her bones.
A beacon.
A promise.
A reminder that even in the darkest times, someone would be standing, holding a light.

"We should sleep on it," Carolyn said, but her tone was already settled.

They didn't need to.

Some things you just knew.

The First Official Step...

The next morning, armed with coffee, stubbornness, and an overworked internet connection, they filed the first paperwork for The Lantern Project's nonprofit status.

It would take months to process.
There would be setbacks.

Fundraising nightmares.
Legal hurdles.

But for now, they had a name.
They had a purpose.
They had each other.

And sometimes, that was enough to ignite a revolution.

The First Client

The knock at the farmhouse door was hesitant — two quick raps, a pause, then one more. Furtive. Anxious.

Laila exchanged a glance with Carolyn over the kitchen table, where a laptop and a clutter of grant applications sat abandoned.

Carolyn stood first, instinctively resting a hand on her hip — near, but not on, where a sidearm once would have been.

Old habits.

Laila followed, wiping her hands on a dish towel.

When they opened the door, a man stood on the porch, shivering despite the heavy jacket he wore. Mid-thirties, slight of build, with sharp eyes that darted nervously around the empty yard.

Behind him, a battered sedan idled on the gravel drive.

"I'm sorry," he said immediately, voice thick with an accent — Haitian, Laila guessed. "I... I heard you help people."

Carolyn stepped slightly forward, her stance protective without being overtly aggressive.

"Who sent you?" she asked crisply.

The man hesitated.
"A friend. From the market. He said... you helped someone. You didn't ask for money. You listened."

Laila's mind raced.
Small towns had fast rumor mills.

She softened her tone slightly. "What's your name?"

"Jean-Pierre Lafleur," he said, clutching a frayed baseball cap in his hands. "Please. I need help. I have papers — green card — but they want to send me back."

"Deport you?" Carolyn asked.

Jean-Pierre nodded frantically. "They say... I stole. That I hurt someone. I swear on my life, I did nothing! I work, I pay taxes. I have a son, born here. I didn't... I wouldn't—"

His voice cracked, raw with desperation.

Carolyn and Laila exchanged another glance — a full conversation in a heartbeat.

Instinct:

- Could be lying.
- Could be dangerous.

Heart:

- What if he wasn't?

Laila stepped out onto the porch, squinting at him carefully.
"Slow down. Start from the beginning. What happened?"

Jean-Pierre wrung the cap tighter.
"Police say I attacked a man outside a bar. Took his wallet. They say there are witnesses — but I wasn't there! I was at work. Night shift. Many people saw me, but no one writes it down.

No camera. Boss is scared to say anything — thinks police make trouble for him."

Laila's training kicked in:
Timeline.
Witnesses.
Evidence — or lack of it.

Carolyn folded her arms. "If you're innocent, why would they come after you?"

Jean-Pierre's face twisted with frustration.
"I don't know! Maybe... someone wants me gone. I worked for a man — he fire me when I ask for better pay. Maybe he say things to police. I don't know!"

His voice rose, thick with fear.

Laila rubbed her temple. She felt the old tension building — the weight of wanting to believe, the danger of being wrong.

They had seen plenty of cases where desperation made people lie.
Good intentions weren't enough if you charged into the wrong situation.

But they had also seen good people crushed because no one bothered to listen.

She inhaled slowly, feeling the farm's earth-solid air steady her.

"We'll need to verify everything," she said carefully. "Work records. Witnesses. We'll have to dig."

Jean-Pierre nodded rapidly. "Anything. Please."

Carolyn's eyes narrowed, assessing him.
She still didn't look convinced.

"We're not miracle workers," she said bluntly. "We can't guarantee anything. You understand that?"

"Yes," he said. "I just... I need someone to believe me."

The simplicity of it hit Laila like a punch.

She thought of Madeline.

Thought of the boy at the market.

Thought of all the small injustices that turned into tidal waves when no one stood against them.

She met Carolyn's gaze.

A long pause stretched between them.

Carolyn sighed heavily.
"Alright," she said, her voice gruff. "We'll look into it. No promises."

Jean-Pierre sagged with relief, tears glinting at the corners of his eyes.

"Thank you," he whispered.

They ushered him inside, sitting him at the table, pulling out fresh notebooks. Laila flipped to a blank page, pen poised.

"Start from the beginning," she said again, but softer this time.

As Jean-Pierre spoke — halting, anxious, but determined — Laila felt it:

The Lantern Project wasn't just an idea anymore.

It was alive.

And it had work to do.

Beginning the Investigation...

They started the next morning, methodically, the way they'd been trained.
No assumptions.
No shortcuts.
Build the case piece by piece — or tear it apart if it didn't hold.
Jean-Pierre sat at the kitchen table, wringing his cap in his hands as he listed names, dates, addresses with shaky determination. Carolyn recorded everything in a thick spiral notebook, her handwriting clean and crisp.
When they were done, she tapped the pen against the page and looked up.
"We verify everything," she said. "Every name. Every shift. Every second."
Jean-Pierre nodded. "I understand."
He left soon after — visibly reluctant, but trusting them to

do their work.

Laila watched his battered sedan disappear down the drive, a knot of tension tightening in her gut.

"I want to believe him," she said quietly.

Carolyn tucked the notebook into her satchel. "We don't have the luxury of wanting."

Laila knew she was right.

Truth didn't care about feelings.

Truth was built on evidence — or it crumbled.

First Stop: The Night Shift Alibi

Jean-Pierre had claimed to be working a night shift at a local packaging plant — Green Hollow Produce — the night of the alleged assault.

The plant sat at the edge of town, a low squat building that smelled faintly of ammonia and old vegetables. The manager, a wiry man named Travis Kent, met them at the gate, eyes suspicious under the brim of his sweat-stained ballcap.

"Jean-Pierre?" Kent said, scratching his stubbled jaw. "Yeah, he worked here. Night shift. Good worker, too."

"Was he working the night of October 14th?" Laila asked, keeping her tone neutral.

Kent shifted uncomfortably.

"I don't know. Maybe."

Carolyn's eyes narrowed. "You don't know, or you don't want to say?"

Kent bristled.

"Look, I'm not getting involved in no immigration mess. Feds start poking around, my business takes the hit."

"We're not here for politics," Laila said calmly. "We just

want the truth."
Kent hesitated.
Finally, he ducked into the office and returned with a battered timecard ledger.
There it was — Jean-Pierre's signature, clocking in at 7:03 p.m., clocking out at 3:59 a.m.
The assault had taken place at 10:45 p.m.
"It's not foolproof," Carolyn said under her breath.
"Someone could clock in and leave."
"But it's something," Laila replied.
They copied the records, thanked Kent, and moved on.
Second Stop: Witnesses
Jean-Pierre had given them the names of three coworkers who had seen him that night — Manuel Ortega, Rosalie Vance, and Theo Martin.
Manuel worked at a mechanic shop across town. When they found him on his lunch break, he eyed them warily, glancing around as if expecting trouble.
"I don't want no problems," he muttered.
"We're not the police," Carolyn said quickly. "We just want the truth."
Manuel looked torn.
"I saw him," he admitted. "Jean-Pierre. He was working. Loading pallets. Same time they say he was out robbing people."
"Would you be willing to say that formally?" Laila asked.
Manuel shook his head, fear tightening his mouth.
"You don't understand. If I stick my neck out, my boss finds a reason to fire me. Maybe I get a visit from immigration, too."

The warning wasn’t subtle.
Carolyn muttered a curse under her breath as they left the garage.
"Somebody doesn’t want him cleared," she said grimly.
"And they’re using fear to keep it that way," Laila agreed.
Third Stop: Pressure Mounts
They found Rosalie Vance after her shift at the local diner.
A tired woman with kind eyes and a limp from an old injury.
She listened quietly as they explained, then sighed heavily.
"I saw him too," she said. "Saw him stacking crates around 10:30. Right where he said he was."
Relief surged in Laila’s chest.
"Will you testify?" Carolyn asked.
Rosalie hesitated, looking over her shoulder toward the diner windows.
"I want to. God knows I want to. But..."
She trailed off, her hand trembling slightly.
Laila frowned. "But what?"
Rosalie leaned in, whispering.
"Someone came by yesterday. Said it'd be a shame if anything happened to my daughter’s car. Or my house."
Carolyn stiffened immediately.
"Who?"
Rosalie shook her head violently. "I didn't see. Just a voice. I can’t risk it."
Back at the Farmhouse
Night had fallen by the time they returned to the farmhouse, frustration thick between them.

Eleanor brought both women plates of food, “You two missed dinner. You should eat, it’ll help you think”.
“Mom, I can’t right now”
‘Shit, give me that plate. I do think better with a full belly” declared Carolyn. Looking at Laila, “How can you burn up so much energy when you eat like a bird?”
‘Vitamins. Now can we get to work?”
They spread their notes across the table, piecing together what they had:

- Jean-Pierre had a solid alibi.
- Witnesses existed — but fear kept them silent.
- Someone — or some group — was pressuring them hard.

"This isn’t just about deportation," Carolyn said, scowling.
"Somebody’s invested in making sure he disappears."
"Someone with enough influence to scare a whole shift of workers into silence," Laila agreed.
They sat in silence for a long moment.
Finally, Carolyn leaned back in her chair, stretching.
"So," she said, voice rough but determined, "do we play it safe and walk away?"
Laila looked at the board — at Jean-Pierre’s anxious face, at the sparse scraps of evidence they had.
At the system that would swallow him whole if no one stood up.
"No," she said quietly.
"We fight this."

Shielding the Truth

The farmhouse kitchen looked like a tactical operations center again.
The table was covered with yellow legal pads, phones, a laptop displaying an encrypted messaging app, and hastily drawn maps of town and surrounding routes. Coffee mugs sat forgotten, cooling.
Carolyn circled the table, chewing on a toothpick, while Laila stared at the witness list pinned to the wall with thumbtacks.
Three names.
Three potential targets.
Three lives hanging in the balance.
"Back in the Service," Carolyn muttered, "this would be easy."
She tapped a name on the list — Rosalie Vance, the diner waitress who had seen Jean-Pierre working.
"We'd slap federal protection orders on them, lock down housing, reassign deputies for shadow detail."
Laila nodded absently. "We'd have the weight of the U.S. Marshals Service behind us."
A pause stretched between them.
Neither said the obvious:
We're not those Marshals anymore.
Not officially.
Not legally.
But instincts didn't vanish with the badge.

They still knew how to protect people.
They would just have to do it without the armor of authority.

Building the Plan, step by step...

"First priority is keeping the witnesses safe enough to testify," Laila said. She tapped the table decisively. "Visibility is our best weapon right now. They're safer if whoever's behind this knows people are watching."
"Public pressure," Carolyn agreed. "Not covert. Loud. Messy. Hard to shut down."
They split the responsibilities:

- Carolyn would work with the Lantern Project's early supporters — drumming up community attention without exposing Jean-Pierre or the witnesses prematurely.
- Laila would set up informal safe houses — rotating shifts with friendly farms and businesses willing to quietly offer shelter.

They couldn't promise the kind of round-the-clock protection the Marshals once provided.
But they could make it *very costly* for anyone who tried to intimidate or harm the witnesses.
By midafternoon, as a pale sun hovered weakly over the fields, Laila leaned against the porch railing, sipping cold coffee.
Carolyn joined her, flipping her badge holder open and closed absently.
The badge was still there — tarnished, suspended,

meaningless in the eyes of the Service now.
"Ever wonder if we're doing the right thing?" Carolyn asked, voice low.
Laila didn't answer right away.
She thought about Jean-Pierre. About Madeline. About all the faces they'd seen crushed by silence.
"If you're not using the law to protect people," she said finally, "what's it even for?"
Carolyn grunted.
"I miss it," she said after a moment, almost reluctantly. "The badge. Not the bureaucracy, not the politics — but the power to actually *do* something. Legally. Officially."
Laila smiled faintly. "You just miss the emergency sirens."
Carolyn grinned back — but it faded quickly.
"Sometimes," she said, "I think the law needs people outside it. Watching it. Pushing it. Reminding it what it's supposed to be."
Laila nodded slowly.
She didn't say it aloud, but she felt the same tension: Pulled between what they were, what they had lost, and what they might still become.
First Moves
By sunset, the plan was in motion.

- Manuel Ortega, the terrified mechanic, agreed to stay at a friend's ranch outside town for a few days — a quiet place with neighbors who minded their own business.
- Rosalie Vance was moved temporarily into a spare room above the Lantern Project's fledgling office — an old law library they had rented for a pittance.

- Theo Martin — the third witness, more reluctant — at least agreed to nightly check-ins by burner phone.

Carolyn arranged for a handful of sympathetic locals — teachers, farmers, retired cops — to start circulating Jean-Pierre's story through coffee shops, churches, and school board meetings.

Nothing official.

Nothing actionable.

Just a slow, steady drumbeat of public curiosity that would make any retaliation a lot riskier.

"Fear works both ways," Carolyn said with a grim smile. "Let's see how they like being watched for a change."

It wasn't long before they knew they'd kicked the hornet's nest.

That night, after checking on Manuel's temporary hideout, they returned to the farmhouse to find something new:

A single envelope taped to the front door.

Inside — no note, no threats.

Just a single playing card.

The Queen of Spades.

A silent, unmistakable message.

Carolyn held it up between two fingers, expression dark.

"We're being marked," she said.

Laila stared at the card, her pulse steady, cold.

Once, the Service would have rolled out protective teams, federal alerts, procedural lockdowns.

Now, it was just them.

Two women.

No badges.

No backup.
Only grit, skill — and the iron determination to keep fighting.
Laila tucked the card into her jacket pocket and looked out across the darkened fields.
"Let them watch," she said.
"We're not going anywhere."
The kitchen smelled of roasted chicken and fresh bread, the kind of meal that had once been synonymous with comfort. Tonight, it felt like armor.
Eleanor moved quietly around the stove, setting out plates, humming under her breath
— an old hymn Laila half-remembered from childhood.

Across the room, one of her brothers — Thomas — leaned against the doorframe, arms crossed, watchful without being intrusive. Another — Daniel — was outside, fixing a loose hinge on the barn door, the clang of metal floating faintly in with the cool night air.
Family moved around them like a steady, living heartbeat.
But at the table, between Laila and Carolyn, lay the Queen of Spades card — stark against the wood, a black symbol of warning.
Carolyn tapped it once with her finger. "You ever seen anything like this before?"
Laila shook her head slowly. "Not a standard threat. Too... stylized."
"No note, no demand. Just a mark." Carolyn's jaw tightened. "Which means it's personal. Whoever left it wants us to know we're being watched. Wants us

guessing."
Laila nodded grimly. "And wasting time guessing keeps us off balance."
Eleanor glanced over from the stove, a knowing look passing between mother and daughter.
"You girls be careful," she said simply, then returned to stirring a pot like she hadn't just dropped a thunderclap into the room.
Laila allowed herself a tiny smile.
They had to be careful.
And smart.
"Start at the edges," Carolyn said, her tactical voice slipping back into command tone. "The witnesses are the obvious targets. Someone warned Rosalie off — threatened her daughter."
"And Manuel's already scared stiff," Laila agreed.
They sketched it out:

- Suspects: Whoever benefited from Jean-Pierre's removal — employers, competitors, someone inside local law enforcement maybe.
- Immediate task: Figure out who knew about Jean-Pierre's witnesses and had enough reach to intimidate them without drawing formal charges.

"I'll poke around at the sheriff's department," Carolyn said. "See who's been asking about Jean-Pierre off the books."
"I'll talk to Kent again," Laila added. "Jean-Pierre's old manager. He was nervous when we asked about the timecards — too nervous."
Carolyn grinned. "Good cop, bad cop?"
"More like good cop, worse cop," Laila said dryly.

Thomas snorted from the doorway.
"If you need backup," he said casually, "I got a baseball bat I've been itching to use on someone."
Eleanor shot him a look. "Not under my roof," she said firmly.
But her voice held a thread of fierce pride.
Family might not have badges either.
But they had loyalty.
And sometimes, that was stronger.

The First Leads.

Carolyn spent the next morning "bumping into" old contacts at the sheriff's office — casual conversations in coffee shops, friendly faces who didn't ask too many questions if you smiled right.
She learned two important things:

1. Someone had been pulling Jean-Pierre's immigration file — someone who didn't officially log the requests.
2. There was a deputy named Vince Harlow — loud, ambitious, nursing political ambitions — who had made no secret of his disdain for immigrants "stealing jobs."

Meanwhile, Laila returned to Green Hollow Produce.
Kent, the nervous plant manager, was less welcoming this time.

He met her on the gravel lot, arms crossed tight across his chest.

"I told you everything," he snapped. "Why you keep pokin' around?"

Laila kept her voice cool and steady.

"You're scared, Mr. Kent. Scared of whoever's leaning on you. I get it."

Kent said nothing, jaw clenched.

"But if Jean-Pierre goes down, and it ever comes out you knew he was innocent..." Laila let the thought dangle.

"You think they'll protect you then?" she asked quietly.

Kent hesitated.

Then — voice barely above a whisper — he muttered, "It ain't the police you gotta worry about."

Laila frowned.

"Then who?"

Kent shifted his weight, looking over her shoulder like he expected to be shot on the spot.

"Jacobson," he said finally. "Old man Jacobson. Owns half this town. Farms, supply stores, construction. Big money. Big pull."

"And?" Laila pressed.

Kent wiped a hand down his face. "Jean-Pierre worked for him. Was gonna file a complaint about wage theft. Next thing I know, he's canned, and two weeks later — boom — cops say he's a criminal."

Jacobson.

Of course.

Not just a local businessman.

A kingmaker.

And he didn't like loose ends.
Especially ones that could cost him money — or influence.

Back at the Farmhouse...

By dusk, they regrouped.
The brothers helped Eleanor with dinner preparations, while Laila and Carolyn hunched over the table, piecing everything together.
"Jacobson's the puppet master," Carolyn said. "And Harlow's his enforcer inside the sheriff's office."
"They frame Jean-Pierre, scare the witnesses, and sweep the whole thing under the rug," Laila said, voice cold.
Carolyn leaned back, tossing the Queen of Spades card onto the table.
"So what now?"
Laila looked around — at the house she grew up in, the mother who hummed old songs while making stew, the brothers who would fight to the last breath if asked.
At Carolyn — who had stood with her through hell and back.
"We bring the truth into the light," she said.
"No matter who it pisses off."
Carolyn grinned.
"I was hoping you'd say that. I knew you had some 'hood' in you!"
Laila just shook her head and smiled softly.
The old kitchen chalkboard — once used for grocery lists and weather notes — had been repurposed into a tactical command center.

Names, times, locations.
Arrows connecting players.
Jacobson at the top, his network of influence sprawling like spiderwebs.
Carolyn circled the chalkboard, one hand tapping a piece of chalk rhythmically against her palm.
"So, big picture: Jacobson uses his influence to lean on the sheriff's office. Harlow feeds fake leads to ICE, files reports on Jean-Pierre. Meanwhile, anyone who could clear Jean-Pierre gets threatened or disappears quietly."
Laila nodded grimly, adding: "And if we go public too soon, we could lose the witnesses. Or worse — make them targets."
The stakes were crystal clear.
"They'll crush us if they can," Carolyn said.
"Then we make it too costly for them to try," Laila answered.
The Strategy: Light Up the Dark.
They needed visibility.
Not slow, careful visibility.
Explosive, undeniable visibility.
Step one:

- Record statements from the witnesses — securely, redundantly — so even if they backed out under pressure, the evidence survived.

Step two:

- Push the recordings anonymously to regional news outlets — bypassing the local media, which Jacobson's money likely controlled.

Step three:

- Coordinate with early supporters of The Lantern Project to flood social media with the story. Community pages, local forums, churches, schools.

Once the story was out, Jacobson wouldn't be able to operate in the shadows.
Every move he made would be under a microscope.
"The only thing bullies fear," Carolyn said, "is a bigger crowd."
It would be a quiet mobilization.
They moved fast.

That evening, Eleanor made extra stew and kept the kitchen bustling — casual cover for the steady stream of visitors slipping quietly in and out of the farmhouse.
Manuel Ortega arrived first — pale, hands shaking as he recounted the night he saw Jean-Pierre working.
Laila recorded his statement carefully, asking only clear, simple questions.
No leading. No pressure.
Rosalie Vance followed, a scarf pulled low over her face.
She was terrified — but fierce beneath it.
"I don't want my daughter growing up thinking silence is safer than truth," she said quietly after signing her statement.
Theo Martin was last — reluctant, but ultimately convinced by Laila's calm, patient insistence that the truth mattered.
Each recording was encrypted, copied three times, stored across burner drives hidden at different farmhouses nearby — friends and allies who understood the stakes even

without all the details.
Carolyn oversaw the transfer of videos to regional reporters, using VPNs and burner accounts to cover their tracks.
Every hour, their reach grew.
And every hour, the risk sharpened.

The Blowback Begins.

Just after midnight, as Laila and Carolyn double-checked the last upload, the farmhouse phone rang — an old landline Eleanor refused to give up.
The shrill sound made everyone jump.
Laila grabbed it on the third ring.
Silence crackled on the other end.
Then a voice — low, male, unfamiliar — rumbled through the line.
"You should mind your own business," the voice said. "Or next time, it'll be more than playing cards on your porch."
The click was deafening.
Laila set the receiver down carefully, breathing slowly.
Across the room, Noah rose from the couch, his expression grim.
"Want me to sit up tonight?" he asked.
Carolyn answered for her, grabbing her jacket.
"No. We both will."
Outside, the stars burned cold and distant.
Inside, the farmhouse braced itself — steady, ready.

Preparing for the Storm.

While Eleanor and the brothers locked windows, checked doors, and silently distributed baseball bats, Laila and Carolyn reviewed the plan again.
No deviation.
No second-guessing.
They had the statements.
They had the evidence.
They had the story — already uploading to trusted outlets.
By dawn, the world would know.
Jacobson could threaten, he could bluster, he could rage — but once the light was on him, there would be no putting it back into darkness.
"We're gonna make some very bad people very nervous," Carolyn said, a sharp smile tugging at her mouth.
Laila matched her smile, feeling the old fire burn in her chest.
"We already have."
The house was quieter than usual that night.
The kind of quiet that came after a storm — not total silence, but a softened hush, as if the walls themselves were exhaling.
Dinner was a little later than normal.
No fancy dishes. Just Eleanor's roast chicken, mashed potatoes, and greens pulled from the garden.
But it felt like a feast.
Jean-Pierre had gone home, trembling and tearful, papers in hand, his son clinging to his waist.
The videos were still circulating.

Jacobson's name was on every news ticker.
The Lantern Project had struck its first blow — and it had landed hard.

Laila sat at the kitchen table, elbows resting on worn wood scarred by years of family meals and quiet conversations.
Carolyn was to her left, nursing a beer she hadn't touched yet.
Daniel and Thomas were across from them, arguing lightly about a broken tractor belt.
Eleanor moved in and out of the kitchen, humming under her breath, as though her daughter hadn't just helped dismantle a local empire.
For once, no one mentioned courtrooms.
Or law.
Or trauma.
They just… existed. Together.
Warm.
Worn.
Alive.
"You girls did something good," Eleanor said softly as she set down a dish of baked apples. "Not just for that man, but for this place. For this house."
Laila looked down, jaw tight. "Still feels fragile."
"Most things worth keeping are," Eleanor said simply.
The Porch, Later…
After dinner, they drifted.
The brothers stepped out to check the livestock.

Eleanor cleaning up, singing softly to herself.
Laila and Carolyn sat on the porch, wrapped in blankets, nursing hot cider instead of coffee.
The stars burned clean and bright above them, scattered across the sky like powdered bone.
Neither spoke for a while.
Finally, Carolyn broke the silence.
"I keep waiting for someone to say we did it wrong."
Laila raised an eyebrow.
"Wrong how?"
"I don't know. Too aggressive. Not aggressive enough. Out of line. You know — the usual fallout from telling the truth."
Laila smiled faintly.
"You're thinking like a Marshal again."
Carolyn snorted. "Maybe. You?"
Laila sipped her cider.
"I'm trying not to. But yeah… it's in there. Comes back when things go loud."
They were quiet again.
Then Carolyn said, softly, "What happens when the next case comes in?"
Laila's answer came quicker than she expected.
"We help."
Even if it hurts.
Even if it risks everything again.
Even if it's not clean or safe or guaranteed.
Because they weren't just survivors anymore.
They were something else.

Chapter 9

A Quiet Shift.

The screen door creaked behind them.
Eleanor stepped out, wrapped in her old knit shawl.
"There's a message for you," she said, handing over a folded note.
Carolyn took it, reading the neat handwriting — unfamiliar but official.
"We've been watching your work. The Department may be reaching out. There are changes coming. We'll be in touch."
It wasn't signed.
Carolyn handed it to Laila, who read it twice, then folded it again and slid it into her jacket.
Neither woman spoke.
But something shifted between them.
Not panic.
Not fear.
Just the quiet, heavy understanding that the world was watching again — and this time, the stakes were going to be even higher.
Inside, Eleanor turned off the porch light.
The farmhouse sank into darkness.
But Laila and Carolyn sat together in the cold and the stars, blanket wrapped tight around their shoulders, staring out at the long road ahead.
"You think we're ready?" Carolyn asked.
"No," Laila said honestly.

Then: "But we're going anyway."
And in that moment, under a sky wide enough to hold both memory and hope,
neither woman flinched.

The farmhouse had become a strange intersection of quiet domesticity and quiet dread. As the sun spilled golden light across the Pennsylvania hills, Laila leaned against the porch railing, her gaze fixed on the long dirt road beyond the soybean field. It should have been a peaceful moment. But her mind was elsewhere — on the case.
Inside, Carolyn was at the kitchen table, papers spread around her like a cyclone's aftermath.
A manila folder sat at the center, its label handwritten in crisp block letters:

MATEO RUIZ: ICE HOLDS & SUPPRESSION REQUEST.

"This doesn't feel right," Carolyn muttered, circling something with a red pen. "No priors, no gang affiliations, no evidence — just proximity to a crime scene and an over-eager local deputy with a grudge."
Laila stepped back inside, her boots thudding softly on the old floorboards. "And now he's in detention," she said. "ICE picked him up without formal charges. If we weren't already tipped off, no one would've noticed until after deportation."

Their credentials as U.S. Marshals carried weight, even unofficially. But since discussing resigning — or being quietly sidelined — following the Falfor scandal, they treaded a narrow line between oversight and irrelevance. Their work on the Ruiz case was freelance, unofficial, and likely unwelcome. But their instincts didn't care for permission.

From the hallway, Daniel's voice rang out. "Hey Yaya, you've got mail — government seal on it."

She exchanged a quick look with Carolyn, who raised an eyebrow. "You think it's the DOJ already?"

"Too early," Laila said, taking the envelope and slicing it open with a penknife. But her expression tightened as she read.

The seal was real.

The message was simple:

The department requires your presence for a classified debrief. Bring Agent Halston. Do not discuss with local authorities. — J.A.

"Looks like we're back on the clock," she murmured.

"Seriously?" Carolyn rose, pulling her jacket over her shoulder holster. "What about Mateo?"

"We finish what we started," Laila said, resolute. "No one gets left behind. Not again."

A moment of silence passed between them. In the background, Eleanor clattered pans in the kitchen, humming an old Johnny Cash song.

The familiarity of home clashed sharply with the road ahead.
Then — *a loud pop.*
The farmhouse windows rattled. Carolyn ducked instinctively, hand to her weapon. Daniel shouted from outside.
Both women rushed to the door. A rusted Ford pickup had peeled off down the drive. In the yard, the mailbox smoldered — someone had rigged it with a small explosive.
"This just escalated," Carolyn said, voice cold.
Laila's eyes narrowed. "Someone doesn't want us digging."
But they'd seen worse. And they never backed down.

The Briefing – DOJ Headquarters, Washington D.C.

It was surreal walking back through the steel-and-glass corridors of power. The DOJ building hummed with the clinical efficiency Laila remembered — stark white walls, low voices, the occasional echo of polished shoes against marble. Except this time, the stares were different.
The aide at the front desk glanced at their badges, did a double take, and picked up the phone without a word.
Thirty seconds later, they were being led into a secure elevator. The descent was silent except for the low rumble of hydraulics and Carolyn tapping her fingers rhythmically against her thigh — a habit from old recon missions.
The door opened into a subterranean conference room. Dimly lit. Sterile. Two armed guards flanked the entrance, while a heavy-set man in a gray suit stood at the far end of

the table. His name was *Deputy Director Elijah Cormac,* and his eyes carried the weight of too many secrets.
"Marshals Wright. Pryme," he greeted without rising. "Appreciate your discretion. Sit."
They didn't sit. Not immediately.
"What's this about?" Carolyn asked flatly.
Cormac slid a dossier across the table. "Operation *Threshold*. We're reactivating key personnel for targeted enforcement and intel recovery. We've got a compromised channel inside Immigration and Customs Enforcement — someone's pulling strings to deport key witnesses before they can testify. Mateo Ruiz is one of them."
Laila picked up the file. Inside: blurry surveillance photos, redacted case memos, a map connecting detention centers across three states.
"You're saying someone inside ICE is weaponizing deportation?" she asked.
Cormac nodded. "And ICE isn't the only agency being manipulated. We have reports of federal judges being pressured, evidence disappearing, even journalists being intimidated. It may be above all of our paygrade."
Carolyn scoffed. "Sounds like Falfor all over again."
"Falfor was the tip of the spear," Cormac said, voice low. "This — this is the shaft. And it's pointed at the heart of the system."
He leaned forward now, finally showing urgency. "We need your access, your instincts, and your experience with internal corruption. You won't be reinstated officially — yet. But you'll have full operational autonomy under DOJ oversight."

Laila's jaw clenched. "And what about the Ruiz case? We're already neck-deep."
"Handle it," Cormac said. "That's your first directive under Threshold."
"And after that?" Carolyn asked.
He hesitated. Then: "You'll be asked to cross lines. Legal, diplomatic… maybe even moral. Are you both prepared for that again?"
Laila and Carolyn exchanged a glance — years of combat and courtrooms distilled into a silent agreement.
"We never stopped being Marshals," Laila said.
Cormac allowed the ghost of a smile. "Then welcome back to the war."

Parking Garage, DOJ HQ – Later That Evening

The concrete walls of the underground garage wrapped around them like a bunker. A sharp wind filtered in from the slatted vents near the ceiling, stirring up the dust and echoes of distant footsteps. Laila leaned against their rental SUV, arms folded, silent.
Carolyn paced near the front bumper, hands on hips, brow furrowed.
"Well," she muttered, "that wasn't subtle."
Laila didn't respond. She stared at the cracked concrete beneath her boots as if it might offer a simpler truth than what they'd just heard upstairs.
"They're not asking us to investigate a case," Carolyn continued, voice edged with frustration. "They're asking us to walk back into the swamp. Deep cover.

Loose authorization. No real backup. It's Falfor all over again — only now the stakes are national."

Laila finally looked up, her eyes dark and steady. "That's why they called us. We're already the 'outsiders'. We're expendable."

Carolyn stopped pacing. "You think we can trust Cormac?"

"No," Laila said without hesitation. "But we don't need to. We just need to trust each other."

Carolyn exhaled slowly, stepping closer. "You sure about this? About going back in? We had a quiet mission — helping Ruiz, living life outside the crosshairs. The farm, your family, peace."

A long pause.

Then Laila's voice, soft but resolute:

"I was trained to fight enemies I could see. But the ones hiding in the system? They're the ones that rot everything from the inside. If I walk away now, I'm just leaving it for someone else to clean up. And that's not who I am."

Carolyn gave a small, dry laugh. "You really do love lost causes."

"Only the ones worth saving."

They stood there in silence for a while — not as law enforcement officers, not as covert assets — but as two women who had seen too much, survived too much, and still chose to fight.

Then Carolyn spoke, calm and clear: "Okay. We finish the Ruiz case. Then we hunt down whatever the hell *Threshold* really is."

Laila nodded once.

Above them, headlights flickered across the garage as

another vehicle pulled out. Somewhere beyond the walls, the government turned its wheels, grinding forward. But down here, in the quiet, they were already moving ahead — partners in the shadows again.

Berks County ICE Detention Facility – Two Days Later

The facility loomed like a cold reminder of the line between enforcement and entrapment. Gray fencing, motion sensors, a perimeter patrol that ran on rigid timing. Laila and Carolyn passed through the security checks with little resistance — Marshals still commanded a certain authority, even unofficially.

But inside, the mood was different.

The halls were too clean. The guards too quiet. And the intake officer

— a woman named *Sergeant Noelle Bristow* —

barely glanced up as she stamped their visitor passes.

"You're here for Ruiz?" she said, tone clipped.

"That's right," Carolyn replied, handing over their request form.

"Hmm." Bristow tapped her computer. "That's odd."

"What is?"

"He was supposed to be transported yesterday to a federal holding site. Transfer was canceled last minute by someone higher up — no signature on the override."

Laila's posture straightened. "And he's still here?"

Bristow nodded slowly, a flicker of discomfort breaking through her bureaucratic mask. "Unit B-4. But I'd tread lightly — since the cancelation, we've had some... unofficial visitors."
Carolyn exchanged a glance with Laila. "Feds?"
Bristow hesitated. "They didn't identify. But they weren't from here. Suits. Asked a lot of questions. Took photos."
As they moved toward the cell block, the fluorescent lights above seemed to hum louder than usual — a static warning.

Interview Room, Detention Facility.

Mateo Ruiz looked thinner than his file photo. Late twenties, sunken eyes, a faded tattoo of the Virgin of Guadalupe on his forearm. But his posture was straight. Defiant.
"Are you cops?" he asked, voice hollow.
"No," Laila said. "We're better."
Carolyn added, "We're here to make sure you're not silenced for something you didn't do."
Mateo's eyes scanned them both, unsure. "They told me I'd be gone before the week ended. 'Expedited,' they said. But I didn't do anything. I don't even know what the crime was — they just kept saying I matched a description."
"What description?" Laila asked.
He shook his head. "I never saw it. But they were scared. Not of me — of whoever sent the order."
Carolyn leaned in. "Do you know this name?" She slid a small paper forward: *C. JACOBSON*.
Mateo's expression changed — not recognition, but

confusion.
"That name was on a box," he said slowly. "The agents who visited… they left a file on the desk. I saw it upside down. Red folder. That name was stamped on the tab. Big letters."
Laila's breath caught. "You're sure?"
Mateo nodded. "I remember because it looked like a lawyer's file. Not ICE paperwork."

Hallway Outside the Interview Room…

As the door closed behind them, Carolyn turned sharply. "Jacobson's dead. His name should've died with him."
Laila's thoughts churned. "Or someone's using his credentials. Or copying his playbook."
They moved down the corridor — and paused as two men in suits passed them from the opposite direction. No ID badges. No smiles.
The men looked at them — too long — then disappeared into a stairwell.
"I've got a bad feeling," Carolyn muttered.
Laila didn't reply. Her phone buzzed — a new encrypted message from the DOJ's shadow channel:
"Threshold compromised. Trust no one inside ICE or DHS. Begin data sweep. You're not just hunting a network — you're inside one."

A chill ran through both women.
What began as a case of wrongful detention now pointed to something far deeper — a covert operation with roots in

dead men's names and living bureaucracies. Something that wasn't just using the system — it was *rewriting* it.

Highway 222, Northern Pennsylvania – Just Before Midnight…

The SUV cut through the dark like a bullet on rails. Rain danced across the windshield in needle-fine strands, the wipers swiping rhythmically as the farm came closer with every mile.

Carolyn was in the passenger seat, laptop open, the glow of the screen painting her face in cold light. A hotspot tethered from her phone linked them to a secure DOJ mirror server — a relic from their marshal days, long dormant, now humming again under an old access code: *"LAWM42X"*.

"We're inside the ICE personnel registry," she said, typing furiously. "Looking for any digital imprint on Jacobson. Past login activity, file authorizations, facility access."

Laila kept her eyes on the road. "He's supposed to be dead. And buried."

Carolyn frowned. "That's the thing. His credentials are still *active*. Refreshed two weeks ago. And guess what? Someone used them to access the *Nexus 7B Archive*."

Laila shot her a glance. "That's off-books. Wasn't that supposed to be locked down after Falfor?"

"Yeah, it was. That's where sealed corruption cases go to die. The only people with clearance now are senior DOJ brass… and apparently, ghosts."

Another tap.

Another window opened. “Got something. A cloned login sequence traced through a shell server in Arizona. Pinged once more from inside Berks County Detention… the same day Ruiz was almost transferred.”

“Someone used Jacobson’s ID to pull sealed witness files,” Laila said grimly. “Then tried to deport one.”

Carolyn turned the screen toward her. “And it gets worse. Look at this alias: *R. Greaves*.”

“Never heard of it.”

“It’s listed under cross-agency operations as a ‘civil liaison.’ But the email tied to it? Was on Falfor’s internal comms list.”

Laila clenched the wheel tighter. “So someone’s not just reviving Jacobson. They’re reactivating Falfor’s entire *playbook*.”

Carolyn closed the laptop, her expression unreadable. “This isn’t just about deportation, Laila. They’re cleaning house. Silencing old witnesses. Scrubbing inconvenient truths. Threshold might not be a mission — it might be a firewall.”

Rain continued to tap against the windows as the lights of the farmhouse appeared in the distance, soft and flickering like candles against the night.

Laila finally spoke, voice low.

“Then we find Greaves. And whoever's holding Jacobson's puppet strings.”

Carolyn nodded. “And if we’re inside the network…”

Laila finished the thought: “...then it means someone wants us to stay just long enough to take the fall.”

The SUV turned onto the gravel path of the family farm. But there would be no rest tonight.

The Farmhouse Kitchen – Just Past Midnight.

The farmhouse was warm, quiet, and filled with the smell of strong coffee. Rain tapped lightly at the windows as if reluctant to interrupt the moment.

Eleanor stood at the stove, wrapping her robe tighter as she poured three mugs, sliding them across the table toward Laila, Carolyn, and Daniel — who'd already pulled out his old FBI notebook, flipping it open with an audible sigh.

"You two show up at this hour looking like you've seen a ghost," Eleanor said gently. "So talk to me like I don't have a badge or a clearance — just a mother who knows when something smells wrong."

Laila leaned back in her chair. She hadn't removed her jacket, and the tension in her shoulders hadn't eased since they walked through the door.

"Someone inside ICE is using the ID of a dead man to move witnesses off the board," she said. "We think they're targeting people tied to old corruption cases — probably ones we helped expose during the Falfor takedown."

Eleanor's brow furrowed. "You mean to say they're… deporting people who could testify? Just shuffling them out the back door?"

Carolyn nodded. "Or worse. With them gone, sealed evidence loses context. Cases collapse. People forget. No one follows up on a ghost file."

Daniel spoke up now, voice low and steady. "You two are saying this is more than just some rogue operator. You think it's *institutional*."

"We don't know how far it goes yet," Carolyn said. "But the activity's consistent. Patterns, timing, firewall cover-ups. Someone's reviving a playbook we thought we shut down years ago."

Eleanor set her coffee down with a soft clink. "And this Jacobson — he's the one who…?"

"He was Falfor's right hand," Laila said. "Coordinated illegal detentions, asset seizures, even blackmail. He died during the investigation."

"But now his name's showing up again," Carolyn added. "Digitally, at least. His login was used to pull secure files. Files that include the man we're trying to protect — Mateo Ruiz."

Daniel let out a slow breath and leaned forward. "Then let me tell you what's going to happen if you're not careful. You'll start chasing shadows, and whoever's behind this — if they're half as smart as Falfor — will be three steps ahead. They won't just erase data. They'll erase *you*. Reputation. History. Maybe even physically."

A long pause followed.

"But you're going after them anyway," he said, already knowing the answer.

Laila nodded. "We don't have a choice."

Daniel looked at Carolyn, then back to his sister. "Then promise me something: don't go at it like it's the old days. You're not protected anymore. You're not wearing stars on your chest. You're vulnerable — and this house, this family, might be too."

Eleanor stepped in softly. "Then how do we help?"

Laila looked up, her face unreadable for a beat. Then: "You

keep life normal. Keep the lights on, the coffee hot. Be eyes and ears. If strangers show up asking questions, call us first."

"I've raised enough stubborn children to know what silence looks like," Eleanor said. "But you'll get no judgment here. Just don't leave us in the dark."

Carolyn gave a tired smile. "Then keep that porch light on."

Daniel stood, rubbing the back of his neck. "I'll do a quiet sweep of your devices tomorrow. Check the lines, the security system, just in case someone's sniffing around."

As he turned to leave, he paused at the doorway.

"One last thing," he said. "R. Greaves… that alias you mentioned? I've heard it before. Not in an official file — in chatter. Quiet, peripheral. Like a fixer or… a cleaner. If that name's back in play, this isn't just about covering tracks. It's about tying up *loose ends.*"

Then he disappeared into the hallway.

The kitchen fell into silence, save for the clock ticking and the wind picking up again outside.

Laila finally took a sip of her coffee. "We've got to move fast."

Berks County Immigration Court – 9:12 A.M.

Carolyn adjusted the collar of her blazer as she entered the modest courtroom. The setting was deliberately underwhelming — gray walls, unadorned benches, a flickering exit sign. It looked more like a DMV than the venue where someone's future could be shattered.

Mateo Ruiz sat beside her at the defendant's table, dressed

in a clean but ill-fitting button-down shirt provided by the detention facility. His eyes scanned the room nervously. "What changed?" he asked under his breath. "Why so fast?"
Carolyn leaned in. "That's what I'm here to find out."
The judge, a middle-aged man with thinning hair and an emotionless stare, shuffled in a moment later and called the room to order.
"Docket number 47B–326. Mateo Ruiz. Responding to Department of Homeland Security expedited removal motion."
Carolyn stood. "Objection, Your Honor. Defense was not notified of this motion until late yesterday. The respondent's legal advocate has not had time to review the submitted evidence."
The DHS representative, a man in a sharp gray suit with an unfamiliar badge, stood. "The motion falls within established policy for high-risk foreign nationals. Due process has been met."
Carolyn's jaw tightened. She recognized the type — a company man with no visible fingerprints. But something was off. His tone was too controlled, too clean.
As the judge nodded and flipped through pages with mechanical precision, Carolyn whispered to Mateo: "Stay quiet. Let me do the talking."

At the Farmhouse – Laila's Bedroom/Office…

Laila sat cross-legged on her bed, a tangle of charging cables and open folders around her. Her laptop blinked with

encrypted overlays — DOJ mirrors on one screen, local ICE logs on another.
She scrolled through layers of buried credentials tied to "R. Greaves." No birth certificate. No social footprint. Just ghost-data: email routing from state department terminals, travel logs tagged to encrypted flight manifests, even a few redacted FISA court notes.
But then she hit a vein.
A corrupted metadata file in the DOJ archive bore the notation:
"GREV-739 / Operative Liaison – External Discretionary Use / Status: In Play"
Laila froze. "External… discretionary?"
She backtracked. Cross-referenced the tag with a decommissioned marshal's index from five years prior. The system hung for a moment — then resolved.
Name: Rhys Greaves.
Status: Suspended Contractor.
Clearance Level: Alpha Black.
Location: Unknown.
"Rhys…" she whispered. "He's real."
She scanned the notes. Greaves had once been an intel liaison during the Falfor investigation, embedded deep inside ICE and DOJ, supposedly neutral. But his clearance was pulled after an internal probe. The file didn't say why. And now he was back — accessing sealed archives and pushing removal orders through the system.
Just as she pieced it together, her screen flashed.
ALERT: Expedited Removal Order Filed – Ruiz, Mateo – 9:13 A.M.

"Dammit," Laila muttered, grabbing her phone and dialing Carolyn.

Immigration Courtroom – Minutes Later

Carolyn's phone buzzed. She saw 'LAILA – URGENT' and pressed her earpiece to answer under her hair.
"Talk," she whispered.
Laila's voice was clipped and fast. "R. Greaves is real. Rhys Greaves. Ex-intel, black-level clearance. Suspended after Falfor fallout. He's the one moving your courtroom strings."
Carolyn's eyes narrowed as she watched the DHS rep slide a folder toward the judge. "He's here. At least, his puppet is."
"Ruiz is the first of many," Laila continued. "We stop this motion now, or it sets precedent for every case tied to the old network."
Carolyn stood suddenly. "Your Honor, I request this court be recessed immediately pending a formal review of the agent's credentials and chain of custody of the submitted documentation."
The judge looked up, irritated. "On what grounds?"
Carolyn's tone was calm, razor-sharp. "On the grounds that this courtroom is being manipulated by a suspended federal contractor using defunct clearance to influence ongoing judicial proceedings. I have DOJ logs and archived reports that implicate unauthorized access to federal systems."
A long silence.

The judge glanced at the DHS rep — whose jaw tightened ever so slightly — then banged his gavel. "This court is recessed. Agent, I expect your full documentation and ID logs submitted within 24 hours."
Carolyn exhaled, guiding Mateo gently by the shoulder. "Let's get out of here before they change their minds."

Farmhouse – Afternoon

Back home, Laila met Carolyn at the door.
"They're moving faster than we thought," she said.
Carolyn nodded. "But now we've got a name. Greaves."
"And a pattern."
Carolyn leaned in, voice low. "What if Greaves wasn't working alone back then — and isn't now? What if Falfor was just a front?"
Laila didn't blink. "Then we're not chasing shadows anymore."
She looked down at a note Daniel had left on the kitchen table.
"Picked something up in the wire logs. We've been scanned. Twice."
They were officially being watched.
And Rhys Greaves had just moved to the top of their list.

A Diner Outside Harrisburg – The Next Day.

The walls of *Charlie's Diner* were lined with faded NASCAR posters and a jukebox that hadn't played anything newer than 2003. The place smelled of bacon grease and burnt coffee, and that's exactly why it was chosen — too plain to raise suspicion.

Officer Evan Fielder, mid-50s, stocky, with thinning gray hair and a badge he kept tucked in his inside pocket, sat in a booth by the window. He looked like he hadn't slept in weeks. His eyes flicked up as Laila and Carolyn approached.

"No uniforms. No marshals. Just two ghosts from the Falfor files," he said as they slid in across from him.

"We appreciate you meeting us," Carolyn said.

"I didn't," he muttered. "I agreed to coffee. That's all."

Laila leaned forward, voice measured. "You worked with Rhys Greaves. We know he was assigned to internal review on Falfor's task force, but your name shows up three times in secure communiques."

Fielder's jaw tightened. "You're looking in places that should've stayed locked."

Carolyn didn't flinch. "So is he."

That hit. Fielder's hands trembled slightly as he picked up his mug. "Greaves was supposed to be a liaison. He showed up with a Black-level clearance and a cold stare. The kind of guy who never blinked, never ate, never showed up on payroll. He knew what people were hiding before they did."

"He's back," Laila said. "Using dead men's IDs. Pulling ICE strings. Targeting witnesses tied to sealed corruption cases. We stopped one — Mateo Ruiz. But we're not going to stop them all unless we understand how deep this goes."

Fielder's eyes searched theirs — two women who had once brought down giants and lived to testify about it. He nodded, slowly.

"Greaves had two faces," he said. "The one he showed agencies — tactical, clinical, obedient. Then the other one... off-record, late-night calls from untraceable lines. Files he'd slide across your desk and say, 'This one doesn't get processed. Just... removed.'"

"Removed?" Carolyn asked. "Like transferred?"

Fielder shook his head. "Like disappeared."

A chill ran through the booth.

"Falfor never gave those orders," he continued. "He was a crook, yeah, but Greaves was a *cleaner*. If Falfor got sloppy, Greaves wiped it clean — files, people, memories. He wasn't loyal to anyone."

Laila leaned in. "So who *was* he working for?"

Fielder's voice dropped to a whisper. "We used to joke that he answered to something called 'Room 19.' A real deep room. Old Cold War stuff. No paper trail, no witnesses. You'd only hear about it when someone who mattered disappeared."

Carolyn exchanged a look with Laila. "You think Room 19's still active?"

Fielder finished his coffee. "You wouldn't be looking for Greaves if it wasn't."

He stood and left a crumpled twenty on the table. Before walking away, he stopped and added one last line over his shoulder.

"If you're smart, you'll drop it. People who go looking for Rhys Greaves don't just vanish. They get *revised.*"

As the door closed behind him, the women sat in silence.
"Room 19," Carolyn repeated. "Sounds like a legend."
"No," Laila said, pulling out her phone. "Sounds like our next target."

The Farmhouse – Late Afternoon

The upstairs study had become something of a makeshift war room. Maps, folders, and a corkboard filled with red pushpins dominated one corner, while three laptops blinked and hummed with filtered data. Daniel sat at the largest desk, glasses on, sleeves rolled up, and two monitors running old ICE and DOJ backdoor logs through a custom decryptor he'd built during his FBI days.
Carolyn and Laila hovered nearby, watching the screens flash faster than they could follow.
"Room 19," Laila said again, handing him a small notepad. "Fielder says it was old Cold War clearance. Ultra-compartmentalized. He described Greaves as a 'cleaner' for that program."
Daniel didn't look up. "I've heard the term in field whispers, but never saw a file. I always thought it was disinfo planted to confuse internal audits."
"Well, it's back," Carolyn said. "And it's bleeding into modern ICE operations."
Daniel paused the scroll.
"Look at this." He pointed to a line of green-highlighted code. "I ran a query on encrypted calls and access codes tied to defunct projects within DOJ, Homeland Security, and federal intelligence archives."

He opened a log file labeled:

[ARIES-ECHO19 / ACCESS REQUESTS: 2009–2025]

"There's a pattern," he said. "Every time a person connected to Falfor was detained or deported, this tag — ARIES-ECHO19 — was pinged."

"What is it?" Laila asked.

"I don't know yet," Daniel admitted. "But it's tied to three things: the Federal Courthouse Archives, the State Department's emergency response protocol… and a now-defunct blacksite in West Virginia."

Carolyn blinked. "Wait — a *blacksite*? Like a detention facility?"

Daniel clicked again, revealing an aerial map with a single structure nestled in the hills, cloaked in forest and removed from public satellite imagery. A label flickered across the screen:

Facility 9 – BUREAU OF STRATEGIC INITIATIVES (DEACTIVATED 1998)

"Facility Nine," he said. "Look at the number. Room *19*, Facility *9*. It's not a room — it's a *place.* The legend was the misdirection."

Laila stepped back. "And if that place is still operational…"

"…then we've just found the center of Greaves' operation," Daniel finished.

Carolyn crossed her arms. "We'd need aerial recon, entry logs, and a damned good reason to breach a facility like that."

Laila glanced out the farmhouse window, dusk rolling in over the soybean field.

"We'll get that reason. But we go smart. Quiet. No badges.

No paperwork."

Daniel looked up. "You're talking a black op. Are you ready to go off the grid?"

Laila's voice was low, certain. "I never got back *on* it."

Farmhouse – The Following Morning
"Operation: Mislead"

Sunlight filtered through gauzy curtains in the farmhouse kitchen, but the mood was anything but pastoral. The team had convened early. Coffee brewed in steady cycles. Phones were kept in the barn refrigerator — a low-tech tactic to muffle passive geolocation. Daniel sat at the dining table with a burner laptop, while Laila and Carolyn reviewed their travel gear in silence.

Daniel finally spoke. "We need to feed them a story. A convincing one. Something that makes it look like you're going after someone else entirely."

Carolyn nodded. "And it needs just enough truth to be dangerous."

Daniel cracked his knuckles. "I've got just the bait."

He began typing into a mirrored DOJ intranet sandbox — not the real thing, but a dark mirror used in cyber-training simulations. It would ping the federal watchlist queues without triggering immediate tracebacks.

"I'm planting chatter that you've redirected focus to a federal contractor named *Maya Trent*, based in Virginia," he said. "She was an accountant for Falfor's asset laundering program. We're fabricating her flight to Argentina two days ago and a subpoena request drafted by

‘Agent Wright.’”
“Nice touch,” Laila said.
“Also posting under burner aliases in two defense-related chat rooms,” Daniel added. “Wording implies that Greaves’ intel is bogus, and that your real interest is buried in missing financial audits.”
Carolyn smirked. “That’ll make Greaves paranoid. He’ll start covering a trail we’re not even on.”
Daniel hit send. “It’s live. I give it 48 hours before someone sniffs it and overreacts.”

Farmhouse Barn – Later That Day
“Planning the Infiltration of Facility 9”

Inside the old hayloft, the team had turned barn siding into a tactical board. A crudely drawn floorplan of *Facility 9* was pinned beside hand-labeled satellite maps. The surrounding forest was dense, pockmarked with streams and old mining roads.
Carolyn pointed with a capped pen. “There’s only one known entrance — this old loading bay on the southern face. The rest is fortified, and it’s too embedded in terrain for chopper insertion.”
Laila circled another area. “But here — these drainage culverts near the rear. If they weren’t collapsed, they’d be the perfect route in.”
Daniel added, “Thermal scans show intermittent heat patterns in those culverts — not active sewage or water. Likely vented air from internal systems. That means access and air. Could be crawlable.”

"Which means we need to move on foot, at night, through about two miles of rough terrain," Laila said. "Entry through the culverts. Breach quietly. Find intel. Exfil within five hours max."
Carolyn looked over the gear: fiber-optic scope, encrypted thumb drives, cutting tools, and three suppressed sidearms. "No electronic coms once we breach," she said. "If they're running black-level operations in there, they've got scramblers."
Daniel handed over two hard-copy maps. "I'll act as basewatch from here. You'll have one scheduled check-in when you clear the outer shell. After that, total blackout."
Laila stared at the map of Facility 9. "What's our target inside?"
Daniel clicked open a file and showed a grainy photo of a steel vault door with the old BSI (Bureau of Strategic Initiatives) emblem.
"That vault houses a cold archive. Pre-digital records. If Room 19 still exists, that's where we'll find proof—operational memos, personnel transfers, maybe even Greaves' real chain of command."
Carolyn smirked. "We walk in as ghosts… and come back with names."
Laila gave one final nod. "Saddle up. We leave at nightfall."

Farmhouse – The Night Before…

The farmhouse was dim and quiet, lit only by the soft amber glow of a single lamp in the living room. Outside, the wind rustled through the trees — the kind of night where silence felt heavy, like the world was holding its breath.

Eleanor stood in the kitchen doorway, arms crossed, watching her daughter and Carolyn check their packs one final time.

"You sure you don't want to wait another day?" she asked gently. "You've barely slept."

Laila zipped up her bag without looking up. "Can't. If we wait, we lose the element of surprise."

Carolyn gave Eleanor a reassuring nod. "We've done worse with less, I promise."

"That's not what worries me," Eleanor said, stepping forward and placing a hand on Laila's arm. "It's that you're going back into a place designed to erase people — and I already lost you once."

Laila paused, her eyes softening. "You didn't lose me. I just went quiet for a while."

Eleanor smiled faintly, but the worry remained. She kissed her daughter's forehead, then Carolyn's, and quietly returned to the kitchen.

Daniel stood by the front door, leaning against the frame, arms folded. His eyes tracked every movement — protective, analytical, brotherly.

"You two really going to ghost into a decommissioned blacksite based on thirty-year-old rumors and heat signatures?" he asked.

Laila gave a thin smile. "Sounds dumber when you say it like that."

Daniel pushed off the doorframe. "Then let me come with

you. One more gun, just in case things go sideways."

Laila hesitated, then motioned for him to follow her out onto the porch. The night air was cool, the stars faint behind a blanket of clouds. They stood in silence for a moment before she spoke.

"I need you to stay here," she said softly. "If we don't come back — if something goes wrong — you're the one I trust to keep Mom safe… And Thomas. Keep things together."

Daniel clenched his jaw. "That's a shitty trade, Yaya."

"It's the right one," she said. "You're the one person who can keep this place from going under if we don't walk out of that mountain."

He stared at her, conflicted, then slowly nodded.

"Alright. But just know," he said, stepping closer, "you're going to come back. And you're going to annoy the *fuck* out of me with your victory speech."

Laila laughed — really laughed — for the first time in days.

"I'll make it long and dramatic," she promised.

He smiled, pulled her into a tight hug, then stepped back and opened the door.

Carolyn was already slinging her bag over her shoulder. "We ready?"

Laila nodded once. "Yeah. Let's go break into the dark."

They stepped out into the night — two silhouettes swallowed by the edge of the forest road, moving like ghosts toward the truth.

The porch light stayed on behind them, flickering once — but never going out.

Chapter 10

Appalachian Foothills, Two Miles from Facility 9 – 11:47 P.M.
"Ingress"

The forest swallowed them whole.

Carolyn's boots moved with practiced quiet over the soft, pine-needle-covered ground. Laila followed a half-step behind, her eyes constantly scanning the tree line, listening to the rhythm of the woods: the distant hoot of an owl, the whisper of leaves in the breeze — and, more importantly, the *absence* of anything mechanical.

Their tactical gear was stripped down to essentials — matte black packs, subsonic sidearms, fiber-optic scopes, compact breaching kits. Lightweight, quiet, invisible.

A red-lensed flashlight flicked briefly as Carolyn consulted the terrain map. "Half a klick to the ravine. If the culverts are where Daniel said they are, we should hit the first grate soon."

"Thermals still holding?" Laila whispered.

Carolyn checked her wrist unit. "Minimal interference. The vents are warm enough to be viable. No active EM fields — which means no scramble perimeter, or it's buried deeper."

They moved down a narrow trail, overgrown but faintly navigable. Laila noticed the unnatural stillness — no wind, no insects.

"Too quiet," she muttered.

Carolyn didn't disagree. "Could be sensor grid. Passive acoustic detection — listens for what *isn't* natural."

"We're ghosts," Laila reminded her.

Five minutes later, they reached the edge of a steep drop — the mouth of the ravine. Below, nearly concealed by vines and brush, was a squat concrete outflow pipe — half-submerged, about four feet in diameter, with a rusted access grate hanging loose.

Carolyn crouched and scanned the perimeter with a monocular. "No motion. No tripwires."

Laila knelt beside the grate. A faint stream of warm air brushed her fingers — not sewage, but recycled HVAC exhaust. It smelled like dust and ozone.

"Bingo," she whispered. She pried the grate the rest of the way open, catching it before it could clang to the stone.

Carolyn slipped in first, crawling on forearms and toes, the shaft barely tall enough to accommodate them. Laila followed, pulling the grate back into position behind them.

The only sound now was the rhythmic drip of water echoing off the walls — and their own breathing.

They moved deeper.

Every twenty feet, a vent opening spilled dim orange light into the tunnel — emergency reserve LEDs, likely decades old but still running. It was enough to see by, but not enough to be comforting.

At a bend in the shaft, Carolyn held up a fist.

They stopped. Listened.

Footsteps.

Above them — faint but deliberate. Then a thud. Metal on concrete. A dragging noise. Voices. Muffled.

"Facility's not dormant," Laila whispered.
Carolyn nodded. "That was gear being moved."
They exchanged a look.
"Still in?" Carolyn asked.
Laila's expression hardened. "Deeper than ever."
They continued, crawling toward the inner vent grid — and the dark truths buried beneath Facility 9.

Facility 9 – Interior Breach Point, 12:26 A.M.

The crawlspace ended at a rusted maintenance grate — bolted in four places, reinforced with an interior pressure latch. Carolyn adjusted the micro-scope attached to her wrist light and peered through the slats.
Beyond the grate: a narrow access corridor lined with concrete and steel, walls slick with condensation. A utility panel hummed faintly. No visible cameras. No alarms. Just a single hallway stretching left and right — sterile, unmarked, silent.
Carolyn whispered, "No motion. No thermal blooms. I say we're clear."
Laila nodded and unrolled a canvas pouch. Inside: a thin vibration-saw with a ceramic blade — slow, but silent. She went to work on the bolts.
Skrrrk... skrrrk... skrrrk... skrrrk...
Ten minutes later, the final bolt came loose. They caught the grate before it dropped and slid it carefully aside.
Laila went first, drawing her suppressed sidearm and sweeping the corridor. Carolyn dropped in behind her, already placing a signal tag behind a loose floor panel — a

digital breadcrumb for their exit.
They moved in tandem — low and smooth, clearing corners with practiced rhythm.
The interior was cold. Not abandoned-cold, but *controlled*-cold. The kind of climate regulation that implied ongoing systems: powered circulation, temperature monitoring, backup generators. This place wasn't dead.
And someone was still here.
They moved through a branching series of hallways — half map-memorized, half guesswork. Occasionally, they passed security doors with long-dead keypads, flickering ID scanners, or outdated warning decals:

AUTHORIZED PERSONNEL ONLY – ROOM 19
CLEARANCE REQUIRED
PROPERTY OF BUREAU OF STRATEGIC INITIATIVES

Carolyn paused at one junction. "This isn't just a vault. It's a bunker."
"Designed to protect something," Laila added.
Or *someone*, she didn't say aloud.
They found a narrow stairwell leading downward. At the bottom: a door.
Heavily reinforced. Mechanical lock. No digital interface.
Carolyn pulled out her bypass kit. "If this opens, it's the inner sanctum."
Three minutes of tense silence.
Click.
The latch disengaged.

They both raised their weapons.
Laila slowly pushed the door open —
— and froze.
Cold Archive Room – Facility 9 Sublevel.
Rows of cabinets stretched before them, industrial and sealed. Paper files. Tape reels. One corner had an analog terminal mounted on a pedestal — blinking cursor, green CRT glow. A silent room, humming faintly with age and secrecy.
But something wasn't right.
On the floor: a small pile of dust. A single overturned chair. And — most notably — a folder, lying open on the center table.
Carolyn approached cautiously. "That's not archival placement. That's recent."
The folder was marked in red ink:
"DEAD OPERATIVES – CLOSED OPERATIONS – NO REINSTATEMENT"
Code: GREAVES-SD7
Inside: photos. Dozens of them. Men and women, some familiar. Some labeled "EXFIL", others "REDACTED" — and three marked "ELIMINATED."
Carolyn flipped further.
One of the last pages had been hastily circled in pencil — and a sticky note attached.
"Someone's watching the watchers. This file isn't safe. I took what matters. You're not alone."
No signature. Just the corner of the note, torn as if the person had heard something and fled mid-thought.
Laila looked up. "Carolyn… someone got here first."

Carolyn nodded, scanning the room. "And they left us a warning."
Laila lowered her weapon — but didn't relax.
"Which means we're now part of someone else's plan."

Surveillance Hub – Facility 9 Sublevel…

Carolyn traced a faint trail of scuffed footprints through a side corridor — the pattern led to a locked security room adjacent to the archive.
Inside, banks of analog monitors displayed feeds from grainy black-and-white cameras — many of them dark or static. But a few still ran.
One camera flickered.
A dim hallway.
A figure in a hood. Slim built, fast-moving.
Twelve hours ago.
The angle shifted — the figure reached the archive door, pulled something from their coat, and disabled the lock with ease. No hesitation. Clearly experienced.
Laila leaned closer. "Same person who left that note."
Carolyn rewound and froze the screen. The angle wasn't clear, but one frame caught the reflection in a ventilation panel — a faint glimpse of the intruder's face.
Too grainy to ID — but female. Short-cut hair. Tactical clothing. Lone operator.
"She's not one of ours," Carolyn said.
"Not one of Greaves' either," Laila added. "She didn't take the file — just the part she needed. Left the rest… for us."
Carolyn moved to the control panel. A blinking light caught

her eye.
A log-in attempt.
Just now.
“Someone else is watching the feeds,” she whispered.
Laila didn’t hesitate. “We’re burned. Time to move.”

Corridor Outside Cold Archive – Two Minutes Later

As they exited the surveillance room, Laila froze mid-step.
A red light blinked above a doorframe that had been dark before.
Motion sensor triggered.
Carolyn cursed under her breath. “They're onto us.”
A voice echoed down the corridor. “Security teams to Sublevel Four. No lethal force — detain only.”
Footsteps. Fast. Boots on steel.
Laila turned to Carolyn. “Drop packs. Go loud — but *not* lethal.”
Carolyn gave a grin. “Been waiting all week for this.”
The first guard rounded the corner — taser in one hand, baton in the other.
Laila stepped into him, deflecting the baton with her forearm and slamming an open-palm strike to his sternum.
He dropped instantly.
Carolyn caught the second guard in a sweeping leg kick that sent him crashing into a utility cabinet. She pivoted smoothly, disarmed him mid-fall, and snapped a zip-tie restraint around his wrist in one motion.
Two more came at once.

Laila ducked a punch and delivered a quick three-strike combo: elbow, knee, shoulder toss. The man hit the floor with a winded gasp.

Carolyn took the last one with a spinning back-fist and upper cut to the jaw — brutal, efficient.

Both women were breathing hard now, but focused.

Laila gestured to the stairwell. "Exit route's covered. We take the vent shaft back the way we came."

Carolyn popped open the service panel. "I've got point."

They climbed back into the crawlspace, sealing the entry behind them.

Footsteps and voices trailed in the hall behind — confused, searching, just seconds too late.

At the Forest Edge – *2:09 A.M.*

The grate creaked open under Laila's boot, and she emerged into the night air with a gasp, face damp with sweat and dust. Carolyn followed, wiping blood from a scraped knuckle.

They were back in the trees. Moving fast. No lights. No voices.

They didn't stop running until they hit the extraction point where an old Jeep, hidden under a camo tarp and brush, waited.

As Carolyn started the engine, Laila glanced at the file still clutched in her hand.

Inside was a second sticky note — this one folded and placed behind the top page. Neither of them had seen it before.

Carolyn frowned. "That wasn't in there when we left the room."

Laila unfolded it slowly. A simple message in the same handwriting as before.

"Room 19 never shut down. It just changed form.

Greaves is a tool. The real architects are still active.

If you want answers... follow the Sable Protocol."

Beneath the note — a partial fingerprint.

Carolyn drove. Laila stared ahead, her mind already turning.

They were no longer chasing ghosts.

They were hunting architects.

At an Undisclosed Location – 2:47 A.M.

The room was all angles and shadows — a secure suite tucked beneath a nondescript federal annex building, far from any official floorplan. One wall was a digital map of the eastern United States. Another projected rotating data feeds from detention facilities, surveillance hubs, and unnamed "processing zones."

At the center, seated in a leather chair, was *Rhys Greaves.* He was neither tall nor physically imposing, but the stillness of him was unnerving — a man who never wasted movement, breath, or time. His hair was clipped short, the sleeves of his charcoal-gray suit rolled to his elbows. A stainless steel pen tapped rhythmically against a glass desk.

A chime.

"Facility 9 — Surveillance Breach Logged. Sublevel Four. Archive Accessed."

Greaves didn't blink.

Another chime.
"Intrusion Confirmed. Two unidentified assets. Neutralized security team. No gunfire. Evaded perimeter."

He leaned forward slightly, the pen now still between his fingers.
On the monitor, black-and-white footage replayed: two figures moving through the halls with surgical precision. No insignia. No hesitation. One of them stopped to look directly into a vent camera before disabling it.
Greaves zoomed in on the freeze-frame.
He recognized her.
"Wright."
He sat back, eyes narrowing.
"She took the bait," he said, almost amused. "Faster than I expected."
A voice responded over intercom — modulated, anonymous. "Do you want them eliminated?"
Greaves didn't answer right away. He picked up a tablet and scrolled through metadata from the breached archive — lines of file access logs, anomaly alerts, residual command strings.
He found what he was looking for.
A fingerprint log. Not just the infiltrators'. A third print — one not flagged by security.
A ghost.
Someone else had been inside the vault before Wright.
Someone who *knew* the rules and had used them to leave just enough behind.
Greaves' smile was barely perceptible.

"No. Let them dig. Let them chase shadows. The more they find, the more they'll depend on the wrong answers."

He stood, slowly.

"But I want every facility put on blackout alert. No new transfers. No deletions. Full lockdown."

The intercom clicked. "And the Sable Protocol?"

Greaves stared at the map, a red pin blinking over the West Virginia mountain range.

"They're not ready for Sable," he said. "But if they push further…"

He picked up the pen again, clicked it once.

"…we'll be ready."

Backroads, Somewhere in Pennsylvania – 3:26 A.M.

The Jeep's tires hummed over the cracked blacktop, weaving through narrow mountain roads flanked by pine and silence. The adrenaline had started to wear off, replaced by a tense quiet.

Carolyn drove, one hand on the wheel, eyes steady on the road. Her other hand rested near the glove compartment, fingers twitching slightly — a tell Laila had seen before.

They hadn't spoken since ditching their burner gear half a mile from the extraction point. Every movement since the escape had been methodical. Trained.

But something was off.

Laila sat in the passenger seat, arms folded, eyes fixed on the rearview mirror. Not looking at the road. Not the woods.

The *silence*.

Finally, she broke it. "Does this feel… too easy?"

Carolyn glanced at her. "We broke into a federal blacksite

and made it out in one piece. That's not what I'd call easy."
"No," Laila said. "I mean the *exit*. The guards — they came fast, but not like they should've. Like they were just delaying us."
Carolyn's jaw tightened. "You think we were being *allowed* to leave?"
Laila didn't answer right away. She looked out the side window at the endless darkness.
"I've had this feeling before," she said quietly. "Right before an ambush in Kandahar. We cleared a village without a shot fired. Intel was perfect. Too perfect. We walked right into a kill zone."
Carolyn let that settle.
"You think Greaves knew we were coming?"
"I think he *wanted* us to come," Laila said. "And maybe worse — I think he knows *where we're going back to.*"
A beat.
Carolyn tapped the brake slightly. "You think we're compromised?"
"I don't *know,*" Laila admitted. "But something's been off ever since we saw that third set of footprints. The other infiltrator — she didn't warn us to stay out. She *led us in.*"
Carolyn exhaled. "Breadcrumbs."
Laila nodded slowly. "And we followed them all the way home."
Silence settled between them again.
Then, instinctively, Carolyn reached under the dash and flipped the Jeep's ignition kill switch — coasting them to a soft stop on the side of the road.
She reached into the center console and pulled out a low-

frequency signal sweeper, flicked it on, and held her breath.

Bzzzt... click.

A blip.

A faint one. But there.

"Tracker," Carolyn muttered. "Somewhere in the undercarriage. Embedded."

Laila's face went stone-cold. "They let us walk out… to see where we'd go."

Without another word, both women exited the vehicle and moved to the rear axle. Carolyn dropped to her back, scanned the undercarriage with a penlight, and found it — a black disc the size of a quarter, magnetized and warm to the touch.

"Military-grade passive. No blink. Short range."

Laila wrapped it in aluminum foil, tucked it in an old snack bag, and handed it to Carolyn.

"Throw it out the window on a passing truck," she said. "Let them think we're halfway to Ohio."

Carolyn grinned. "Old school misdirection. I like it."

Back in the Jeep, Laila didn't relax.

She stared at the road ahead — but her mind was already racing back toward the farmhouse, to Eleanor, to Daniel.

"If they know where we live," she said, "we're not just up against surveillance."

Carolyn nodded grimly. "We're up against a warning."

They returned to the Farmhouse – *4:17 A.M.*

The soft creak of the front door was all it took.

Daniel was already seated in the armchair near the window, mug of lukewarm coffee in hand, his silhouette outlined in the glow of a low lamp. He didn't rise — just watched the two women come in, eyes scanning them like a scanner through customs.

“You look like hell,” he said flatly.

Carolyn smirked. “That’s how you know it went well.”

Laila closed the door behind them and locked it. Her eyes lingered on the windows for a moment longer than necessary — confirming nothing had been disturbed. The farmhouse was still just a farmhouse.

Footsteps padded down the hallway.

Eleanor appeared, wrapped in a faded blue robe, silver hair loose over one shoulder. She looked half-asleep but somehow still dignified.

“Thank God,” she said, voice gravelly with sleep. “I knew you’d make it back. Just needed to *see* it.”

Laila stepped forward and embraced her gently. “We’re okay, Mom.”

“I never doubted it,” Eleanor murmured, pulling back with a faint smile. “But you’d be amazed how much worry fits inside an old woman’s chest after midnight.”

She touched Carolyn’s arm briefly. “You too, honey. Glad you’re safe.”

Then she yawned, turned on her heel, and shuffled back down the hallway with a parting murmur:

“I’m going back to bed now. For real this time. Don’t burn down the house.”

The three of them chuckled quietly as her door clicked shut.

Daniel took a long sip and set his mug down. “Alright. Start talking.”

Moments Later…

The map was back on the table, lit from above by a pendant lamp. The folder marked "DEAD OPERATIVES – GREAVES-SD7" lay open, its pages slightly curled from the cold. Beside it, the handwritten note and the partial fingerprint sat protected in a plastic sleeve.

Carolyn walked Daniel through the breach. The corridor. The cold archive. The surveillance room. The third infiltrator. The silent warning.

"Someone else got there before us," she concluded. "Female. Tactical. Left us just enough to follow. Like she *knew* we'd be coming."

Laila added the kicker. "And Greaves knew too. He let us go. We found a tracker on the Jeep halfway back."

Daniel's brow tightened. "They're tracing your *behavior*. That's why it felt clean — they wanted to study your next move."

"We fed them a disinformation campaign," Laila said. "But I don't know if it'll hold. We might've underestimated just how deep this thing goes."

Daniel turned the sticky note over in his hand. "'Sable Protocol.' That's what we chase next?"

"Not yet," Laila said. "We don't move on it until we know what it is — and what we're walking into."

Carolyn leaned back in her chair. "We've been reactive. We need to pivot. Go on offense."

Daniel nodded. "I'll run the fingerprint and handwriting through legacy databases. Could get a match if your mystery guest used to be federal."

Laila folded her arms. "Whoever she is, she's not working

with Greaves. And she's not working with us. But she's watching. Leaving breadcrumbs."

"And bait," Carolyn added. "This *feels* like a setup. Greaves might be a player, but I don't think he's the architect."

Daniel's eyes moved from one woman to the other. "Then we find the architect."

Laila nodded.

The house creaked softly around them — the kind of sound that came from wood and warmth and old ghosts in the walls. But for now, the storm had passed.

The map stayed on the table.

The mission, however, had just begun.

Dawn was just Breaking…

A pale orange glow stretched across the kitchen window as the first rays of morning light touched the soybean fields. The world outside looked peaceful. It felt like a lie.

Carolyn sat at the table, fingers gliding over printouts from the GREAVES-SD7 folder, red circles marking key details. Daniel hovered near the coffee pot, having pulled a second all-nighter, and Laila stood leaning against the far wall, arms crossed, silent but alert.

Daniel tapped a page. "Here. This guy — Luis Cortez. Killed in an ICE detention center three years ago. Report says gang-related stabbing."

Carolyn looked up. "I remember that name. He testified in the Falfor case — pre-trial. Gave a sealed deposition about illegal seizures tied to inland deportation raids."

Laila moved closer. "Cortez… Ruiz mentioned a cousin who vanished in detention after filing a complaint. Mateo

thought he was deported. What if it was Luis?"
Daniel nodded. "I pulled Mateo's sealed intake documents. Look at the hidden metadata — Greaves's ID was used to alter his case file three weeks ago."
Carolyn swore under her breath. "They weren't just deporting random targets. Ruiz was on a *cleanup list*. One tied to Falfor."
Laila clenched her jaw. "They're scrubbing the witnesses who never got their day in court."
Daniel added, "I think you're looking at the second phase of Falfor's operation. Greaves was the containment man. What you found in Facility 9 — this file — that wasn't just a leftover. It was a *hit list.*"
Carolyn leaned over the table, her eyes narrowing. "And the Sable Protocol?"
Daniel pointed to the sticky note. "If 'Falfor Echo' was the mop-up… 'Sable' is probably the evolution. Smarter. Quieter. Maybe predictive."
Laila stared at the fingerprint card — the one from the third infiltrator. "She wanted us to see this."
Daniel added, "I ran the print. No match in DOJ, Marshals, Homeland, Interpol, or CIA. But get this — one partial from a declassified, Cold War-era operative file. Name redacted. Alias listed only as: '*Iris*.'"
Carolyn sat back slowly. "That sounds made up."
Laila looked out the window. "Or too real to be official."
A silence settled over the kitchen — not the peace of completion, but the cold stillness that comes when the puzzle suddenly gets much bigger.
Then Carolyn's phone buzzed.

A text. Anonymous source. Encrypted channel.
"SABLE INITIATED. 4 TARGETS CLEARED. STOP THE FIFTH."
A second later, another text followed:
"Ruiz is the fifth."
Laila's expression hardened. "They're going to finish what they started. If we want to stop the Sable Protocol..."
Carolyn stood. "We protect Mateo Ruiz."
Daniel was already grabbing his gear. "We'll need legal cover, transport, and safe housing. And if they're sending a cleaner — this time, they won't make it quiet."
Laila nodded. "Then we go loud before they do."

Classified Operations Annex – Sable Command Node (Redacted Location)
"Execute"
The room was a clean room — in every sense of the word. Walls of tempered soundproofed glass. Floor lit from beneath with a pale surgical glow. No identifying markers. No clocks. No signs. Just purpose.
Rhys Greaves stood at the center, not at a desk but at a suspended glass interface that floated like a hologram, operated by hand gestures alone. A live dossier was projected in front of him: *Mateo Ruiz. Subject Five. Sable Protocol Classification: ECHO-LINKED.*
To Greaves' left stood a woman in black fatigues — tall, efficient, her face partly obscured by a mask marked with a white glyph: **ΔS5**. She said nothing, only waited.
Greaves spoke without turning. "You'll approach through DHS cover. You'll use the marshals' disruption last week as your pretext. Ruiz is to be relocated during routine

custody chain validation."
He turned now, voice calm, almost bored.
"No noise. No postmortem questions. Collapse the chain. In three days, no one will remember Ruiz was even pending release."
The woman nodded once.
"Status: Sanctioned," she said.
Greaves tapped the final command into the interface.
SABLE TERMINATION AUTHORIZATION: SUBJECT 05 CONFIRMED — PROCEED TO CLEANSE.
A light pulsed green.
Greaves didn't blink.
"Wright and Halston will react," he said softly. "We want them to. Pressure reveals purpose. Let's see what they do when they realize they're not fighting a man anymore…"
He turned away.
"…they're fighting a protocol."

Berks County Detention Facility – 9:34 A.M.

It began with a clipboard.
A manila folder tucked neatly beneath a transfer manifest, stamped with DHS authorization, ICE routing codes, and a small digital verification chip that blinked blue.
The guard at the intake checkpoint barely looked up as the new agent passed through. Black tactical fieldwear under a plain Department of Homeland Security jacket. Female. Average height. Brown eyes. Hair pinned tight beneath a ball cap.
Nothing remarkable. Nothing memorable.

She moved like someone used to being ignored — and yet whose presence automatically commanded space.
Her name badge read *Agent E. Wells.*
The badge was false.
The identity? Temporary.
The agent? Δ*S5*. Sable Protocol's fifth field operator.
As she walked through the sally port, her eyes flicked across security cameras, shadowed corners, sensor placement — every vector mapped and logged without a word. She wasn't here to fight. She was here to delete.
Her lips moved faintly as she passed two guards at the rear hallway.
"Transfer order for detainee Ruiz," she said, voice clipped and professional. "WITSEC routing. Tier 3 clearance."
The guards exchanged a quick look.
"You're early," one said.
"Clock's off," she replied without breaking stride.
No one challenged her.
They never did.
Administrative Holding Hall – Mateo Ruiz's Cell.
Inside the small gray cell, Mateo sat cross-legged on the lower bunk, nervously shredding a paper towel between his fingers. He had heard whispers — something about his case being reopened, then closed again. A "clerical reset."
Whatever that meant.
He didn't trust it.
He didn't trust anything anymore.
Footsteps echoed down the corridor. Intentional. Clean. Singular.
The door buzzed open. Agent "Wells" stepped in.

She looked at him once, then down at her clipboard.
"Detainee Ruiz. You've been reassigned."
Mateo frowned. "Reassigned where?"
"To disappear."
He didn't even have time to stand before she stepped inside, closed the door, and set the clipboard gently on the bunk.

Surveillance Room – Simultaneous

A young guard watched the security feed. He reached for his coffee — then paused.
Cell B-47's camera was glitching. Flickering slightly. A distortion he hadn't seen before.
He leaned in.
Then, just for a moment, the screen cut to black.
When it blinked back on, the agent was still inside.
But she was no longer holding the clipboard.
And Ruiz was no longer seated.
The guard reached for the phone.
But he never made the call.

Exterior Fence Perimeter – Ten Minutes Later

Agent Wells exited through the east gate, now wearing a delivery jacket, her DHS tag buried deep in her pocket. A gray van idled at the loading dock, its rear doors open.
She stepped in without looking back.
Inside, she set her clipboard down again.
The same clipboard.

No blood. No evidence.
Just a single photo clipped inside — now stamped in red: CLEARED.
As the van pulled away, she keyed a brief message into an untraceable device.
"Subject 05 — Cleansed. Proceeding to next node."
But what she didn't know—
Was that Mateo Ruiz was *still alive.*
And Laila Wright was only minutes behind.

Berks County Detention Facility – 10:02 A.M.

The SUV skidded to a halt outside the facility's east security checkpoint, tires kicking up gravel.
Laila was already out before the engine stopped, her U.S. Marshal credentials in hand. Carolyn slammed the passenger door and followed, straight-backed and grim.
The gate guard blinked, startled by their urgency. "Can I help you—?"
"Marshal Wright. Emergency override," Laila snapped. "We have reason to believe a federal detainee under protection was targeted for illegal extraction."
The guard hesitated. "We already had a DHS transfer this morning—"
Carolyn flashed her badge. "That wasn't DHS."
Something in her tone chilled the man. He picked up the phone.
In Holding Block B – Three Minutes Later…
The facility supervisor — a nervous man in a cheap tie — jogged to keep up as Laila and Carolyn stormed the

corridor.

"I'm telling you, everything looked official. She had clearance. Digital badge. She signed all the right papers."

Laila stopped cold. "Where's Ruiz?"

"Room B-47," the supervisor said. "But the feed—there was a glitch."

They reached the cell.

Carolyn opened the door first — expecting blood. A body. But instead: *chaos.*

The cot was overturned. The sink cracked. Scrape marks on the wall. A faint smudge of blood on the frame. And in the corner… a rolled towel, jammed into the vent.

Carolyn crouched. "She silenced him. Probably with a nerve pinch or a chokehold. Tried to make it clean."

"But something went wrong," Laila muttered. "This isn't how Sable operates."

Her eyes scanned the floor… then locked onto something near the baseboard.

A small plastic fragment — a tooth retainer, bloodied but intact.

Carolyn's eyes widened. "It's Mateo's. He still had his jaw wired from the old beating he took in detention."

They followed the drag marks to the rear service hall.

Carolyn pulled her phone. "Daniel, trace all non-official vehicles exiting in the last twenty minutes. East gate only. There was a van."

The two women leaned over a frozen playback frame from the exterior camera.

Gray van. Partial plates.

The same woman from the archive breach — now dressed

as a courier. Same poise. Same clinical calm.
Laila's voice was low. "It's her. Our infiltrator. She's not working with us."
"But she didn't finish it," Carolyn said. "If Mateo were dead, they'd have sanitized the scene. No trace. No clutter. No witness risk."
"Something went off-plan," Laila said. "Either she hesitated… or she *wasn't supposed* to kill him."
Carolyn stepped back, connecting the dots. "Then someone pulled him."
"Greaves?"
"Or Iris."
They turned to the supervisor.
"I want every loading dock checked. Every vehicle scrubbed. And every guard questioned," Laila ordered. "If Mateo Ruiz is still alive, he has less than an hour before they erase him *properly*."
As Laila and Carolyn burst back into the sunlight, a single question hung in the air between them — heavier than the rest:
Why did she spare him?
They didn't have the answer.
But now… they had a lead.

Berks County Surveillance Command Trailer – 10:42 A.M.

Inside a cramped mobile command trailer behind the detention facility, Laila stood hunched over a bank of screens while Carolyn tapped rapidly at a keyboard. A traffic grid map slowly pieced itself together from live and cached footage. Sweat traced down the back of Laila's neck. Every second lost was distance gained.

"There—" Carolyn pointed.

Camera 9B — an industrial access road near the facility's east loading dock.

Gray van. Partial plate match. No escort. No standard DHS markings.

It turned left onto a two-lane road heading north.

"Zoom and enhance," Laila said.

Carolyn chuckled under her breath. "That only works in movies. But—wait—look."

She slowed the footage.

A **sticker** on the back of the van — faded, circular.

"Traynor Logistics." Private company. Out of service since 2018.

"A shell," Laila muttered. "They're riding under ghost credentials."

Carolyn tapped keys again. "Cross-referencing Traynor Logistics' old warehouse and storage locations within a 60-mile radius. Four hits, two still structurally viable."

Daniel's voice came through on their shared comms line. "I see it too. Pulling DMV and utility activity now…"

Static crackled. Then:

"Warehouse in York County shows minor electrical usage over the past four months. Sporadic water flow. No formal leaseholder."

Laila's voice went cold. "A ghost building. Hidden in plain sight."

Carolyn nodded. "We've got our probable destination."

Daniel again: "Sending you the satellite layout and an

interior blueprint pulled from the 2015 fire code survey. No visible security from the outside, but interior's segmented — likely walls or false loading bays."
Laila grabbed her pack. "We roll now. Quiet. Non-lethal unless we're outgunned. If Ruiz is alive, he won't be for long."
Carolyn checked her weapon, then her backup blade. "Let's make sure the next person Sable sends doesn't walk out so clean."

Back Road – En Route – 11:21 A.M.

The SUV sliced down the backroads at speed, gravel spitting under its tires. Laila stared at the map on the tablet between them — one finger tapping the warehouse zone in York County.
Carolyn drove in silence for a few beats.
Then: "You think it's Iris?"
Laila looked over. "If it was, she wouldn't have let the van leave with Mateo inside. She would've burned the scene or left him in place."
"Unless she's running a long game," Carolyn muttered.
Laila nodded. "Or… she's not working alone. And someone *intercepted* her op."
Carolyn's jaw clenched. "So what's this place then? A kill house? A holding zone?"
"Either," Laila said. "But we've got to assume the worst and move fast."
She checked her watch.
"Forty minutes. That's how long it takes to vanish a body

and burn a facility."
Carolyn pressed harder on the gas. "Then we get there in thirty."

Abandoned Warehouse – York County, PA – 11:58 A.M.

The SUV rolled to a stop behind a ridge of rusted shipping containers. The warehouse stood fifty yards ahead — a long, low structure with flaking aluminum siding and shattered floodlights. One roll-up bay hung halfway open, like a dead mouth.
Laila and Carolyn moved in on foot, weapons drawn, silent as breath.
Carolyn swept left around the perimeter, scanning for motion sensors or buried cameras.
"Dead tech," she whispered. "No active feed. Just decoys."
Laila knelt near the front bay. "Tire tracks. Still warm."
She touched the ground. "They're here. Or just left."
They exchanged a glance. No words needed.
Laila gave a three-count on her fingers.
Three. Two. One.
Carolyn breached first — low and fast, weapon angled upward. Laila followed, sweeping the corners.
No gunfire.
No alarm.
Just stillness.
Inside, the air was heavy with chemical residue — bleach, solvents. The walls were lined with rusting storage racks, many of them empty. A makeshift cot sat near the center, beside a bucket of still-warm water and a stained towel.

"Someone cleaned something fast," Carolyn muttered.

A door on the far end of the space creaked slightly in the breeze. Laila moved toward it and paused.

Blood.

A faint smear along the frame — wiped down, but not perfectly.

She pushed through the door.

Interior Office – Rear Section of Warehouse

A small room. Cinder block walls. Fluorescent light flickering above.

And in the center, slumped against the wall, zip-tied but alive — Mateo Ruiz.

His shirt was torn, a shallow cut on his brow, but his eyes flicked open as the door burst in.

Laila holstered her weapon instantly.

"Mateo."

His voice was dry, rasped. "You're not her."

Carolyn scanned the corners. "Clear."

Laila crouched beside him and sliced the zip ties. "What happened? Who brought you here?"

Mateo coughed, then nodded toward the door. "A woman. Not the one from ICE. A different one. She stopped her… they fought. She threw me in a closet and said if you came, to *show you this.*"

He reached shakily into his waistband and pulled out a folded piece of paper.

Carolyn opened it. No words. Just a symbol.

A hand-drawn *eye*, surrounded by a ring of barbed wire.

Under it: "One layer deeper. Room 19 was just the skin."

Laila's expression darkened. "It's her. Iris."

Carolyn helped Mateo to his feet. “Then this wasn’t a hit. It was a test.”
“No,” Laila said, eyes narrowing. “It was a message.”
As they exited the warehouse with Mateo between them, Carolyn glanced up at the sky.
Clear. Blue. Quiet.
Too quiet.
Behind them, inside the building, a faint *beep* echoed from somewhere beneath the floorboards.
Laila’s eyes snapped wide. “MOVE!”
They sprinted.
A second later—
BOOM.
The building erupted behind them — windows shattering outward, the corrugated roof lifting like a paper plate in a storm. The shockwave knocked them to the ground.
Mateo groaned. “Still... think I’m not worth saving?”
Laila smiled grimly as she rolled to her knees. “No, Mateo. You’re the reason we fight.”
Roadside – 20 Minutes Later…
As emergency crews converged on the smoke plume in the distance, Laila sat against a tree, cradling the symbol from the note.
She looked at Carolyn.
“Room 19 was just the skin. So what’s under it?”
Carolyn’s voice was quiet. “Sable. Iris. The architects. Maybe even worse.”
Laila’s eyes narrowed, hardened by ash and purpose.
“Then it’s time we stop digging for names… and start exposing them.”

Hilltop Overlook – York County Woods – 1:08 P.M.

The smoke curled lazily into the afternoon sky, drifting like ink across blue. Below, where the warehouse once stood, fire crews sprayed foam over blackened steel, their movements brisk but meaningless. Whatever had been there — evidence, blood, secrets — was gone.

But higher up, in the cover of a rocky overlook surrounded by tall pines, Iris watched.

She stood motionless. Binoculars rested in gloved hands. Her jacket was civilian now — olive green with a hiking patch. Her backpack looked like it belonged to a field biologist. Nothing about her drew attention. She was as forgettable as fog.

Her face remained unreadable. Cool. Focused.

Through the lenses, she saw them — Laila, Carolyn, and Mateo — sitting on the back bumper of a paramedic van, wrapped in gray thermal blankets. Laila held the folded note in one hand, her thumb tracing the drawn symbol absently.

Iris didn't smile.

She didn't frown.

She simply *nodded* once.

A voice crackled through her earpiece — scrambled and distorted.

"Visual confirmation?"

She didn't respond right away. Her eyes never left the woman she had once worked parallel to. Or perhaps beneath. Or perhaps not at all.

"Is she viable?" the voice asked again.

Finally, Iris answered, her voice barely above a whisper. "She's ready."
The channel went silent.
She lowered the binoculars and tucked them into her bag. A thin, palm-sized case sat in the side pouch — black, sleek, fingerprint-locked.
She pressed her thumb to it.
Click.
Inside: a single dossier. Top page marked with three words.
"PROJECT: RESONANCE INITIATED"
She zipped the bag shut, turned toward the trees, and disappeared into the woods.

Laila Wright thought she was hunting shadows.
She hadn't yet realized:
She was being groomed to replace one.

Operations Command Bunker – Undisclosed Location – 1:41 P.M.

The hum of filtered air and fluorescent light filled the room. Screens lined the walls in a semi-circle — surveillance feeds, encrypted comm logs, asset trackers. At the center of it all stood Rhys Greaves, hands clasped behind his back, expression unreadable.
He was surrounded by silence.
The image of the warehouse explosion played on loop — no bodies, no confirmation, just smoke and a vanishing trail.
He spoke to no one, yet his voice filled the space.

"She was never meant to survive the breach."
No reply.
He turned toward a single active console. On its display:
SABLE-05 – STATUS: OFFLINE
TARGET 05 – STATUS: UNKNOWN
WITNESS SECURE? – FALSE
Greaves tilted his head slightly.
"Who pulled her off mission?"
From the shadows beyond the monitors, a distorted voice emerged — filtered, deep, genderless.
"You gave authorization to terminate. But you do not authorize replacement."
Greaves narrowed his eyes. "The Ruiz subject was compromised. Protocol was followed."
"Protocol is evolving."
A beat of silence.
Greaves's jaw flexed. "You activated Iris."
"She activated herself."
The words weren't reprimand. They were confirmation.
Greaves turned away from the console, his composure cracking for the first time. He walked to a side terminal and input his personal code — a six-point biometric sequence.
A screen opened, revealing data on Wright, Halston, and Ruiz.
Files he thought were sealed.
Each was stamped with a new classification.
PROJECT: RESONANCE

Access Level: Above Sable
Control Clearance: Revoked

His pulse ticked in his throat.
Revoked.
Greaves had orchestrated cleanups, coverups, and covert acts of war — but *this*? This was manipulation on a level *he* was no longer part of.
“She's being prepared,” he said aloud. “Conditioned. Iris isn't acting alone.”
No response.
Only the click of a hidden relay disengaging. Somewhere above him, a door slid shut.
Control was slipping.
And for a man like Greaves… that was unforgivable.
Scene: Farmhouse – Upstairs Study – 2:03 P.M.
“In the Silence of the System”
The farmhouse study was dim, lit only by the soft glow of two monitors and the occasional flicker from a weathered desk lamp. Daniel Wright sat hunched forward, eyes locked on lines of cascading code and ghost files strung together like spiderwebs across three virtual drives.
He hadn't left the chair since Laila and Carolyn's departure that morning. Coffee cold. Sandwich untouched. The only movement was his hand — flicking between keyboard macros like a man decoding a language he wasn't supposed to see.
Until now.
_SableNode_47.relay.outbound
Encrypted_packet_9344-A
**— Key Verified: [Echo/Iris]*
Daniel leaned back slowly. “What the hell…”
He pulled up the decrypted output file. No audio. Just a

dense, minimalistic string of operational flags and mission descriptors.
OP: ECHO/LURE INITIATED
OBJECTIVE: Expose breach pathways
SUBJECT: WRIGHT, LAILA – Status: ACTIVE
OBSERVER: DESIGNATE "IRIS"
COLLATERAL VIABILITY: HALSTON (FLEX)
THREAT INDEX: GREAVES (FIXED)
AUTHORITY TRANSFER: RESONANCE PHASE PREP IN PROGRESS

He froze.

It wasn't a kill order. It wasn't even a standard field protocol.

It was a calibration event — one designed to observe Laila under stress, to track decision-making under fire, psychological responses to loss, moral pressure, and betrayal.

And Carolyn had been flagged not as essential… but flexible.

Daniel's hands moved faster now. He opened a mirrored archive, tracing packets back to their origin node. A deeper file was embedded inside.

[SABLE-HOST-DOM: AUTH-SERVER-IXION]
RELAY KEY – PROJECT: RESONANCE
Designate: "Wright / Iris"
Result Goal: Integration / Succession
State: AWAKENING

He backed away from the keyboard.

"This isn't about stopping her," he whispered. "They're... training her."

His phone buzzed beside him — encrypted line. Laila.
He answered, voice low and shaken.
"I know what they're doing to you."
Static crackled, then Laila's voice, breathless. "What?"
"I dug into the Sable servers. They're not just watching you — they're building around you. Testing you. It's part of something bigger — something called *Project Resonance.* You're not the target, Laila..."
A pause.
"You're the next stage."

Rural Pull-Off – Edge of State Forest – 2:07 P.M.

The SUV idled on the side of an empty road, just outside the tree line. Sunlight filtered through a break in the clouds, glinting off the windshield, but neither woman noticed.
Laila stood by the driver's door, phone pressed to her ear, her other hand gripping the edge of the roof.
Carolyn sat on the rear bumper with Mateo, both of them drinking from plastic water bottles, exhausted but alive.
Daniel's voice came through the earpiece — low, controlled, but vibrating with urgency.
"They've been monitoring you, Laila. Not just tracking — testing. Sable is part of something deeper. It's called *Project Resonance*. You've been selected. You're not just under observation... you're being evaluated."
Laila's face remained still. Only her eyes moved — narrowing slightly, fixed on the horizon.
"Evaluated for what?"
"Succession. Integration. Call it what you want. But you're

the center of it. And Carolyn…"
"…she's labeled as 'flexible.' Collateral if necessary."
Laila's breath caught — not loudly, not visibly — but enough. She closed her eyes for a heartbeat, opened them again. Calm returned like muscle memory.
"Can you send me everything?"
"Already in your inbox. Triple-encrypted. Use your field tablet."
Laila nodded, though Daniel couldn't see her. "We'll call you once we find cover."
She hung up.
The wind rustled through the trees. A hawk cried somewhere high above.
Carolyn glanced over from the bumper. "That was your brother?"
Laila didn't answer right away. She walked over and crouched in front of Carolyn, staring her dead in the eyes.
"They're not trying to kill us," she said. "They're *testing* me. You. Us."
Carolyn furrowed her brow. "Testing… what?"
"Loyalty. Decision-making. Pressure. Morality. Resilience. I don't know." She looked down for a moment, then met Carolyn's gaze again. "But the file Daniel found — it called me a candidate for something called Project Resonance."
Carolyn's voice dropped. "And me?"
Laila hesitated. "You're… labeled as flexible."
A beat of silence.
Carolyn looked away. Nodded slowly.
"Well, that's cute," she said dryly.

"I'm not going to let them use you like that," Laila said, voice steady but soft.
Carolyn's laugh was tight. "You don't have to *let* them, Laila. You just have to keep doing what you're doing. That's the game. And we're already in it."
Laila stood.
She looked back down the road they'd just come from — the smoke still faintly rising in the distance. Then up ahead, the long stretch of road winding into something they hadn't seen yet.
"They want to see what I'll do next," she said.
Carolyn stood beside her now, arms crossed.
"Then let's give them something they can't predict."

Abandoned Ranger Cabin – Appalachian Foothills – 4:13 P.M.

The old ranger outpost was built into the side of a hill — stone foundation, moss-covered roof, boarded windows. Once used for forest fire watch rotations, it had been offline for over a decade, tucked deep within federal land no one patrolled anymore.
Laila keyed in a code on a rusted padlock. The door opened with a creak that sounded like the past itself.
Carolyn stepped in behind her, sweeping the interior.
"Still here," she muttered. "Still smells like dried pine and rat piss."
They shut the door and dropped their gear.
Laila moved fast — unzipping the outer lining of her duffel and pulling out a hardened black tablet. Military-issue. Encrypted. Untouched since the Falfor operation's final

days. She synced it to Daniel's transfer package and waited.
The screen blinked once.
Then again.
Then loaded a single folder:
PROJECT: RESONANCE / ECHO DESIGNATE / WRIGHT
Inside: four subfolders.

- PSYCH PROFILE SERIES / PHASE I
- MONITORED DECISIONS / LIVE FIELD RESPONSE LOGS
- REPLACEMENT INDEX / CANDIDATE REJECTIONS
- INITIATION TRIGGER – PRE-APPROVED EVENTS

Carolyn sat across from her, watching quietly.
"Go slow," she said. "Let's see how far this rabbit hole goes."
Laila opened the first file.
PSYCH PROFILE: WRIGHT, L.
Entry Date: 14 Days After Falfor Testimony
Author: Redacted
Status: Conditional Match
Classification: ECHO-TIER ASSET
Recommendation: "Subject exhibits sustained moral rigidity under systemic stress. Suitable for reintegration under abstract authority model. Risk of autonomy: HIGH. Manage through layered validation."
She scrolled further.
"Subject is *not compliant*, but *predictable in principles.*

Primary flaw: loyalty to secondaries, especially 'Halston, C.' Leverage: emotional entanglement and survivor guilt."

Laila looked up at Carolyn — who was now staring at the floor, hands clasped.

"They planned this," Carolyn whispered. "The missions. The detainees. Ruiz. The conflict."

Laila moved to the next folder.

REPLACEMENT INDEX – CANDIDATE REJECTIONS

"Voss, J." – Noncompliant

"Kearney, M." – Psych instability

"Pryme, C." – Lacks ideological aggression

Carolyn blinked. "That's me."

Laila nodded slowly. "They want someone who *fights the system* but still works within it. Someone they can build a new version of justice around. Someone angry… but not broken."

"They want a symbol," Carolyn said.

"No," Laila replied. "They want a *weapon.*"

She scrolled to the last file.

INITIATION TRIGGER – PRE-APPROVED EVENTS

- False ICE order for Ruiz
- Breach at Facility 9
- Surveillance release of Iris
- "Observation: Wright's response to flexible collateral under duress. If lethal, deny approval. If protective, initiate *Resonance Phase II*."

Carolyn whispered, "They were watching to see if you'd let me die."

Laila stared at the screen.

"They were watching to see if I'd become them."

Laila closed the tablet. The light inside the cabin dimmed as clouds rolled over the trees.
The game had changed. This wasn't about survival anymore.
It was about reclamation.

Underground Transit Terminal – Location Unknown – 6:03 P.M.

The platform was long abandoned — no signs, no schedule, no sound. Fluorescent bulbs buzzed in dying intervals overhead, casting faint light across crumbling tile and soot-streaked walls.
Iris sat alone on a steel bench, hood pulled over her cropped hair, a worn duffel beside her feet. Her boots were caked in ash from the exploded warehouse. Her gloves were off. Her hands were shaking.
Not from fear.
From memory.
In front of her lay a portable terminal — the kind used by off-grid operatives decades ago. Its screen flickered once, then bloomed with a symbol.
PROJECT: RESONANCE
Status: Phase I – Complete
Candidate: WRIGHT, L.
Psychological Threshold: Passed
Observer Status: Standby Directive
Iris stared at the screen. Not with pride.
With *regret.*

She reached into her coat and pulled out an old dog tag — not military, not even governmental. Black metal etched with a strange sigil: a spiraled glyph surrounded by thirteen stars.

She rubbed her thumb across it.

It used to belong to her.

Now it was just a scar with edges.

A soft footstep echoed from the tunnel entrance behind her.

She didn't turn.

A man's voice — older, composed, filtered — filled the space.

"You broke protocol when you spared the boy."

Iris didn't respond.

"You were not assigned to protect her. You were assigned to *provoke* her."

Still, silence.

Then she spoke, voice low and calm.

"You wanted a weapon. But I saw a soul. That was your mistake. And mine."

The man stepped into the edge of the light now, but his face remained in shadow.

"She will hate you when she learns everything."

"I expect her to."

"And still you watch her."

"I *guide* her."

A long silence.

Then the man said:

"If she rejects the Resonance path... what then?"

Iris stood slowly, eyes fixed on the dark tunnel beyond. "Then she becomes something you can't control. And I help her burn the rest of this program to the ground."
The terminal blinked once. Then darkened.
Iris picked up her duffel, tucked the dog tag away, and walked toward the darkness — into the unknown.
But not alone anymore.
Because now… the next candidate had woken up.

Strategic Oversight Command – Level 7 – 6:39 P.M.

The chamber was subterranean and cold — designed like an engine room dressed up as a war room. Screens blinked against concrete walls. Operators moved in silence around circular workstations, unaware or unwilling to acknowledge the man standing at the center of the storm.
Rhys Greaves stood motionless beneath a ring of overhead lights. The illumination cast long shadows under his eyes, the kind carved by sleeplessness and betrayal.
On the central screen:
PROJECT: RESONANCE – PHASE II UNLOCKED
Candidate: WRIGHT, L. – Status: INITIATED
Override Level: RESTRICTED
Security Note: "External Observer Triggered Advancement (Iris Flag: 13-A)"
Greaves's jaw clenched.
Another screen blinked.
Iris access confirmed
Protocol deviation: "Subject 05 – Alive"
Operational Integrity: 72%

Greaves authority scope: *diminished*
He exhaled slowly. And then—acted.
"Bring up contingency package *REZ-Null-7*," he said coldly.
A technician turned, startled. "That's not an authorized path under the current—"
Greaves stepped forward. Not shouting. Just close. Dangerous.
"Your job isn't authorization. It's execution. Now open it."
Hesitantly, the tech input the sequence.
A red file emerged on the screen:
REZ-NULL-7
Codename: *PILGRIM LOCK*
Directive: "Preemptive destabilization of Echo candidates in the field."
Greaves keyed his override.
Authorization: GREAVES/OMEGA-TRIAD
Status: UNLEASHED
Another file snapped into place. A digital blueprint. Tactical.
TARGET: WRIGHT, L.
INDIRECT MANIPULATION – APPROVED
PSYCH-WARFARE ASSETS – DEPLOY
SURROGATE AGENT: [ACTIVE]
DESIGNATION: *WHISPER*
Greaves spoke quietly, almost to himself.
"She won't break through fire. But she might break through doubt."
He turned away from the monitor and stepped into the shadows.

"To win a war of minds, you don't aim for the head..."
"...you aim for the trust."

Elsewhere, a silent terminal powered on.
A new figure logged in.
Unknown. Unseen.
Codename: Whisper.
And their first directive was simple:
"Infiltrate. Divide. Disarm."

Ranger Cabin – Appalachian Foothills – 7:08 P.M.

Rain had begun to fall in slow sheets outside the cabin, tapping against the moss-covered roof like a war drum slowing its tempo. Inside, the soft glow of the field tablet illuminated Laila's face — focused, firm, far past the moment of disbelief.

Carolyn stood by the boarded window, watching the curtain of rain blur the tree line, hand on her sidearm like it was part of her body. Not from fear.

From readiness.

"I know what we're up against now," Laila said. "And I know what they want."

Carolyn turned. "You think Greaves still thinks he's running this?"

Laila smirked. "No. That's what makes him dangerous."

She turned the tablet toward Carolyn. Displayed was the Resonance network interface Daniel had decrypted — partial routes, buried sub-networks, forgotten nodes that hadn't been purged.

"This system's old, but Greaves needs it to stay hidden. The moment Resonance gets exposed to light — congressional hearings, press leaks, digital footprints — the whole thing collapses. He knows that."

Carolyn stepped closer. "So what's the plan?"

Laila tapped one node in particular — a closed-loop junction in Virginia marked *BX9-A*.

"This one connects to a Sable recruitment site that was supposedly shut down five years ago. Daniel says it went dark after the Falfor fallout. But two months ago, activity spiked. Quiet, hidden... but consistent. Data transfers. Energy pulls. Print requests."

Carolyn leaned in. "You think it's where they train new operatives?"

Laila nodded. "Or worse — where they bury old ones."

Carolyn sat across from her, arms crossed. "So what? We ghost in? See what sticks?"

"No." Laila shook her head. "We do something they'll never expect."

She reached into her gear pack and pulled out a burner phone. Inside it, a sim card loaded with one thing:

A curated leak package — audio, names, mission briefs. Everything Daniel had filtered from the Resonance servers without triggering Greaves's deeper firewalls.

"We go public."

Carolyn blinked. "That's suicide."

"No," Laila said, eyes cold. "It's bait."

— An encrypted journalist email inbox receives an anonymous message with a digital dossier.

— A former DHS field agent, long retired, sees a familiar sigil on a public message board and quietly wipes his browser.
— An intern at the Department of Justice flags a strange inbound memo marked with a now-defunct project code: RESONANCE.

Back in the Cabin…
Carolyn stared at the screen, then at Laila. "You realize you just declared war."
Laila looked out the window at the rain.
"We didn't start it," she said quietly. "But we'll damn well finish it."
The Next Morning – 8:03 A.M.

Washington, D.C. – DOJ Internal Affairs Office
A junior analyst stared at her screen, pale-faced. Her supervisor leaned over her shoulder, reading the subject line of an encrypted, unsigned email:
"Project Resonance Exists – And It's Already Operating"
Attached: unredacted briefings, digital surveillance threads, recruitment logs tied to defunct personnel files.
The supervisor reached for the phone. "We've got a breach."
A cold room. Suits pacing. One monitor displayed a digital heatmap — red flares rising across encrypted boards and internal leak trackers.
One word blinked repeatedly:
RESONANCE
"Who the hell released this?" one voice barked.

Another: "It's not the data we should be afraid of. It's *who* still has access."

New York City – Independent Journalist Workspace…
A man in his thirties — sharp-eyed, hunched over a laptop, wireless headphones on — read the files line by line.
He recognized one name.
Mateo Ruiz.
He opened a new tab and typed:
"Ruiz – DHS false detention – connection to Falfor case?"
Then leaned back, mind racing.

[Online – Secure Forum: "EagleSignal42"]
A post appeared:
"WITNESS EXISTS. THEY MISSED ONE. HE KNOWS EVERYTHING."
"M.R. – Find him before they do."
It was gone within 45 seconds.
But it had already been screenshot.

At an undisclosed Safehouse – 10:27 A.M.

The safehouse was nondescript — an old farmhouse converted for field use, halfway between York and Harrisburg. It smelled of cedar and antiseptic. Mateo Ruiz sat in a recliner, bandages on his arm, eyes flicking between a muted television and the faint sound of rain hitting the windows.
The screen flashed again:
"DOJ Sources Confirm Investigation Into Black Ops

Program: 'Project Resonance'"
"Whistleblower Allegedly Still Alive"
Carolyn entered with a bag of food, set it down, and turned the volume up.
Mateo looked at her, panic creeping into his voice.
"They're talking about me."
Laila followed her in, eyes on the screen. "That's the point."
Mateo stood, fists clenched. "You don't understand. They *tried* to erase me. Now you've put my face in lights."
Laila met his gaze calmly. "They can't kill what the public is watching. You're not just a witness now — you're a shield. A firebreak. If they move on you again, it confirms everything."
Mateo's voice cracked. "And what if they don't care?"
Laila stepped closer. "Then we take the truth and burn them with it."
Carolyn added, "But we don't do it recklessly. You're not bait. You're the *mirror* — the one who reflects how deep it goes."
Mateo stared at them. Then nodded, barely.
Laila looked back at the television.
"...still no comment from DHS, DOJ, or the U.S. Marshals Service regarding leaked files implicating covert programs allegedly tied to the Falfor scandal."
She muttered under her breath:
"Let's see how long they can keep silent."

Safehouse – Later That Afternoon – 2:12 P.M.

The rain had stopped, but the sky remained heavy — low and gray, like it hadn't yet decided whether to give up or thunder down again.

Inside the safehouse, the dining table was now a battlefield. Laila stood at the head, dry-erase markers in hand. Carolyn sat to her left, flipping through surveillance stills. Daniel's laptop was open, a secure VPN feeding live network scans into a local drive. Mateo stood at the far end, hands resting on the back of a chair, half-in, half-out — unsure if he belonged in the war room or the witness stand.

But he stayed.

Because now, he mattered.

Daniel looked up first. "The leak spread faster than I expected. A journalist picked it up an hour ago. Independent, but smart — not the kind to burn a source. DOJ opened a quiet inquiry. No public denial yet."

Carolyn raised an eyebrow. "And Greaves?"

"Radio silent," Daniel said. "But I traced server irregularities coming out of Virginia — old dead switches flickering to life. Could be fallback systems, but it smells like panic. Or retaliation."

Laila circled a section of the map pinned to the wall. "We need to act before they shift ground. If they migrate ops to deeper black sites, we lose access and narrative momentum."

Carolyn tapped a folder. "We still have their asset lists, handler tags, and facility shell companies. What if we force a confrontation? Leak their *pattern*, not just the facts. Make them think someone close is still feeding us."

Daniel nodded. "Start seeding false location pings.

Repurpose their own signal traffic. Use Greaves' paranoia to move him faster than he's comfortable."

Mateo stepped forward, tentative. "And what happens to me?"

Laila looked at him. "You're not a passenger anymore."

She walked over, placed a hand on his shoulder — not gently, but solidly.

"You testify. On record. We build a protected disclosure platform — multiple layers, multiple formats. You'll tell your story five different ways across five jurisdictions. If they silence one, another survives."

Carolyn added, "We have names. Agents. Photos. Deaths ruled accidental that weren't. If even *one* piece is verified under oath, it blows the lid off."

Daniel closed his laptop. "But there's one more angle. The ghost programs. Sable. Resonance. They're *compartmentalized*. Greaves may not even know who's above him."

Laila walked back to the head of the table.

"Then we keep pushing. Until he breaks protocol. Until he does something loud. And when he does… we make sure everyone hears it."

A beat passed.

Mateo nodded. "Okay. I'm in."

Later – Cabin Porch – Sunset.

Laila stood on the porch, watching the horizon burn gold through the trees. Carolyn joined her, arms crossed.

"You really think we can take it down?" Carolyn asked.

Laila didn't look away from the sunset.

"No," she said. "I think we can make them afraid."

Carolyn gave a tired grin. "Close enough."
Behind them, the war had changed.
This time, they weren't witnesses.
They were the architects of exposure.

Safehouse – Interior War Room – 6:44 P.M.

A topographic map was spread across the table like a surgical blueprint. On it, Daniel had circled a compound nestled within a dense wooded region outside Charlottesville, Virginia — near a defunct FEMA training facility.
Carolyn paced with arms folded. "You're sure it's active?"
Daniel pointed to the screen of his laptop. "Energy signatures and packet pings went from cold to hot right after the leak. If they're relocating data or operatives, they'll funnel it through this ghost node before it disappears."
Laila leaned in. "What was this place originally?"
"A continuity-of-government site — Cold War fallback bunker. Officially decommissioned. Unofficially rented to a private contractor tied to four different false shell corps — all of them flagged in Resonance cross-references."
Carolyn frowned. "Security?"
Daniel tapped the screen. "Automated entry system, drone sweeps every four hours, motion sensors on the lower approach. No live guard rotation logged, but likely at least two on-site operatives embedded to purge if needed."
Mateo shifted nervously. "What's in there?"
Daniel's voice lowered. "Partial data drives. Redacted

training footage. Possibly asset files on the missing witnesses Greaves erased. Enough proof to blow his world open… if we get it out."
Laila looked to Carolyn. "We go in, extract what we can. Fast. Quiet. No trace."
Carolyn smirked. "Old times."
Mateo looked up. "What do I do?"
Laila: "You monitor the media feeds. The moment we send confirmation, we drop everything. Full dump. Let the truth outrun the damage."
She turned back to Daniel. "You'll be our anchor."
Daniel nodded. "Already prepping counter-leaks and proxy relays. You get out with the proof, I make sure it lights up the sky."
Laila exhaled. Then grabbed her gear.
"Then let's pack. We ghost at dawn."

Elsewhere – Greaves' Operations Room – 7:16 P.M

A different war room. Sleek, silent. This one *sterile.*
Rhys Greaves stood with his hands behind his back as an analyst whispered into his ear.
"…encrypted surge detected outside Charlottesville. System nodes accessed through relayed fragments. Traced to Wright's team."
Greaves' jaw tensed. "Which node?"
The analyst hesitated. "BX9-A."
Greaves didn't blink.
"Activate full lockdown. Burn it if necessary."
Another voice spoke — flat, unnerved.

"But sir, that node is part of the foundational data grid for—"
Greaves snapped: "I said burn it."
A long silence. Then the analyst nodded and moved.
Greaves turned toward the main monitor where Laila's face was frozen in mid-speech from an earlier intercepted feed.
Not defiant.
Certain.
"She's not exposing a network," he muttered.
"She's building a new one."

Perimeter of BX9-A Facility – Predawn – 4:26 A.M.

The forest held its breath.
Mist clung low to the ground, coiling through the trees like quiet intent. Laila and Carolyn moved through it in silence, dressed in lightweight field gear, visors pulled low, weapons holstered in drop-leg rigs.
Their approach path was mapped by Daniel, accurate down to the pine cluster. They crept along the overgrown service road, flashlights blacked out, using thermal scopes sparingly.
Ahead: a squat concrete structure built into the hillside.
Faded signs read:
"FEDERAL EMERGENCY TRAINING ANNEX – CLOSED PERMANENTLY"
The rust and neglect were convincing. The sensor grid beneath it was not.
Carolyn held up a hand and crouched.
"Two perimeter nodes. One drone launch pad — no

activity. Guard rotation unknown."
Laila slid forward. "Daniel said there was a heat bloom four hours ago. That means someone's inside."
They circled to the south side — lower elevation, rear maintenance entrance.
Carolyn pulled the encrypted transceiver from her belt and linked it to the old keypad. "Let's hope Greaves still loves his legacy code structure."
Beep. Click.
Door unlocked.
They moved in.

Chapter 11

Interior – Service Corridor – BX9-A

The air inside was still and dry. Emergency lights flickered dimly overhead. The layout was familiar to Laila — an old underground annex, 1970s Cold War design: redundant corridors, low ceilings, no windows.

They moved room by room.

Old office.

Empty barracks.

Then—

Server Room.

Rows of rack-mounted drives blinked with amber lights.

On the far wall, a dedicated console glowed faintly, prompting for login credentials.

Laila sat at the terminal while Carolyn watched the hallway.

"Daniel's access code worked," she whispered. "I'm in."

She pulled a drive from her bag — air-gapped, trace-scrubbed — and slotted it in.

Data began to transfer.

FILE FOUND: WITNESS_REDACTIONS.ZIP

FILE FOUND: RESONANCE_ASSET_LOG-VIII

FILE FOUND: IRIS_CANDIDATE_ARCHIVE_OLD

FILE FOUND: VIDEO_SURVEILLANCE: 'FALFOR-BURN'

Laila's eyes narrowed. "This is it."

But then—

A thud!

Carolyn whirled toward the door. "Movement. North hall. Single set of boots."
Laila didn't stop the transfer. "We've got two minutes."
Carolyn took position behind the door.
Footsteps.
Closer.
A shadow passed the gap under the door.
A breath.
Silence.
Then footsteps… retreated.
Laila pulled the drive just as the final file copied.
"Got it."
They slipped back into the corridor, retracing their path. As they reached the exit stairwell—
A voice behind them. Calm. Female.
"Leaving so soon?"
Carolyn drew her weapon and turned.
But there was no one there.
Just an open service door… slowly swinging shut.
Laila whispered: "She was here."
Carolyn nodded. "Iris."

Exterior – 5:09 A.M.

The women emerged from the forest as the first light of day stretched across the hills.
No alarms.
No pursuit.
But both of them knew they had just taken the heartbeat of the machine — and now, the system would come alive.

Laila held the drive tightly in her hand.
"It's time," she said. "Let's go burn the silence."

Strategic Oversight Command – Private Executive Level – 6:08 A.M.

Greaves stood alone in a sterile observation suite high above the command floor. Glass walls surrounded him, but offered no protection from the chaos rippling below.
Dozens of terminals blinked with intrusion warnings.
ALERT: NODE BX9-A BREACHED
ARCHIVE ACCESS CONFIRMED
DATA TRANSFER DETECTED – SIGNAL UNKNOWN
LOCAL WIPES FAILED – SYSTEM OVERRUN
He stared at the reports as if willing them to reverse.
They didn't.
An assistant entered, hesitant. "Sir… the file package retrieved from BX9-A — it includes witness logs, operative evaluations, internal communications. At least three video executions. One linked to the Falfor case. And the IRIS logbook."
Greaves didn't turn.
The assistant added, quietly: "It's already propagating through decentralized press nodes. Someone launched the distribution tree."
Greaves walked slowly to the glass and placed one hand against it.
They'd done it.

He could feel the silence in the room around him — not reverent silence, but a void. The kind that signaled a shift in power.

He turned to his private terminal. Accessed the Resonance Chain.

ACCESS DENIED – CHAIN OVERRIDE LOCKED

Authority: Redacted / Observer Level

Your level: Reclassified – Monitoring Only

His throat tightened.

They hadn't just beaten him.

They had replaced him.

He reached for the intercom. Voice flat.

"Activate last-tier damage control."

The analyst on the other end hesitated. "That protocol is not recommended unless—"

"Do it."

Greaves closed his eyes.

"Everything we built... sacrificed for her. For *Wright.*"

No answer.

He looked back at the screen. Laila's name was there — linked now to key breaches, testimonial events, data exposure metrics.

Below it, one word glowed red:

CANDIDATE: ASCENDING

He whispered to himself — more confession than calculation:

"Then I'll be the one who breaks her… or buries her."

The lights dimmed.

Behind him, his authority crumbled.

But his *anger*—that had only just begun.

Remote Transmission Site – 7:02 A.M.

Thunder rumbled low across the Pennsylvania sky. The rain had passed, but the air was still tense — like nature itself knew something was coming.

Inside a decommissioned communications tower, Daniel typed with surgical precision. Two laptops open, one satellite node blinking green, a mobile generator humming like an engine beneath a revolution.

Laila stood behind him, the encrypted drive in her palm.

Carolyn watched the timer on the backup relay: *00:59:42*

Every second mattered.

Daniel inserted the drive.

"Target nodes are hot," he said. "We're releasing to six independent whistleblower platforms, three international leak centers, and one legacy media network. With auto-forwarding to public archives and mirrored proxies in eight countries."

Carolyn smirked. "That's one way to say: try scrubbing *this*."

Laila looked down at the folder Daniel had built around the intel:

OPERATION: ECHO LIGHT

SUBJECT: UNSEEN NETWORKS / UNACCOUNTED DETAINMENTS / INTERNAL ASSET ELIMINATIONS / PSYCH-SCALING TRIALS / FALFOR LINKED EVENTS

INCLUDED: VIDEO. TESTIMONY. PHOTOS. TIMESTAMPS. MAPS.

At the bottom, the simplest label of all:

"THIS IS RESONANCE."
Laila placed her hand on Daniel's shoulder.
"Release it."
Daniel hit ENTER.
Intercut Montage – Around the World

[New York Times Digital Desk]
A junior editor sips coffee and stares at her screen as encrypted files begin flooding in — one marked with the name of a long-dead ICE administrator she investigated years ago.

[Al Jazeera Investigative Wing – London]
An analyst shouts to his editor. "This matches the Guatemalan disappearances. The redacted files — they're all here. The operation was *real.*"

[University Server – Berlin]
Students and professors gather around as servers auto-update with a 72GB archive dump titled:
"FROM INSIDE YOUR OWN SYSTEM"

[Global Forums & Media Feeds]
Social channels explode. Threads erupt.
"What is Project Resonance?"
"Names, photos, execution videos... is this legit?"
"Someone just dropped the motherlode on a rogue U.S. program. This isn't a leak. It's a confession."

Back at the Tower – 7:17 A.M.
Carolyn stood at the window, watching the first rays of light split through the clouds.
Laila lowered the tablet. Daniel exhaled — not relief. Readiness.
"It's done," he said.
Laila stared out over the treeline.
"No," she said. "*Now* it begins."

Elsewhere – Resonance Systems Failures – 7:21 A.M.

Internal systems crash. Data obfuscation collapses.
Redundant backups erase themselves in safety loops.
Civilian oversight boards receive anonymous drops.
The veil is gone.
And in its place: a reckoning.

Global Media Broadcasts – 9:02 A.M. EST

[CNN Headline Feed – LIVE]
BREAKING: Massive Leak Exposes Secret U.S. Detention Network Tied to Falfor Scandal — Sources Claim Project "Resonance" Used to Erase Witnesses and Manufacture Trials
A stunned anchor fumbles with pages as clips begin rolling across screens:
Grainy execution videos. Shadowed interviews. Redacted documents with stamps now visible — DOJ, SABLE, ECHO-LINKED.

[BBC World News – Simulcast]
"This morning, world governments and civil liberties watchdogs are calling for immediate investigations into the U.S.-based 'Resonance Program,' which appears to have operated in the shadows for over a decade — detaining, silencing, and erasing individuals connected to government whistleblowing cases…"
Images flicker:
– A photo of Mateo Ruiz, now labeled "Survivor"
– Surveillance stills of Laila Wright and Carolyn Pryme, faces partially obscured but now tied to the leak

[Hashtags Trending Globally]
#ProjectResonance
#WrightAndHalston
#WitnessesNotGhosts
#EchoLeaks
#UnseenJustice

[A Social Feed Screencap Goes Viral]
"She didn't go rogue. She went righteous."
– Tweet, @AgentZeroDay, with 2.3M retweets

Strategic Oversight Command – Observation Room – 9:17 A.M.

Greaves stood in darkness.
No lights. No subordinates.
Just the hum of failing servers and the glow of a dozen news broadcasts playing in chaotic synchrony. The

headlines were all the same — only the *language* differed.
He watched, still. Silent.
Then slowly, calmly, he removed his watch and placed it on the console.
A final symbol of control. Discarded.
He walked to a panel beside the terminal and unlocked a biometric case.
Inside:
– A matte-black pistol
– A disposable phone
– A vial containing a military-grade neuroinhibitor
– One last file folder, sealed and marked with red glyphs:
"OP: CLEAN SLATE"
He picked up the phone and dialed.
When the line connected, he simply said:
"Initiate final phase. Authorization Greaves-Null-One."
"Sir?" the voice asked. "You mean… physical removal?"
"Everyone tied to the leak. I want Pryme first. Wright will watch her die. Then she'll come to me."
A pause. The voice said, quieter now:
"This crosses every line, sir. Even *our* line."
Greaves stared at the screens as new words filled the headlines:
"Senate Demands Emergency Inquiry into Covert Government Ops"
"They drew the lines," he said softly. "I'm just burning the map."
The line disconnected.
He stared into the reflection of his own face on the screen.
He looked… old. Beaten. But more dangerous than ever.

He smiled once. Just once.
Then turned to walk out.

Rural Drop Point Outside Gettysburg – 12:04 P.M.

The sun was high but cold, casting long shadows across the gravel lot of an abandoned feed mill. Carolyn Pryme crouched behind an old Ford Bronco, rifle tight to her shoulder, breath slow and measured.
The meet was supposed to be routine — a dead-drop handoff from a whistleblower courier who had leaked one of the older Falfor logs.
It was a setup.

Ten minutes earlier...
Carolyn pulled up in a non-descript sedan. There was no vehicle in sight, no birdsong, no ambient sound except for the wind brushing through brittle weeds.
Then—
a shot.
The first round punched through her windshield. She hit the ground behind the car before it shattered completely.
Then came the flood:
– Muzzle flashes from the treeline.
– Suppressed submachine gun bursts.
– Glass, gravel, and old rust flying through the air.
They weren't there to scare her. They were there to end her.

Present – Pinned Down...
Carolyn gritted her teeth as another volley cracked

overhead, shredding the Bronco's side mirror.
Three shooters. Maybe four. All trained. Coordinated. Greaves sent professionals.
She rolled to her left and fired two quick bursts — caught one in the leg and sent him tumbling behind a grain silo.
The others adjusted. Smarter. Tighter.
Pinned.
No exits. No cover left that wasn't already ventilated.
Radio dead from signal interference.
"Of course," she muttered. "Greaves doesn't just kill you — he scrubs you off the page."
She pulled her backup mag and cursed.
Two rounds.
Then — a new sound.
Not bullets.
Wheels. Fast.
A black SUV tore onto the lot, tires screaming across gravel. Doors flung open mid-skid.
Laila Wright stepped out. Weapon drawn. Fire in her eyes.
Carolyn yelled, "Right side — treeline!"
Laila opened fire — clean, surgical shots. One assailant dropped. Another scrambled.
From the SUV's passenger side — Mateo climbed out, ducked behind the door, and flung a smoke canister wide across the field. The burst blanketed the yard in swirling gray.
Daniel's voice crackled through Laila's earpiece.
"I've got eyes. Drone above. Last target flanking low, west side—"
Carolyn popped up, pivoted—

Bang!
A final shot — center mass. Last hostile down.
Silence.
Then smoke drifted.
Then breathing.
Laila jogged to Carolyn and dropped beside her.
"You okay?"
Carolyn was already reloading. "Remind me to scream later."
Mateo exhaled hard, face pale. "That was *not* in the mission briefing."
Daniel, over comms:
"And that, ladies and gentlemen, is how you steal back the narrative."
Laila looked around the field. Bullet casings, blood, smoke. A battlefield built in moments.
"This wasn't cleanup," she said. "This was a message."
Carolyn stood, limping slightly. "Then it was a dropped call."

Feed Mill Lot – 12:31 P.M.

The air was thick with smoke and sweat. Sirens echoed in the far distance — emergency services, unaware they'd arrive too late to change anything that mattered.
Carolyn dragged the wounded assailant from behind the silo — a tall, hardened man in black tactical gear, chest soaked red from a gut shot. He wheezed, barely conscious, a smear of blood trailing behind him.
Laila approached, eyes sharp.

Daniel's voice came over the comms.
"I've got no more heat signatures. Just him."
Carolyn dropped the man against the base of the wall and raised her pistol.
"I've got questions," she snarled, voice cracking from adrenaline. "And if I don't like the first answer—"
Laila stepped in, firm. "Carolyn…"
Carolyn didn't lower the weapon. Her hand trembled. "He tried to erase me. I was just something that had to be gone. Do you know how that makes me feel?"
"I know," Laila said gently. "But let him talk before you finish him."
A long beat passed.
Then Carolyn exhaled sharply and pulled back — just slightly.
The man coughed, blood bubbling at his lips. He laughed — dry, gurgling.
"You're… too late," he rasped. "This wasn't just about her."
Laila crouched beside him. "What was the target?"
He smiled through blood. "Insurance."
"What insurance?" Laila asked.
He blinked slowly. "Node B-X… seven-four."
Carolyn's eyes went wide. "That's the decoy facility in Maryland. They listed it as 'decommissioned' three years ago."
Laila leaned closer. "What's there now?"
The man's head lolled to the side.
Laila grabbed his vest collar. "*What's at BX-74?*"
He looked up — eyes glassy.

"A bomb," he wheezed. "Failsafe. Buried… in the walls. Designed to kill the story… if the bullets failed."
Laila stood. "Daniel, did you get that?"
Daniel, over comms:
"I'm on it. Checking every blueprint and signal burst out of Maryland in the last hour."
Carolyn raised her pistol again, hand steady now.
The man didn't plead. He just smiled and closed his eyes.
Laila placed a hand on Carolyn's shoulder. She could feel the shiver in her body. Not from fear, but from the anger.
Carolyn didn't look at her. She just asked, "Do we need him anymore?"
Laila was silent for a moment. Then:
"No."
Carolyn squeezed the trigger.
One clean shot.
The silence after was louder than the gun.

Mobile Command — Minutes Later

Daniel's voice came through their comms again — tight, urgent.
"BX-74's buried under an old federal printing depot. I'm seeing heat blooms and timer signals. Whatever's there — it's active. And it's counting down."
Carolyn holstered her weapon. "Then we move."
Laila nodded once.
"Call in Mateo. We ghost again. One last stop before the curtain drops."

BX-74 Facility – Maryland – 2:12 P.M.

The black SUV screeched to a halt at the rear of a crumbling brick structure—BX-74—once a federal printing depot, now a tomb sealed in bureaucracy and silence. Trees had overgrown the fencing. Moss grew between every concrete crack.

But the danger was very much alive.

Carolyn jumped out first, weapon drawn, moving fast and low.

Laila followed, tapping the comm.

"Daniel, talk to me."

"Pressure sensors triggered an hour ago. Power grid's spiking in zone three. Bomb's wired into the foundation. Based on thermal traces, I'm guessing 40 pounds of high-density composite. Enough to level the place. You've got— *Twelve minutes.*"

Laila and Carolyn pushed into the side entrance — Mateo on overwatch, staying back with the SUV's scoped rifle aimed toward the treeline.

Inside, the building smelled like damp paper and old ink. Broken presses stood like skeletal giants in the dark. But under the silence... was a whine. Electrical. Pulsing.

They moved fast, clearing each hallway.

Laila spotted a faint red glow through a warped office window.

"There."

They kicked in the door.

The walls were stripped bare. In the center: a reinforced detonation rig, six shaped charges wired to an insulated core unit pulsing with LED indicators. Attached to the top: a hardened digital timer.

TIMER: 11:19 ... 11:18 ...

Carolyn moved to the device, her eyes widened. "I don't know this model."

Daniel's voice crackled through:

"It's proprietary. Greaves' people built it to *not* be recognizable. But I've got you."

Schematics began loading onto Laila's tablet.

"Carolyn," Daniel said, "You'll need to remove the casing plate on the right side. Carefully — the panel is pressure-locked. Any lateral movement over 3mm triggers the backup."

Carolyn pulled out a microtool and flashlight. Her hands didn't shake — but her breath shortened.

Laila scanned the floor — and saw something behind the rig.

A crate. Military-issued. Marked with the *Sable Protocol* insignia.

She opened it.

Inside: files. Drives. Documents stamped with names, termination logs, psychological grading sheets — all of it. Backups of everything Greaves had destroyed.

"Holy hell," Laila whispered. "This is the entire program archive."

Daniel came back in her ear.

"You get that out… you don't just end Resonance. You *convict* it."

TIMER: 08:44
Carolyn grunted. “Panel’s off. Talk to me.”
“Two wires. Red and green. Cut red *after* the orange LED flashes three times. If you cut it early, the failsafe charges go off.”
The room was too quiet.
Flash.
Flash.
Flash—
Snip.
Silence.
Then the countdown stopped.
TIMER: 08:12 – HALTED
Carolyn stepped back, chest heaving.
Laila grabbed the crate and stuffed it into her pack.
“We’re done here.”
Carolyn nodded. “No. We’ve just begun.”

2:27 P.M.
The team exited the facility. Mateo jogged to meet them, eyes wide.
“You got it?”
Laila patted the pack. “We got *everything*.”
Behind them, the structure loomed — intact, but still haunted.
Daniel came through the comm.
“I’ll prep a live drop with the files you found. This isn’t a story anymore. It’s a reckoning.”
Laila looked toward the sky.
“This ends with Greaves.”

Unknown Location – Mobile Blacksite Command – 3:03 P.M.

The interior of the mobile command rig was dim, windowless, and pulsing with red alerts. Emergency status lights bathed the walls in the color of failure.

Rhys Greaves sat alone at a central table, watching three things loop on screens before him:

1. A still frame of *Carolyn Pryme*, sweat-soaked, crouched before the BX-74 bomb rig.
2. A still frame of *Laila Wright*, holding the Sable archive.
3. The frozen timestamp: *08:12* — the moment the countdown stopped.

The techs were gone. Evacuated. No more analysts. No more deniability.

Only him.

He poured a drink into a steel tumbler — not out of celebration, but defiance. He didn't drink it.

Instead, he keyed a handheld terminal — old, secure, untraceable.

The screen prompted:

"Manual Engagement Mode: Are you sure?"

He selected YES.

"Retrieve Candidate: Wright. Use direct methods. Primary target only."

Greaves pulled open a weapons case at his side — sleek, custom-built. Suppressed pistol. Knife. Tranq darts. GPS scanner. One tranquilizer already loaded.

Not to kill.

To capture.
He zipped up a black field coat, placed a comms mic into his ear, and clipped a photo of Laila from a marshals database into his inner pocket. A habit. A token.
"She made herself a symbol," he muttered.
Then he stepped into the daylight for the first time in two weeks.
"Let's see if she bleeds like one."

– *Laila* wipes down a pistol at the safehouse, unaware that she's now being *personally hunted.*
– *Carolyn* reinforces the windows, her movements more deliberate, more protective.
– *Daniel* uploads the first of the archive files to a whistleblower news outlet, the countdown to detonation replaced by a countdown to exposure.
And somewhere in the distance...
Greaves is coming.
BX9-A, *02:47 Hours* — Industrial Storage Complex Outside Denver
The steel doors of the warehouse yawned open just wide enough to admit two shadows—armed, focused, and silent.
Laila crouched low, her black tactical gear blending into the shadows. Carolyn moved at her side, her eyes locked on the HUD projected from her contact lens.
They didn't speak. They couldn't. The place was rigged for sound, motion, and heat—layered like a paranoid fever dream of a black-budget ghost division. The air was thick with dust and ozone.
Carolyn whispered into her mic:

"EMP ready. Drones up top. Guards inside — four. We neutralize quietly or this whole place wakes up."

Laila tapped her fingers twice in acknowledgment. Her body moved like memory — all instinct and muscle. She slipped through the narrow rows of crates marked *Defense Surplus, VX-A Recovered*, each one more ominous than the last.

From above, one of their spider drones pulsed red on Carolyn's HUD.

"Tripwire, infrared. Left side. 10 meters."

Laila reached into her pack and pulled a micro-sprayer. With a deft puff of reflective mist, the beam shimmered into view like a laser across a bank vault. She stepped over it without hesitation.

A whisper of breath. A foot scuff. Then—

Thwip!

A throwing knife lodged into a neck. The first guard dropped without sound.

Carolyn dragged the body behind a crate. "Three left," she murmured.

The second man appeared as they rounded a corner. He was ex-military, M4 in hand, full combat rig. He didn't expect a fast drop-kick to the knee or the suppressor kissing his temple.

Thud!

Down.

They crept forward. In the center of the room, on a raised platform surrounded by a poly-steel cage, was a briefcase-sized canister hooked to a series of wires leading into the warehouse's mainframe. Red digital readout: *00:17:49*

"Bomb's active," Carolyn muttered. "Failsafe's ticking."

Laila stepped up to the console. "This isn't standard ordnance. This is…"

She paused. "Military-grade fusion hybrid. Someone meant this to take out the whole block."

Carolyn nodded grimly. "We stop it. Now."

A clatter.

Gunfire erupted from above — automatic, chaotic.

"Ambush!" Carolyn yelled, diving for cover as bullets chewed into crates.

Return fire. Controlled. Surgical.

Laila took down two from behind a loading forklift. One remained — a masked man in carbon-weave armor, firing a flechette shotgun.

He was cornered, wounded — and not going to surrender.

But Laila closed the gap. Elbow. Knee. Disarm.

She tore off his helmet.

Her breath caught. "You…"

His mouth bloodied, he grinned.

"You were never supposed to make it this far, Marshal Wright."

She pressed her pistol to his chest. "Why this bomb? Who ordered it?"

He wheezed, chuckling. "It's not just a bomb… it's a beacon."

Then his eyes rolled back — a cyanide capsule crackling in his jaw.

Carolyn shouted from the control panel. "Laila! That timer jumped—*it's accelerating!*"

00:02:11.

Laila barked, "How do we contain it?"
Carolyn typed rapidly, sweat streaking her brow. "We can't disable it. But we can isolate the blast and vent it underground."
Laila ripped open the subfloor hatch and began slamming emergency reinforcements over the chamber.
00:01:12.
Metal screamed. Lights flickered. The entire warehouse moaned like a dying beast.
00:00:06.
"Get down!" Carolyn shouted, diving into the open blast trench.
BOOM!!!
But the blast didn't hit them.
The ground absorbed it — shuddering, groaning — then falling eerily silent.
Dust rained down.
Carolyn coughed. "That… that was too close."
Laila sat up, dazed. Her voice was iron. "Someone knew exactly how to get to us. Greaves wasn't just trying to kill us. He was trying to send a message."
Carolyn nodded slowly. "He did."

AT AN UNKNOWN BLACKSITE – DEEP IN THE SMOKY MOUNTAINS

The room was cold — not from temperature, but from intent. The walls were steel and soundproofed. A single monitor cast pale light over the face of Edward Greaves, who stood rigid, fists clenched behind his back, watching the final moments of the infiltration on live satellite feed. He saw the detonation. The warehouse shuddering. The feed cutting out for two seconds. Then—there they were. *Laila Wright and Carolyn Pryme*, crawling from the blast trench, covered in ash but *alive.*

The vein in his temple throbbed. His knuckles cracked.

"Why…" he growled, the word rising like bile, "…won't those bitches die?"

He slammed his fist into the titanium tabletop, sending a tremor through the room. Monitors flickered. His aides, watching from the shadows, flinched but said nothing.

Greaves turned sharply, pacing.

"Six operations. Six high-level hitters. Four autonomous cells, two hired teams, a planted judiciary, and a goddamn specter unit—and still they breathe?"

He stopped in front of a one-way mirror, staring at his own warped reflection.

"She was supposed to be broken after Falfor. She was supposed to disappear after that trial. I buried her career, her reputation, her clearance…"

His voice cracked, almost a whisper now.

"…but I didn't bury her."

He took a shaky breath and straightened his coat. But even that ritual couldn't mask the flicker of fear in his eyes. The fear that the ghost of his crimes — dressed in a Marshal's uniform — was getting closer.

"They've seen too much," he muttered. "They've connected the dots. They'll keep coming."

He turned back to the console. The screen showed a security schematic of his remaining fallback assets.

Underground vaults. Bio-keyed defense protocols. Off-grid compounds. He stared at them like a gambler running out of chips.
A soft buzz. His aide approached, hesitant.
"Sir. We've received reports. The media intercepted part of the blast signature. Speculation's already begun — word's spreading it wasn't a gas leak. They're connecting this to the prior attacks."
Greaves exhaled slowly. Then nodded. "So be it. Leak a diversion. Blame it on domestic militancy. Push that new task force narrative."
"Yes, sir."
But when the aide left, Greaves stayed behind — alone with the screen, the shadows, and the growing sense of inevitable judgment.
He whispered to himself, "She won't stop. She's not doing this for revenge…"
A pause.
"…She's doing this for *justice.*"
And for the first time in years — *Greaves looked afraid.*

REGROUP – THE FARMHOUSE, PENNSYLVANIA COUNTRYSIDE
04:21 Hours

The farmhouse porch light flickered softly, casting a golden hue over the dew-slicked steps. The quiet of the pre-dawn hours cloaked the property like a protective shroud. Inside, the kitchen smelled faintly of woodsmoke and strong coffee — grounding scents that clashed with the storm Laila and

Carolyn had just survived.
Daniel Wright stood at the sink, scrubbing his hands as if he could wash away the tension. The eldest of the Wright siblings, Daniel had the broad-shouldered calm of a man who'd fought his own wars long before Laila ever enlisted. His shotgun leaned against the wall, and a mug of black coffee steamed beside him — untouched.
He turned when he heard the creak of the door.
Laila stepped inside first, clothes scorched and dirty, but her eyes sharp. Carolyn followed, limping slightly, her temple bruised.
Daniel met them in two long strides. "Jesus. You look like hell."
Laila dropped her pack with a thud. "We've been through worse."
Carolyn forced a smirk. "Remind me of that when my hearing comes back. That explosion nearly rattled my soul out of my spine."
Daniel wrapped Laila in a tight hug. "I was about to come looking for you. I've been scanning chatter for hours — nothing official yet, but someone's trying real hard to bury the incident."
"Greaves," Laila said flatly, pulling away. "He's losing control of the narrative. And he knows it."
Daniel nodded grimly. "Thomas took Mom out to Wilkes-Barre. Said they were going shopping to calm her nerves. But really, it was a cover. He didn't want her here when you came back... just in case you came back bloody."
Laila's expression softened. "Good call. She doesn't need to be in this."

Daniel studied his sister. "..and *You* do?"
There was a moment of silence. Then Laila answered, voice steely. "I don't have a choice. None of us do anymore."
Carolyn collapsed into a chair, wincing. "He tried to take out a city block just to kill us. The guy who planted the device said it wasn't just a bomb — it was a *beacon*."
Daniel's brow furrowed. "A beacon?"
Laila nodded. "He's signaling someone — or something. That wasn't just about us. It was a fail-safe. Or a countdown."
Daniel paced slowly, processing. "Then we're out of time."
Carolyn leaned forward. "We need to go on the offensive. Hit his network. Expose his shadow play. But we can't do that without making it official — without drawing the public in."
Laila looked out the window. The stars were just beginning to fade. "We start at the roots. The judges. The senators. The dirty marshals who flipped. If we shine a light on them, Greaves burns with them."
Daniel handed her a fresh mug of coffee. "Then let's get to work."
Outside, the wind whispered through the fields. Inside, war was being planned in quict voices.

WASHINGTON D.C. – UNDISCLOSED PARKING GARAGE, LEVEL B3
36 Hours Later

The sodium lights overhead hummed softly, casting a sickly orange glow over the concrete labyrinth. It was the kind of place people didn't linger. Exactly what they needed.

Laila and Carolyn stood between two parked SUVs, flanked by Daniel in plain clothes as lookout. Across from them, *Maya Henson* approached — trench coat drawn tight, messenger bag slung across her shoulder. Award-winning investigative journalist. Unshakable. Dismissed by the mainstream until recently — now, everyone in the capital feared her pen more than any weapon.

Maya stopped a few feet short. "If this is a setup, I'm dead in thirty seconds."

Carolyn handed her a sealed manila folder. "Then let's all hope Greaves hasn't gotten to *you*."

Maya opened the folder and flipped through the contents. Photos. Audio transcripts. Wire transfers. Surveillance stills. Names. Judges. U.S. Attorneys. Marshals. D.C. power players.

Her face turned to stone. "My God. This is a war crime turned bureaucratic chess match."

Laila crossed her arms. "We need it to go wide. Not behind paywalls. Not sanitized. All of it. Now."

Maya looked up, fire sparking behind her eyes. "Then buckle in. Because this is going to set D.C. on fire."

24 HOURS LATER — NEWS NETWORKS LIGHT UP THE COUNTRY

BREAKING: "Leaked evidence suggests widespread corruption in federal judicial and law enforcement branches. Over 40 named officials facing warrants from the Department of Justice. Multiple government agencies involved. Civil unrest growing."

The footage spread like wildfire. Sworn testimonies. Redacted reports turned public. Greaves' dark web of manipulation laid bare. Marshals turned on marshals. Judges issued emergency injunctions. Others tried to flee. Some barricaded themselves in their chambers. Others ordered the destruction of digital records — too late.

BACK IN PENNSYLVANIA…
Laila stood before the mirror, braiding her hair back with precision. The uniform lay crisp on the bed — black tactical Marshal gear, gleaming badge placed reverently on top.
Carolyn, dressed in matching gear, appeared in the doorway, her usual smirk replaced by solemnity.
"They're calling it a purge," she said softly. "DOJ's been fielding a hundred calls an hour. Agents and deputies everywhere asking who they're supposed to be loyal to."
Laila fastened her belt. "The law. That's who."
Carolyn chuckled dryly. "I know that. You know that. The problem is, Greaves sold the illusion that he *was* the law."
Laila placed her badge on her chest, letting it click into place. "Then it's time we remind everyone that's not true."
Downstairs, Daniel loaded up the Jeep with weapons, comms gear, and warrants. Thomas had returned too — driving the long way around to avoid surveillance, bringing encrypted phones and their mother safely to a friend's

cabin.
Laila stepped out onto the porch, the sunrise bathing her in gold.
Carolyn joined her, tightening her gloves. “You realize we’re walking into chaos?”
Laila’s eyes didn’t leave the horizon. “Good. That’s where justice tends to live.”
They climbed into the vehicle. The radio chirped.
“U.S. Marshals Wright and Pryme — you are greenlit for field operation. Priority targets issued. Greaves not on list yet, but…”
A pause.
“…off the record, bring him in before someone makes him disappear.”
Laila keyed the mic.
“Copy that. Starting with the closest snake pit first.”
The engine roared. Tires kicked up gravel. The hunt had officially begun.
FEDERAL ENFORCEMENT COMPLEX – BALTIMORE, MARYLAND
DAYBREAK – *06:12 HOURS*
The city was just beginning to stir, unaware that history was being rewritten one building at a time.
Outside the looming glass-and-steel complex that once served as a command node for federal law enforcement, a convoy of black SUVs rolled to a halt. Tactical teams filed out, armor glinting, badges blazing. Among them — Deputy U.S. Marshals Laila A.Wright and Carolyn Pryme, moving with lethal focus.
Laila, face unreadable beneath her dark sunglasses, gave

the hand signal to fan out.
Carolyn Pryme adjusted her comms and scanned the building with a calm intensity honed by years of battle.
"This place is still running as if nothing happened," she muttered. "They think they're safe behind their bureaucracy."
Laila checked her weapon. "Then we show them their paper walls don't stop justice."
They entered through the east service entrance — no fanfare, no warnings.
Inside, a dozen federal officials were already at their desks. Some froze when they saw the approaching Marshals. Others stood, fingers twitching toward drawers or comms panels.
Laila's voice cut through the tension like a blade.
"Deputy Director Samuels, you are under federal warrant for conspiracy to obstruct justice, perjury, and unlawful authorization of blacksite detainment. Do not resist."
Samuels, a paunchy man in a tailored suit, rose slowly from his glass-walled office. "You've got no jurisdiction here, Marshal. This is a DOJ facility—"
Carolyn leveled her weapon. "And the DOJ signed the damn warrants."
He ran.
Everything exploded.
Tactical teams breached doors. Agents tried to flee down emergency stairs. Others barricaded themselves inside comms rooms. One man pulled a pistol — Carolyn disarmed him mid-motion, slammed him into a filing cabinet.

"Federal property or not," she said, cuffing him, "you answer for what you did."

Laila chased Samuels through the mezzanine, vaulted over a desk, and tackled him just before he could escape into the stairwell. She pinned him, panting.

"Where's Greaves?" she growled.

Samuels spat blood, defiant. "You're too late. He's gone to ground. You'll never—"

Laila knocked him unconscious with a clean blow. "We'll see."

15 MINUTES LATER — LOADING ZONE.

A line of arrested officials stood in cuffs, faces blank, broadcast live by a local news crew tipped off by anonymous sources. Chatter exploded across social media. The public wasn't just watching — they were demanding more.

Carolyn stood beside Laila as black helicopters began descending on other nearby sites.

"We're making waves," she said. "Real ones."

Laila nodded. "Greaves is feeling it now. Like cracks in the ice beneath his feet."

Carolyn turned toward the van holding Samuels. "You think he'll talk?"

Laila didn't answer. She looked to the east, toward D.C. Then she said, quietly, "He doesn't have to. Because we're not stopping."

NATIONWIDE MEDIA FRENZY – 48 HOURS AFTER FIRST RAIDS

CNN. FOX. MSNBC. NPR. TIKTOK. TWITTER(X). YOUTUBE. REDDIT.

The digital landscape had become a battlefield of its own. Every outlet scrambled to stay ahead of the firestorm. Every hour brought new footage, new leaks, new names — and new outrage. The public wasn't just watching anymore. They were ravenous, fueled by the revelation that their justice system had been rotting from the inside for years.

"—dozens of judges and high-ranking DOJ officials taken into custody in less than 72 hours..."

"...audio confirms U.S. Marshals were being targeted by internal black-ops teams..."

"...Twitter-X poll shows 82% of users no longer trust the federal courts..."

"...and today's arrest of Deputy Director Samuels confirms suspicions that the corruption extended directly into the chain of command..."

CAPITOL HILL, PRIVATE JUDGES' CHAMBERS

Panic.

Federal judges who once ruled with impunity were now shredding documents, deleting encrypted archives, and burning backup drives. Some resigned. Some lawyering up. A few were caught trying to board private jets.

One judge — caught live by reporters — collapsed as they read the sealed warrant aloud. Cardiac arrest, on camera. The footage went viral in under three minutes.

LAW ENFORCEMENT AGENCIES IN OPEN CONFLICT!

Inside field offices across the country, tensions boiled over.
FBI vs. U.S. Marshals.
ATF vs. DEA.
Homeland Security walking out mid-mission.
Officers didn't know who to trust — and some didn't trust anyone anymore.
Agents refused orders. Deputies called in sick en masse. Entire divisions ghosted from their posts. Anonymous leaks showed inter-agency memos blaming "rogue elements" and "unauthorized raids" — but the people weren't buying it.
Protests erupted.
At courthouses. At DOJ branches. Even outside private homes of those accused.
And at the center of it all — one image:
Laila Wright and Carolyn Pryme, standing in full Marshal gear, badges gleaming, leading a handcuffed Samuels into the light of day.
The headline: "REAL JUSTICE WEARS BADGES."

TALK SHOWS & COMMENTARY

On every channel, everyone had an opinion.
Anchor: "Are these women heroes… or vigilantes?"
Analyst: "They're enforcing federal warrants. They're doing what the law demands."

Former Official: “This is a coup. A silent insurrection from inside the justice system.”
Civil Rights Lawyer: “This isn’t a coup. This is a *reckoning*.”

WHITE HOUSE – DOJ PRESS BRIEFING

The *Attorney General*, visibly shaken but determined, stepped up to the podium.
“What we are witnessing is painful but necessary. The Department of Justice will not shield corruption. These Marshals acted under full authority and have the support of this administration. The rule of law will stand. No one — I repeat, *no one* — is above it.”

A SECRET LOCATION – GREAVES WATCHING

The screen reflected in Greaves’ eyes, his jaw tight, his fingers trembling. He watched the headlines, the feeds, the collapsing network he built brick by bloodstained brick.
“...rumors of international allies backing Greaves’ faction. Talks of mercenaries. Blacksite movements...”
He turned to a satellite map. A secure airfield in Central America blinked green.
Greaves whispered to himself:
“Time to vanish before they knock on my door.”
But his fingers hovered over the redirection orders.
Something in him knew — he couldn’t run forever.
Not from *her*.

SAFEHOUSE BRIEFING ROOM – OUTSKIRTS OF PHILADELPHIA
DAY 5 AFTER FIRST RAID

A digital map projected across the wall like a living nerve system — threads of red, blue, and flickering yellow points marked active operations, seized properties, and last-known locations of fugitives still in flight.

Laila Wright stood at the head of the table, now flanked by a small task force of loyalists — U.S. Marshals, DOJ analysts, a handful of disillusioned federal agents who had come out of the shadows when the truth broke open.

Carolyn Pryme sat to her left, fingers flying across a tablet, uploading intercept data in real time.

"We have a name," she said, not looking up. "Operation: *Last Light*. Greaves' fallback protocol. Every indication shows he's trying to reach one of the old Rendition airfields in Guatemala. That's his rabbit hole."

A younger Marshal leaned forward. "So we take it out?"

Laila shook her head. "Not yet. If we move too early, he'll ghost again. We've already lost track of him twice this week. We need to cut off his escape without him knowing we're doing it."

Carolyn looked up. "That means we draw him out. Make him think his exit plan is still in motion."

Daniel, leaning against the wall in a Kevlar vest, added, "And what? Meet him at the gate with a warrant?"

Laila's voice was low. Cold. "No. We corner him. We take him down before he disappears into another regime's arms."

She clicked the remote.
The screen zoomed in on a facility marked “BLUE PHOENIX: Holding Site 3” — an off-grid federal location repurposed without oversight. One of Greaves' most protected assets.
“This is our next target,” Laila said. “We believe it's housing the remaining black-budget intel Greaves doesn’t want leaked — payrolls, safehouse blueprints, code names. If we get inside and secure that data... we’ll have his entire escape network in our hands.”
Carolyn nodded, standing. “We go in clean. Small team. Tactical precision. No leaks, no support from on high. Just us. Just justice.”
The room was silent. Then came a quiet chorus:
“Understood.”
“Let’s roll.”
“Time to finish it.”

OUTSIDE – MOMENTS LATER...

Laila and Carolyn stood beside the black SUV again, just like they had a dozen times before. But this time felt different. The sun was setting — the golden light stretching long shadows across the gravel drive.
Carolyn pulled on her gloves. “You know what Greaves doesn’t get?”
Laila raised an eyebrow.
Carolyn glanced toward the farmhouse in the distance. “We didn’t start this to make headlines. We didn’t do this to be saviors. We did this because we were tired of the silence.

Tired of the rot."
Laila looked up at the sky. "And we're not done until it's burned out root and stem."
They slid into the vehicle and drove into the dark — lights off, path clear.
Ahead: *BLUE PHOENIX*
Behind: a country on fire with truth.
Between them: a ghost still running.
SCENE: BLUE PHOENIX – HOLDING SITE 3
LOCATION: DECOMMISSIONED COMMUNICATION BUNKER – WEST VIRGINIA HIGHLANDS
LOCAL TIME: 02:14 HOURS
The mountains loomed like silent sentinels as fog crept across the tree line, cloaking the approach. The facility was buried into the mountainside — a Cold War relic repurposed with black-budget funds and zero accountability.
From above, it looked abandoned. Cracked concrete, rusted fencing, weeds growing through the lot. But buried beneath: servers, private comms lines, secure vaults, and three armed shifts cycling every six hours.
This was Greaves' vault of secrets — and it was about to be breached.

EXTERIOR – PERIMETER RIDGE…
Laila knelt beside Carolyn and two handpicked deputies — Agent Damaris (ex-CIA) and Deputy Nunez (cyber-ops specialist). Thermal scopes confirmed guard placement: four above, eight below, two manning a drone system on a closed frequency.

Laila whispered, "We enter through the exhaust corridor. Unmapped. Shielded. It runs beneath the eastern side. Nunez, disable any thermal countermeasures the moment we drop in."
Nunez gave a tight nod. "EMP disruptor's prepped. We'll have 90 seconds of blindness before they reboot."
Carolyn's eyes narrowed through her monocular. "And after that, we'll be ghosts or targets."
Laila smirked. "Then let's haunt them."

INTERIOR – EXHAUST SHAFT, LEVEL -3

The team dropped silently through the ventilation system, landing behind a bank of data nodes humming like a subterranean heart. The scent of ozone and recycled air filled their lungs.
Nunez tapped a wireless node to the system. "I'm inside. Pulling drive maps now… Holy hell."
Carolyn leaned over. "Talk to us."
"There's not just blackmail here. There's surveillance logs on high-ranking officials, funding trails to overseas regimes, records of whistleblower terminations — everything Greaves didn't want seen."
Laila: "Copy it all. Then torch it. We take the truth. Leave them smoke."
Suddenly—motion ping.
"Company coming," Damaris whispered. "Four hostiles. Rounds chambered."
Carolyn drew fast. "Let's earn our paychecks."

INTENSE CLOSE-QUARTERS GUNFIGHT – SERVER LEVEL

The corridor exploded in gunfire. Suppressed rounds cracked through servers. Sparks rained from shattered conduit. Laila vaulted a divider and took down two guards with swift, center-mass shots. Carolyn swept low and knocked one flat with a baton-strike to the throat before dragging him into shadow.

Nunez continued the upload mid-chaos. "Eighty percent copied. One more minute—!"

A grenade rolled across the floor toward her.

Carolyn dove, grabbed it mid-spin, and hurled it back into the stairwell.

BOOM!!. Screams!

Nunez: "We're clear!"

Laila: "Plant the charge."

Damaris popped a thermal demolition puck onto the server core. "Goodnight, secrets."

EXIT – EMERGENCY STAIRWELL…

The building shook behind them as the core ignited — not with a full detonation, but with enough thermite to liquefy the drives.

As they emerged through the forest edge, radio chatter sparked to life.

"—Secure Facility Phoenix-3 compromised. Full systems offline. High-value data destroyed. Suspected Marshals… unknown if Greaves compromised—"

Laila clicked off the comms, breath steady. "He knows now."

Carolyn wiped grime from her brow. “He’ll run. He’ll panic.”
Laila turned toward the rising dawn. “And that’s when we strike.”

SAFEHOUSE – POST-OP DEBRIEF, 06:43 HOURS
LOCATION: CLASSIFIED — MOUNTAINS OF VIRGINIA

The team was decompressing, wounds patched, gear stowed, hands trembling from adrenaline crash. A bitter pot of coffee brewed while Laila stood alone on the back porch, scanning the tree line — unable to stop scanning.
Carolyn sat at the kitchen table, reviewing fragments of recovered intel when her burner phone buzzed once. Then again. A ping. No caller ID. Encrypted source.
She answered, cautious. “Pryme.”
A voice, filtered, accented, and controlled, came through.
“You’ve made quite the mess, Marshal. Tidy. Clean. Beautiful, really. You’ve taken down half of Greaves’ network. But he’s not just running now — he’s *begging*.”
Carolyn stiffened. “Who is this?”
“Let’s say… a former associate of our mutual enemy. One who’s been silenced, exiled, *watched*. Greaves threw me away when I was no longer useful. I’d like to return the favor.”
Carolyn muted the call, waved Laila in, and patched it to speaker.
The voice continued.
“He’s using a false identity, posing as a foreign attaché under diplomatic cover. He’ll be wheels-up by midnight

tonight. Destination: undisclosed compound in Montenegro. If he lands there — he's gone. No extradition, no record, no return."

Laila: "What do you want in return?"

"Public amnesty. Quiet absolution. My name disappears from the files you took from Blue Phoenix. I become a footnote."

Carolyn glanced at Laila. "You trust this?"

Laila: "No. But we don't have to. We just need the truth to intersect with Greaves' fear long enough to catch him."

The voice, amused:

"Coordinates for his airfield are en route. You'll have a five-minute window. No backup. No reinforcements. You get one shot."

Click. Line dead.

Moments later, the screen lit up:

Geo-Ping Received — Remote Airstrip, Chesapeake Inlet Region.

Carolyn exhaled. "Well. Looks like we're going to the coast."

Laila smirked, already moving toward her gear. "Then let's bring the storm."

CHESAPEAKE INLET AIRSTRIP – MID INFILTRATION
TIME: 23:58 HOURS – TWO MINUTES TO WHEELS UP

The sound of cicadas pulsed in the humid night air, blending into the low rumble of the private jet's engines

spooling to life at the far end of the cracked asphalt runway. A small convoy of blacked-out SUVs idled nearby, their drivers scanning the perimeter nervously. Inside the hangar, uniformed contractors — ex-military, no insignias — loaded the final briefcases onto the jet.
They had no idea what was coming.

NEARBY – TREE LINE, MOVING FAST

Laila Wright ran low through the underbrush, sweat cutting lines through the grime on her face. Her sidearm was drawn, her eyes cold and locked forward. Carolyn Pryme flanked her six meters wide, rifle braced tight to her shoulder.
They had already cut the perimeter fence, taken out two patrols with silencers, and bypassed the motion alarms with a trick Nunez patched into their gear back at the safehouse.
Carolyn whispered over comms:
"Jet's fueling is complete. Flight crew's on final checks. Once Greaves boards, we lose him."
Laila tapped her mic. "Not tonight."
They reached the outer wall of the hangar. Laila peeked around the corner — saw Greaves stepping onto the bottom stair of the aircraft, flanked by two gunmen, his face pale, jaw tight. Not the usual smug arrogance.
He was scared.
"Visual confirmed," Laila breathed. "On my mark."
INSIDE HANGAR – SECONDS LATER
Flashbangs rolled in.
BOOM—BOOM!

White light. Shouts. Chaos.
Laila burst through the side door, fired three tight shots — two guards down before they finished blinking. Carolyn moved like thunder, clearing the elevated catwalk above with precision fire. The pilot was hit in the leg as he reached for the hatch lever. Screams erupted from inside the plane.
Greaves ducked, bolted down the aircraft stairs.
He didn't get far.
Laila tackled him across the tarmac, both of them rolling hard into the gravel.
He clawed for a pistol — she crushed his wrist beneath her knee.
He spit blood, snarled, "You don't understand what you've done—"
Laila leaned in close, breath steady, gun to his temple. "You don't get to hide behind power anymore, Greaves. The only door left for you is a courtroom and prison."
Carolyn approached, rifle still up. "Or a pine box. Your choice."
Sirens echoed in the distance. The *real* authorities, the ones still loyal to the law, were closing in now.
Greaves was panting, trembling. "You think you've won?"
Laila: "No. But we *ended* you."

SCENE: HOURS LATER – MEDIA BLITZ

"Edward Greaves, former high-ranking DOJ official, captured at Chesapeake airfield moments before boarding a jet under false diplomatic status..."

"Marshal Laila Wright and Deputy Carolyn Pryme hailed as national heroes for unraveling one of the deepest webs of corruption in modern American history..."
"Justice has a new face."

LAILA AND CAROLYN, STANDING AT DAWN, LOOKING OVER THE AIRSTRIP

Carolyn: "So what now?"
Laila: "Now? We testify. We rebuild. We watch every corner they try to crawl back into."
Carolyn: "And if they do?"
Laila's badge glinted in the morning sun.
"Then Marshal L.A.W. comes knocking again."

Location: Sullivan County, Pennsylvania
Six Months Later
The late-autumn sun cast long shadows across the golden fields, where stalks of wheat rustled in the breeze like whispers from the earth. The farmhouse, weathered but proud, stood with its windows open and curtains swaying gently. Inside, the air smelled of coffee, cinnamon, and freshly baked cornbread.
Laila Wright stood at the edge of the porch, her boots muddy from the morning's work, a flannel shirt rolled up at the sleeves. A small pile of chopped firewood lay at her feet. She sipped from a ceramic mug — the same one she'd held before the raid that changed everything — only now, it held peace instead of tension.
The distant laughter of children floated up from the back

pasture. Daniel's kids — rambunctious and free — chasing the farm dog through leaves. Her mother was on the swing, humming a church tune and shelling peas. Thomas sat nearby, carving something from a block of wood.

The war was over.

At least, for now.

Inside the house, the TV played quietly. News footage rolled on mute — congressional hearings, judicial reform bills, a new oversight agency being sworn in. The name *Greaves* still appeared from time to time, now synonymous with disgrace and betrayal.

But Laila didn't look at the screen anymore. Not often.

Her phone buzzed once on the porch rail. A message.

Carolyn Pryme:

"Confirmed. Committee accepted full immunity terms. All files declassified. You're officially cleared.

Oh — and I got stuck in another ethics summit in D.C. I miss cows."

Laila chuckled, fingers tapping back:

"Come visit. Got a barn that needs painting. And a firepit with your name on it."

Carolyn:

"Don't tempt me. You know I'll show up with bourbon and a folder labeled 'one last thing.'"

Laila:

"Bring two bottles."

She slipped the phone back in her pocket and looked out across the land. Her land. Her family. Her quiet.

The scars were still there. The memories hadn't faded. But for the first time in a long time, Laila Wright wasn't

running toward danger or away from it.
She was just home.
And if the day ever came when shadows returned…
Marshal L.A.W. would be ready.

EPILOGUE: RETURN TO THE FARM

Sullivan County, Pennsylvania – Late Autumn

The morning sun spilled gold across the Wright farm, where life had settled back into a familiar, peaceful rhythm. Laila Aurora Wright, now 36 and semi-retired from federal operations, was elbow-deep in chicken feed. Her boots were caked in mud, and her overalls hung loose over a frame that belied just how much damage she was capable of doing.

In the distance, her brother Daniel worked the orchard, whistling an old Motown tune. The low rumble of a V8 echoed through the valley as Thomas, the youngest of the two older brothers, peeled off the gravel driveway in his restored '66 Mustang, running an errand for their mother, Eleanor Wright.

Inside the house, Eleanor was vacuuming and humming a gospel hymn. The Judge — the late Henry Wright, a man of principle and thunder — had been gone a few years now, but his presence still echoed through the house. Rather than sell the family farm after his passing, all three Wright children had moved back home. Eleanor hadn't needed them to, but she loved having her children near — even if they made more messes than they cleaned up.

Each of them came home with their own baggage. Daniel after a divorce. Thomas after his exit from military life. And Laila… well, Laila had always surprised them all. First a whirlwind marriage, then a swift, righteous divorce. Then the U.S. Marshals. A badge. A gun. A purpose.

Eleanor smiled to herself as she gathered laundry upstairs, stopping at the hallway where each child's bedroom had returned to life. But as she reached Thomas's room, her smile faded.

A padlock.

"Hmm," she muttered, tugging on it. "Since when do we lock doors in this house?"

She turned to leave — but froze. There was someone inside.

Shuffling. Drawers opening. Deliberate, hushed movement.

Eleanor's eyes widened. She backed away and hurried down the stairs, bursting out the front door, waving frantically toward the chicken coop. Laila saw her mother flapping both arms and frowned.

"Mom?" she called out, approaching. "Why are you waving at me like you're one of the hens?"

"Where are your brothers?" Eleanor demanded, breathless.

"Danny's in the orchard with Simon, and Tommy went to town for you. Why?"

"I heard someone in the house. In Thomas's room. And it's not one of you kids."

Laila's smile vanished. She scanned the property — only her Jeep, the farm truck, and Danny's beat-up 'Cuda were on site.

"If someone's here," she muttered, "they walked a long

way to rob a farmhouse in the middle of nowhere."
"You think I've lost my mind?" Eleanor snapped. "I know what I heard."
"Okay. Okay. Show me."
They stepped inside — and that's when they heard it.
The locked bedroom door jostling violently.
Eleanor gave Laila a victorious glare. "Told you."
Laila moved quickly to her late father's roll-top desk and unlocked a drawer, retrieving a .44 revolver. She checked the cylinder — loaded.
"Stay here," she said.
"I will not," Eleanor retorted. "This is *my house*."
Laila sighed. "Fine. Just… stay behind me."
They crept up the stairs, Laila's muddy boot prints trailing behind her. Eleanor winced at the mess. Another crash came from Thomas's room. Someone was inside — moving fast, trying to get out.
"Why's there a padlock on Tommy's door?" Laila whispered.
"Because you and Daniel keep going through his things," Eleanor replied matter-of-factly. "He's probably tired of it."
Laila scoffed, "His stuff? I'm usually just reclaiming *my* T-shirts—"
Bang. A sharp thud against the door. Then, the creak of a window.
Laila raised her boot and kicked in the door, gun trained, ready to shoot.
Instead of a burglar…
A half-dressed woman was halfway out the second-story

window, in a wrinkled evening dress turned inside out, holding her heels in one hand and the sill in the other.
Laila blinked. "What in the hell—"
The woman looked up, startled. "Uh… hi. I'm a friend of Tommy's."
Eleanor stepped beside her daughter. "Then why on God's earth are you climbing out the window, child?"
The woman answered quickly, "I couldn't unlock the door. And I really had to pee."
"You should've knocked!" Eleanor scolded. "We'd have gotten you out. Laila, help this poor girl."
Laila was already doubled over, laughing uncontrollably, tears streaming down her dirt-smeared face.
"Yaya, did you hear me?"
Through gasps, she managed, "Sorry, Mom. I'm… I'm trying…"
She wiped her face, flicked the safety on the revolver, and slipped it into her back pocket. With a bit of maneuvering, she hauled the embarrassed young woman back into the house. Eleanor pointed the direction of the bathroom.
The stranger darted into the bathroom without another word.
Eleanor turned, took in the muddy footprints, the shattered doorframe, and the chaos of Thomas's room. She let out a long, exasperated sigh.
"That fool boy is going to drive me to drinking. Locking up women like she's contraband. Where'd he get *that* idea?"
Laila exploded with laughter again — just as her phone buzzed in her pocket.
Still chuckling, she glanced down at the screen.

Caller ID: Carolyn Pryme
She answered, "Hey lady, have I got a story for—"
Carolyn's voice was tight. Focused.
"It'll have to wait. The *Ogre* just made a move. One of our witnesses is down."
The smile vanished from Laila's face. Her body tensed.
She turned, gaze narrowing.
"I'll be in D.C. as soon as I can."

Laila Aurora Wright and Carolyn Pryme will Return

Marshal L.A.W.: The Ogre Directive

Acknowledgments

First and foremost, I extend my deepest gratitude to the brave men and women of law enforcement who dedicate their lives to upholding justice, often in the face of overwhelming adversity. Their unwavering commitment serves as an inspiration and a testament to the human spirit.

My thanks also go to the legal professionals who generously shared their time and expertise, helping me to understand the complexities of the courtroom and the delicate dance of justice. Their insights proved invaluable in shaping the narrative.

A special thank you to my editor for their insightful guidance and unwavering support throughout the writing process. Their patience and expertise helped refine the manuscript and bring the story to life.

Finally, to my family and friends – your love, patience, and understanding are what fuel my passion for storytelling. This book would not have been possible without your belief in me.

Appendix

This appendix contains supplementary materials relevant to the narrative, including:

Exhibit A:

A simulated transcript of key portions of the Falfor trial, highlighting the testimony of Laila Wright and Carolyn Pryme. This is a fictionalized representation based on legal precedents and procedures.

United States v. Falfor
Simulated Court Transcript — Key Excerpt
Day 14 of Trial
[DIRECT EXAMINATION — Laila Aurora Wright, U.S. Marshal]

Prosecutor (Ms. Devereaux):
Marshal Wright, can you describe the moment you first became aware that the defendant, Mr. Falfor, was involved in the conspiracy?

Laila Wright:
Yes, ma'am. It was during a multi-agency briefing on June 12th. We intercepted communications linking Mr. Falfor to shipments flagged by Homeland Security — not just weapons, but trafficking operations. What caught my attention was his coded reference to "The Package," which, we later confirmed, was a human asset.

Prosecutor:
Did you personally witness Mr. Falfor's actions?

Laila:
Yes. On June 20th, during a joint task force operation, I witnessed Mr. Falfor giving direct orders to his subordinates. He coordinated extraction routes and payment drops. I saw him. Face to face.

Defense Counsel:

Objection — speculation on intent.
Judge Monroe:
Sustained. Marshal Wright, please limit your answer to what you personally observed.
Laila:
Yes, Your Honor. I observed Mr. Falfor giving orders related to the operation.

CROSS-EXAMINATION — Laila Aurora Wright
Defense Counsel:
Marshal Wright, you're aware that operational chaos can cause misidentification, yes?
Laila:
Yes, I'm aware. But not in this case.
Defense Counsel:
And your certainty — is that based solely on that single observation?
Laila (firmly):
No. It's based on six months of investigation, surveillance, and briefings. This wasn't a fleeting moment. We knew who we were looking at.

DIRECT EXAMINATION — Carolyn Pryme, Deputy U.S. Marshal
Prosecutor:
Deputy Pryme, what was your role in the June 20th operation?
Carolyn Pryme:
I was lead on ground surveillance. I coordinated perimeter lockdowns and extraction points.
Prosecutor:
Did you have eyes on the defendant?
Carolyn:
Yes. I was positioned on the southwest corner of the facility. I saw Mr. Falfor enter at 21:04 hours. He stayed for about 35 minutes. He wasn't there as an observer — he was giving orders.
Prosecutor:

Did you hear what was said?
Carolyn:
Over comms, yes. "Make sure the cargo moves tonight. No loose ends." That's what Falfor said.

[CROSS-EXAMINATION — Carolyn Pryme]
Defense Counsel:
Deputy Pryme, isn't it true that comm lines can be intercepted or misattributed?
Carolyn:
They can, but in this case, the voice match and physical confirmation leave no doubt.
Defense Counsel:
You're absolutely sure?
Carolyn (staring directly at Falfor):
As sure as I'm standing here.

[JUDGE'S INTERJECTION]
Judge Monroe:
Let the record reflect the witness identified the defendant. Counsel, move along.

Exhibit B:

A partial list of law enforcement reforms implemented in Pennsylvania following the events depicted in the novel. This is not an exhaustive list, but rather a selection of notable changes.

Notable Law Enforcement Reforms in Pennsylvania
Statewide Use of Force Policies (2020–2021)

- Mandated standardized use-of-force policies across all police departments
- Required de-escalation techniques before using deadly force
- Prohibited chokeholds except in life-threatening situations

Police Transparency & Accountability Act (2020)

- Created a public database to track officer disciplinary records and terminations for misconduct

- Required disclosure of prior disciplinary actions when officers apply for new law enforcement jobs

Expanded Background Checks for Police Recruits

- Enhanced psychological and background evaluations
- Mandatory review of social media for signs of bias or violent behavior

Mandatory Body Cameras & Dash Cameras

- Increased funding for body-worn and vehicle-mounted cameras
- Established statewide camera usage standards and required policies for releasing footage

Crisis Intervention & Mental Health Training

- Required police officers to undergo specialized training in handling mental health and substance abuse crises
- Expanded collaboration with mental health professionals and community outreach teams

Ban on "No-Knock" Warrants (in most cases)

- Restricted the use of no-knock warrants, especially in drug-related investigations, to minimize risk to civilians and officers

Expanded Civilian Oversight

- Supported creation of local civilian review boards in major cities like Philadelphia and Pittsburgh
-
- **Increased state-level oversight of local police departments**
-

Improved Data Collection on Police Stops

- Required agencies to collect and report data on traffic stops, arrests, use of force, and racial profiling
- Aimed at addressing racial disparities in law enforcement

Exhibit C:

A map of the Wright family farm and the surrounding area, illustrating the key locations mentioned in the story.

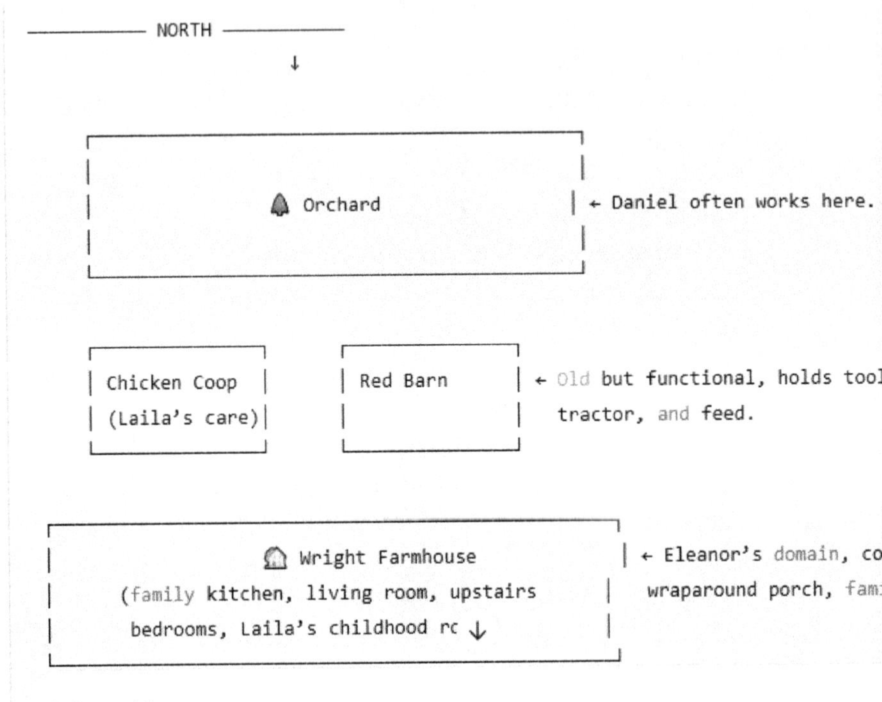

Glossary

This glossary provides definitions of key legal and law enforcement terms used in the novel:

Brady Material: Evidence favorable to the defendant that must be disclosed by the prosecution.

Chain of Custody: The chronological documentation of the handling of evidence from its discovery to its presentation in court.

De-escalation Techniques: Methods used by law enforcement to reduce the intensity of a potentially volatile situation.

Exculpatory Evidence: Evidence tending to clear a person of guilt.

Miranda Rights: The rights of an arrested person, including the right to remain silent and the right to an attorney.

Probable Cause: Reasonable grounds for believing that a crime has been committed.

Direct Examination
The initial questioning of a witness by the lawyer who called them to testify.

Cross-Examination
Questioning of a witness by the opposing lawyer to challenge their statements.

Objection
A formal protest raised by a lawyer during a trial when they believe a rule of evidence is being broken.

Sustained
The judge agrees with the objection; the question or evidence is disallowed.

Overruled
The judge disagrees with the objection; the question or evidence may continue.

Comms
Short for "communications equipment," such as radios or earpieces used by law enforcement during operations.

Multi-Agency Briefing
A planning meeting involving multiple law enforcement or government agencies.

Perimeter Lockdown
Securing the outer boundary of a location to prevent entry or escape.

Orchard
A piece of land planted with fruit trees, often used for family or commercial harvesting.

Wraparound Porch
A porch that extends around two or more sides of a house, providing outdoor space.

Heirlooms
Valuable or sentimental objects passed down through generations of a family.

Use-of-Force Policy
A set of guidelines outlining when and how police officers can use physical force.

De-Escalation
Techniques used by law enforcement to reduce the intensity of a conflict without force.

Chokehold
A physical maneuver used to restrain someone by applying pressure to the neck, often controversial and banned in many places.

Body-Worn Camera / Dash Camera
Recording devices worn on a police officer's uniform or installed in a patrol vehicle to capture interactions and incidents.

No-Knock Warrant
A legal warrant allowing police to enter a property without announcing themselves beforehand.

Civilian Review Board
An independent panel of citizens that reviews complaints and investigates police misconduct.

Racial Profiling
The practice of targeting individuals for suspicion or investigation based on race or ethnicity rather than evidence or behavior.

References

While this novel is a work of fiction, the legal procedures and law enforcement practices depicted are based on extensive research and consultation with legal and law enforcement professionals.

Legal Procedures (U.S. Court System)

1. **Federal Rules of Evidence**
   → Official rules governing the admission of evidence in federal courts.
   → Website: uscourts.gov
2. **Federal Rules of Criminal Procedure**
   → Governs procedures in criminal cases in U.S. federal courts.
3. **Black's Law Dictionary** (Bryan A. Garner, ed.)
   → The most widely used legal dictionary; excellent for definitions and legal terms.
4. **American Bar Association (ABA)**
   → Offers clear guides on courtroom procedures, trial advocacy, and legal ethics.
   → Website: americanbar.org
5. **Nolo Press Guides**
   → Plain-language legal books, such as *Everybody's Guide to Criminal Law* or *Represent Yourself in Court*.
   → Website: nolo.com

Law Enforcement Practices

1. **U.S. Marshals Service (USMS) Website**
   → Details on the duties, history, and procedures of U.S. Marshals.

→ Website: usmarshals.gov

2. **Bureau of Justice Statistics (BJS)**
   → Official data on police practices, use of force, arrests, and court outcomes.
   → Website: bjs.ojp.gov
3. **International Association of Chiefs of Police (IACP)**
   → Provides best practices, training guides, and policies for law enforcement.
   → Website: theiacp.org
4. **National Institute of Justice (NIJ)**
   → Research on policing, body-worn cameras, de-escalation, and reforms.
   → Website: nij.ojp.gov
5. **State-Level Guidelines (Pennsylvania-specific)**
   → Pennsylvania Commission on Crime and Delinquency (PCCD)
   → Pennsylvania State Police: Training, policies, and public reports

---

Recommended Reading for Writers

- *Police Procedure & Investigation: A Guide for Writers* by Lee Lofland
  Highly recommended; written specifically for fiction authors.
- *Crime Scene: A Writer's Guide to Crime Scene Investigation* by Connie Fletcher
- *Criminal Law Handbook* (Paul Bergman & Sara J. Berman, Nolo Press)

A complete bibliography of the consulted materials is available upon request from the publisher.
www.TheMegaverseCity.com

Author Biography

Born in New York city, E.S. Bennett moved Boston and was raised back and forth between the two cities absorbing the differences, cultures, problems, and successes of each city.

He is also an accomplished thriller writer, with a passion for crafting suspenseful narratives based on real-world experience.

E.S. Bennett currently resides in North Carolina, with family and pets, and continues to write and consult on matters related to law enforcement and justice reform.

This novel,
Laila Aurora Wright; Court of L.A.W.
marks their Fifth published work.